Kate and Jack minutes later, the below. Bower's two acres melded into Emily Ann's property. If the wind blew in that direction, the fire would spread unbelievably fast, and the entire hillside could go up in a matter of minutes—the woods, the houses, Eagle Crossing, the animals. Kate prayed as she scampered down the trail after Jack, running as fast as possible. Kate lost her footing going down a steep incline, and, unable to right herself, she tumbled down the rest of the way. Jack was several yards ahead. With adrenaline shooting through her veins, Kate jumped up and didn't stop to check for damage. Not twisting an ankle was all that mattered and, assured that she was okay, she continued after Jack.

The sirens grew louder and seemed to scream with an urgency that became worse with every passing second. Kate willed the noise to stop. She willed the fire to go out, for everything to be under control as soon as she and Jack came down off Chadwick Hill. When they entered the clearing near the road, Kate knew her wishing and praying had been in vain. Emergency vehicles had blocked Watmough Bay Road. What had been a thin trail of gray smoke half an hour ago was now a tower of flames with smoke blackening the sky.

Praise for Eagle Crossing

"Vivid passionate writing."

Eagle Crossing

by

Kathleen Kaska

*The Kate Caraway Animal-Rights
Mystery Series*

Eagle Crossing

Cover Art by *Jennifer Greeff*

The Wild Rose Press, Inc.
PO Box 708
Adams Basin, NY 14410-0708
Visit us at www.thewildrosepress.com

Publishing History
First Edition, 2022
Trade Paperback ISBN 978-1-5092-4527-7
Digital ISBN 978-1-5092-4528-4

The Kate Caraway Animal-Rights Mystery Series
Published in the United States of America

Dedication

To my goddaughter Katie.

Chapter One

Kate felt the pressure on her chest even before he pulled the trigger. She gulped for air and tried to cry out, hoping the sound of her voice would stop him.

"Kate."

She jerked, grabbing at her husband's hand as he shook her shoulder.

"Bad dreams aren't allowed while napping. You've been out since we left Everett."

Kate sat up and stretched her legs just to feel her body move. She took a long drink from her water bottle. "I don't take naps."

Jack laughed. "Then your spirit left your body for the last forty-five minutes."

"Where are we?"

"Just pulling into Anacortes."

The dashboard clock blinked 1:53. "Think we can make the 2:20 ferry?" Kate unfolded the ferry schedule. "The next boat's not until 5:15."

"Even if we get to the ferry landing in time, there's no guarantee that the 2:20 won't be full. We may have to wait anyway. What's the hurry? We can put the car in line and go for a hike. Emily Ann will understand."

Kate smiled at her husband. "You're right. I'm anxious to get there."

"Being anxious is also not allowed. Don't forget, we're on vacation."

Kate and Jack drove through Anacortes and made the left onto Oakes Avenue for the final four miles to the ferry landing. Tourist season was winding down. A month earlier, making the 2:20 would have been wishful thinking. A steady stream of cars flowed in the opposite direction down the narrow two-lane road—the ferry was docked and unloading. Just as Jack turned off the road and approached the ticket booth, a red Grand Cherokee swerved dangerously close and darted ahead of them.

"If he buys the last ticket, I'll put a hex on him," Kate said.

Jack nosed up to the ticket window.

"You're on standby, sir. We may be able to get you on."

The Grand Cherokee rolled into what would have been their space. Kate wanted to slide down her window and shout obscenities. Jack calmly removed the Frank Sinatra from Pandora and clicked on Bruno Mars. "Got your hiking boots on?"

Kate laughed. When her husband left the ballpark, he left as a free man. During games, Jack paced the dugout, too nervous to sit back and let his pitchers go it alone. But when he left the dressing room after a game at Wrigley Field, win or lose, he was as calm as a Sunday morning. If Kate possessed half her husband's patience and laid-back attitude, she'd be able to sleep at night instead of allowing her worries to hold court in the wee hours of the morning.

The ferry attendant called out, "This is your lucky day. We can take one more car. Enjoy your ride." He motioned for Jack to drive on and directed him to pull up within inches of the Cherokee's bumper. The cars were packed so tightly Kate had to crawl over the console to squeeze out the driver's-side door. She edged her way toward the stairs leading to the upper deck just in time to see the driver crawl out of the Cherokee, take off his suit jacket, and throw it in the back seat. He winked at her and gave her a thumbs-up. She rolled her eyes. He threw his head back and cackled. Rather than help unbuckle his struggling child from the safety seat, he came to see how close Jack was to the Jeep's bumper.

"Humane Society, huh?" The man pointed to the license plate on their Land Rover. "I support worthy causes, too, like Ducks Unlimited and the NRA." At the sound of his voice, a golden retriever poked its head out of the Cherokee's back window, erupting in barks and yelps, muffling the man's last words. Several other dogs on board answered. Kenya growled from the back seat, too well-mannered to join the canine ruckus.

Before Kate could comment, Jack grabbed her hand and led her to the back of their car. "What an asshole," Kate said. "Did you see that smirk on his face?"

"Ignoring rude people is another vacation rule." Jack cracked the windows and opened the back of their SUV to rearrange a wad of blankets. "Sorry, girl. Make yourself comfortable. Dogs aren't allowed above the car deck."

Kate patted her greyhound on the head and followed Jack up the stairs to the passenger deck.

The San Juan Islands were experiencing an Indian summer. The ice-blue sky shone bright enough for sunscreen and sunglasses, and with the temperature in the low sixties, the day felt like heaven. Perfect weather after a sticky Chicago summer and a losing season for the Jack's team. Kate was more than ready for two weeks on Lopez Island in the Pacific Northwest.

Kate and Jack strolled the deck to take in the scenery. On their second pass around, Kate said, "I could use a strong cup of coffee. How about you?"

"Sounds good." Jack took his binoculars from his bag.

"Be right back," Kate replied.

The galley line snaked out into the passageway. Kate used the wait time to call Emily Ann and tell her that they'd be on time after all. She edged up closer to the cashier and dropped her phone back into her bag.

"Hey, glad you made it on board."

Kate turned to see the Grand Cherokee's driver behind her. She smiled a thank you and paid for the coffee.

"A pint of light draft," he said to the cashier and turned to Kate. "Usually don't drink in the middle of the day, but I'm trying to gear up for this wonderful weekend with the in-laws, and having a cranky kid doesn't help."

Kate walked to the condiment bar, doing her best to ignore the guy. The bawling coming from the nearby booth gave her an excuse to pretend she hadn't heard his comment. Although her maternal instincts did not extend much further than furry creatures with four legs, the fact that this guy referred to his child as "the cranky kid" made Kate's stomach boil.

"Hope you didn't hold it against me for going ahead of you." He came up behind her and grabbed a napkin. "It's just that waiting three hours with a toddler can be a nightmare."

"I understand. No harm done." Kate added cream to the coffee, snapped the lids on the cups, and turned to leave.

"People who have those license plates, like the one you have. I mean, I think there are more important things in the world."

"Listen, if I choose to pay extra for my license plates so that some of the money goes to the Humane Society, that's my business."

"You're not one of those animal-rights people, are you?"

"Animal-rights activist."

"Woo. I'm not sure what that is."

"Google it."

****

Kate handed Jack his coffee.

"You just missed a bald eagle," he said. "It soared over and landed in those treetops."

When Kate did not respond, he set his binoculars down and looked at his wife.

"Your face is red. Is it too brisk out here?"

"No, I'm rather hot. I just ran into the dickhead."

"Take a deep breath and look around. The scenery is spectacular."

"And I'm on vacation with my favorite husband." Kate laughed. "I was a bit rude to that guy. I should go apologize."

"You're cranky after the nap you didn't have, and there's no need." Jack put down his coffee cup and wrapped his arms around Kate. "Don't ever change. I'm a fool for an outspoken woman."

****

Less than an hour later, the ferry docked at Lopez

Island. Kate and Jack stopped at the Village Market. Jack ran inside to buy a bottle of wine while Kate walked Kenya along the grassy area across the road. The unmistakable cry of a young osprey echoed across the sky. A flurry of sailboats crisscrossed the bay. Kenya raised her head, a bead of moisture dripping from the tip of her nose. Kate laughed. "Smells good here, doesn't it, girl?"

The nine-mile drive through gentle, sloping farmland and up into an evergreen forest that grew thick along the cliffs overlooking the Strait of Juan de Fuca allowed Kate time to release any lingering frustration. She felt halfway normal when they drove up and pulled to a stop at their friend's hideaway.

"Uh-oh," Jack said. "Looks like you'll have your chance."

"Chance?" Kate asked.

"To apologize."

The Grand Cherokee with an RNA bumper sticker sat square in the middle of the drive, leaving little room for another car to park. Jack pulled up behind and cut the engine. "Seems this guy is always one step ahead of us."

"Damn. Dickhead must be Emily Ann's son-in-law. I didn't see Laurie on the ferry. I'm not sure I would've recognized her anyway. She was a teenager when I last saw her. This should make for an interesting evening."

Jack laughed. "Let's face the music."

Kate grabbed the wine and headed down the walkway to the house. Wild roses grew over latticework that framed the porch. Their fragrance filled the air with a heavy sweetness that reminded Kate of funerals. She had looked forward to this visit for weeks. Spending the first evening with a man she'd insulted was not a good omen. The few times Kate had visited Emily Ann when her children, Evan and Laurie, were younger, had been a bit tense. Kate had been part of Emily Ann's life in Austin—before she'd married and had children. As much as Kate wanted to visit her old friend, she felt like getting back into the car and driving away.

Jack released Kenya from the travel kennel and walked her around to stretch her legs and sniff her new surroundings. "Don't look so forlorn," he said. "I'll bet Dickhead has a sense of humor, and you two will hit it off after the initial shock wears off."

"I feel like an idiot. You'd think at my age I'd have learned to keep my mouth shut."

"Well, you haven't. That's why I married you. Let's leave the bags. I'll bring them in later."

Just as Kate reached for the doorbell, the door opened. Emily Ann stood there grinning. Her short blonde hair, now heavily streaked with gray, shone brightly. She had lost some weight, but that mischievous sparkle in her eyes was still there.

"Get your butt in here, already," Emily Ann ordered. "It's been too long." She greeted them with hugs and ushered them inside. Two Jack Russell terriers raced over, followed by a big, bouncing golden retriever, tail wagging and tongue lolling.

"Kate, you remember my two girls, Dotty and Speckle. And this big girl with her tongue hanging to the floor is Laurie and Brian's dog, Mattie." The two terriers were appropriately named. Dotty had a brown saddle across her back, and in the center was one small white spot. Speckle looked as though someone had splattered ink across her face.

"They were slick little balls of fur when I was here before," Kate said. "You'd just brought them home from the pound." She scratched Dotty behind her ears.

"Well, they're full-grown and high maintenance," Emily Ann replied. "Jack, you're looking good. Being back in the game agrees with you." She stood on her toes and kissed him on the cheek. "How was your stay in Seattle last night?"

"Great. I got to leave the city this time without my tail between my legs."

Emily Ann gave him a questioning look.

"The last time we were here, Seattle played my team in an inter-league game. Unfortunately, we got roughed up pretty bad."

"Right. I remember. But the season's over." Emily Ann led them into the den.

"Still have your cats?" Kate asked.

Emily Ann laughed and then rolled her eyes. "Do I ever?! My two *Felis domesticus* are out roaming the woods for lizards."

Suddenly the terriers flew across the room and out the doggie door onto the deck. "Obviously something outside needs investigating," Emily Ann said. "Everyone's outside on the deck. Let's go."

Kate looked up. The view never failed to astonish her. Emily Ann's house sat on the edge of a hundred-foot cliff. One huge window overlooked the Strait of Juan de Fuca with the Olympic Mountains shadowing the horizon.

"It's been ages since you've seen Laurie and Evan," Emily Ann said. "They're both grown and have kids. Laurie's here with her husband, Brian, and their two-year-old, Ben. Can you believe I'm a grandmother?"

"Shall we tell her now?" Jack said to Kate.

"Tell me what?"

"We ran into your son-in-law on the ferry on the way over," Kate said.

"I suspected as much." Emily Ann chuckled. "He told us about running into an animal rights activist with a big mouth. I knew it had to be you."

Emily Ann opened the glass door, and Kate and Jack stepped onto the deck. The sun was still high above the evergreens, but a slight breeze promised a chilly evening.

Brian wasted no time. He walked over and shook her hand. "Wikipedia lists a hundred different animal rights groups. I haven't had time to read each one's mission statement, but it's on my to-do list. Can I offer you a glass of wine?" He flashed a confident smile and cocked his head. Kate recognized the benign apology— a gesture not unlike Kenya's when she knocked the pillows off the sofa—and realized that Brian's bark was worse than his bite.

"Thank you, Brian. Wine sounds good. Hope you forgive my rudeness. I wish I could use travel fatigue as an excuse, but at times I'm too outspoken for my own good."

Brian laughed. "It's a common thing here on the islands. The Washington State Ferry System has caused many skirmishes when it comes to loading those boats."

Laurie lounged on a green Adirondack chair. Evan fiddled with the dials on the gas grill. Neither one looked up when Kate and Jack stepped out.

Kate's eyes widened over how unalike they looked. Laurie resembled Emily Ann—fair, delicate features, hair that lightened easily from the sun, and skin that needed protecting from those same sun rays. Evan's olive complexion must have come from his father. She'd never met Emily Ann's ex-husband. Kate had been no part of that episode in her friend's life.

About a year after Emily Ann had left Austin and moved to San Diego, Kate and her father received a phone call. Ecstatic over hearing Emily Ann's voice, Kate got her hopes up that Emily Ann called to say she was coming home to attend Kate's graduation from the university. Instead, Emily Ann announced that she had gotten married. Five years later, Emily Ann had two children, and her calls became less frequent.

Laurie set down her wineglass and gave Kate a tentative hug. Evan saluted her and smiled stiffly. For the first time since she and Jack had planned their trip, Kate felt that a bed and breakfast might have been a better idea. Then she relaxed. Beginning on Monday, Kate would have Emily Ann all to herself.

Emily Ann made the introductions. After a few minutes of uncomfortable small talk, the conversation turned to baseball, with Evan and Brian quizzing Jack about his career in the major league. Laurie went upstairs to check on her sleeping son, and Emily Ann and Kate went back to the kitchen to prepare the food for the grill.

"I'm glad you and Jack are back in the States." Emily Ann handed Kate a pan of vegetables to clean and slice. "Enjoying your time in Chicago, now that your team is winning and have a second World Series under their belt?"

Kate laughed. "Watching the team win and seeing friends again has been nice, but Chicago's a big city. I had gotten used to my simple life in the bush." She stripped the husks from several ears of corn, peeled and sliced a fat eggplant, and did the same with a huge purple onion. She placed them in a pan, reached for the yellow and red bell peppers, split them down the middle, removed the veins, and sliced each into four sections.

Emily Ann pulled a bowl of asparagus from the refrigerator. Kate smiled at Emily Ann going overboard with the veggies to make sure Kate enjoyed her meatless meal. "How do you think these will do on the grill?"

"Great. Hand them over. You must have cleaned out the market's produce." Kate added the asparagus to the pan, sprinkled salt and pepper over everything, and pronounced them ready.

"You're not done yet." Emily Ann grabbed a tray of Cornish hens. "While I take these out to Evan to start grilling, can you make your famous Caesar salad? I think I have everything you need: Parmesan cheese, anchovy paste, minced garlic. Just help yourself."

Kate cubed several slices of stale sourdough bread to make the croutons, laid them on a baking sheet, brushed them with olive oil, and added garlic salt and cheese. She slid the sheet under the broiler.

Emily Ann came back into the kitchen with a bottle of chardonnay and refilled their glasses. "Evan's a grill master," she said. "How long has it been since you two have seen one another?"

"The last time was right before I left for Africa." Kate gathered the anchovy paste, oil, and vinegar, and whisked them together for the salad dressing. "Evan was helping you set up a computer program for your birds."

"Right. I remember now. That program's been invaluable. I can't believe I resisted computerizing my records for so long." Emily Ann paused as if searching for the right words. "How are you doing? I mean, really. Any chance of you going back to Kenya soon?"

Kate removed the croutons from the oven. She felt that all-too-familiar tightening in her chest that often preceded a panic attack, feeling as if she'd stepped to the precipice of a black abyss. It would be so easy to tumble over. It took every ounce of emotional strength not to give in.

"Hey, forget I brought it up. You don't have to talk about it."

"No, it's okay." Kate took a deep breath. "I think about going back every waking moment."

"I can't imagine having to leave Eagle Crossing."

"The bright side is that I've been able to do quite a bit of fundraising since I've been back, so my time away hasn't been a total loss. My staff keeps me informed. Things are settling down. I'm hoping to return to camp in a few months, but…"

"But?"

"Jack's doing so well with his team. I can't see him giving up that position anytime soon."

"How does he feel about you going back?

"He thinks it's still too soon. Africa's a tumultuous place. On one hand, things never seem to change, and, on the other, change occurs so fast it makes your head spin."

"We haven't had a chance to talk about what

happened, why you left so suddenly."

"I'm not sure I'm ready to talk to you about it. Maybe after another glass of wine." Kate forced a laugh. "Anyway, I'm here now."

"There'll be time later." Emily Ann smiled.

"Hey, how many birds do you have?" Kate was grateful for her friend's understanding and took the opportunity to change the subject. "I'm dying to see your aviary."

"Let's go then. I was waiting for the right moment to give you a tour. Right now, I have seventeen birds in all. Eight are permanent residents: five bald eagles, an osprey, a Merlin falcon, and a great horned owl. Unfortunately, their injuries are too severe to ever return them to the wild."

"Thought about breeding the eagles?"

"Actually, I have been. Over the past several years, I've released fourteen of their progeny right here on this ridge. Remember when I started this rescue facility? Bald eagles had just come off the endangered list. Their numbers have increased so much. I like to think I helped in some small way."

A few feet from the back door, a timber-lined pea-gravel trail led through the woods to the aviary. The cages were not visible from the house, but the screech of eagles could be heard anywhere on the property.

"Except for the birds, it's so quiet," Kate said. "No traffic noise, no neighbors blowing leaves, no car stereos thumping."

"Things change, even here on Lopez. I bought this property after it sat on the market for a couple of years. Now when a for-sale sign goes up, the place sells within a week."

Kate followed Emily Ann up the trail. The path skirted the cliff's edge where the trees had thinned, providing a stunning view of the water below and Whidbey Island in the distance. Years ago, during one of her visits, Kate helped Emily Ann haul several wheelbarrows of timbers and tools to this spot. They sawed, hammered, and sweated for two days until Emily Ann had her bench right where she wanted. For Kate, the entire ordeal was a test of courage. Working so close to the steep edge had given her vertigo until she became used to the area.

Kate smiled. The bench had withstood the elements. In fact, Emily Ann had the entire area landscaped. A grove of rhododendrons, their spring blooms barely evident, bordered a small garden. Two pots of thick lavender, now also fading with summer's end, stood on each side of the bench.

"You've turned this into a garden. Your own paradise."

"What can I say? One thing led to another. Between caring for my birds and sitting on this bench every morning with my coffee, I spend more time out here than I do in the house. Sit down for a minute. We have plenty of time before dinner."

"Thanks for inviting us." Kate put her arm around Emily Ann's shoulder. "It's nice to see Laurie and Evan again. They turned out well."

"I suppose so." Emily Ann shrugged.

"Suppose so?" Kate said.

"I swore that when my kids left the nest, I wouldn't be a nosy, advice-giving parent. I did pretty well with Evan, but it was harder with Laurie. I didn't want her to make the same mistakes I did."

"Laurie seems happy."

"Oh, she is. I just wanted her to finish college before she and Brian married, but they saw things differently. Then Laurie got pregnant." Emily Ann stood, walked over to the ridge, and leaned against a madrone tree.

"I'm really sorry about having words with Brian. That was silly of me."

"I'm sure he asked for it. Brian can be immature. Hey, you haven't met my grandson. Ben's a sweetie."

"I haven't met your granddaughters either. Will they be here?"

"Afraid not. Evan and Susan are separated."

"Sorry," Kate said.

"The truth is, I'm so angry at my son, I could scalp him."

"What happened?"

"Oh, you know. Too much too soon. A hefty mortgage, two car payments. When I was their age, marriage, profession, kids—those things hadn't even crossed my mind."

"Yeah, but you were a product of the sixties." Kate chuckled. "And living in Austin, Texas."

"Are you saying my kids rebelled against my hippie ways?" Emily Ann laughed. "I wish it were that simple."

"It usually isn't."

"Certainly not in this case. Susan found out Evan was having an affair with some woman at work. Can you believe it? My son, acting like…like a horny teenager. Susan was willing to work things out, go for counseling, that sort of thing, but Evan packed his bags and left. He refuses to talk to me about it. Susan calls

15

me often. It's so hard on her with the two girls. She's teaching full-time and handling Melissa and Angie by herself. Evan's pretty much out of the picture. Oh, he visits the girls, but that's different from being with them every day."

A murder of crows carried on in the trees above as if to echo Emily Ann's frustration.

After a moment, Kate said, "Everything here smells so clean, like it's just been washed with rain. I'm sure everything will work out."

"And I plan to see that it does."

Kate stared at her friend. Emily Ann's face looked like a smooth piece of marble, imperfections polished over time. Her sixty-seven years looked good on her. But that challenging look—a telltale sign of something soon to come—Kate had first seen it more than two decades ago when Emily Ann packed up her apartment in Hyde Park and left Austin for good. It frightened Kate then. It frightened her now. "What do you mean?"

"Evan and Laurie have been after me for a long time to sell a few acres on the other side of this ridge. You wouldn't believe the price of land here on the island. Evan has this idea that if I sold about ten acres for home sites, I'd have enough money to take the edge off. Hell, I'd be wealthy. I could also control who my neighbors were. Development has already started down the road. In fact, I have a new neighbor. See this trail?" Emily Ann pointed to the left. "It extends over the hill to Jacob Bower's place. He's a retired engineer from somewhere near L.A. A bit odd, if you ask me. Kind of a hermit, but we hit it off pretty well...I guess."

"You guess?"

"Jacob's a little moody. Anyway, I extended my

trail so he could hike up here to the top of the ridge, wind around the cages, and hike back to his place. It's a good, strenuous mile. He enjoys checking on my birds."

"So you've changed your mind about selling part of your land?"

"I most certainly have. I need every acre now. Come on. I'll show you."

Kate followed Emily Ann down the trail, and as they approached the aviary, Kate stopped dead in her tracks. The last time she had visited the place, Emily Ann had six small enclosures. Now the place looked like something one would see in a first-class zoo. Cages reached twenty feet up into the evergreens. Kate scanned the area, her gaze following one enclosure after another as the structures meandered back into the trees as far as she could see.

"Wow! I knew you had expanded Eagle Crossing, but I had no idea. When did you do all this?"

"In the last few weeks."

"You didn't do this by yourself."

"I had help, a friend of mine, Fred Marlow, and a local I hired named Ray Steiner. Ray's become a permanent staff member."

Kate walked around the cages, peering into them. The great-horned owl hooted as she passed its enclosure. It flapped its one good wing, then tucked it close to its body and walked back into a small wooden box that simulated a nest. The next cage looked empty.

"The osprey lives in here. She's up in the top branches somewhere. She's a bit shy. In this cage are two eagles I'll release in a couple of weeks. The one perched on the lower branch came in after being found on the beach entangled in monofilament. Judging by the deep cuts, she must have been struggling for some time. But she's healing nicely."

"And the other one?"

"Brought in with a broken wing. Who knows what happened? I work with a new vet here on the island. She did an incredible job of pinning the wing. I think the bird will be fine."

Kate stepped back to get a better view, shading her eyes from the sun filtering through the trees. Shadows darkened the top of the cage. She backed up a few more feet. A sudden piercing sound caused her to spin around and freeze. A pair of eyes locked on Kate, and her blood chilled. On a moss-covered rock in the middle of an enclosure, a mountain lion rose to its feet and lowered its head.

"Sorry, Kate. We didn't mean to frighten you." Emily Ann rushed over. "She's still getting used to her new home. Like her?"

She took a tentative step forward. The lion intensified her gaze. If the wire cage had not separated them, Kate suspected she'd be the cat's dinner in a matter of seconds. "She's gorgeous, but when did you start taking in stray cats?"

"I was in Santa Rosa last year at the International Wildlife Rehabbers Conference when I met Fred. He rehabs large mammals. His facility is north of San Francisco, and he's running out of room, so I volunteered my place. Fred's a pilot, and he flew her up here last week. We're keeping a low profile. Some folks on the island won't be pleased about me adding a mountain lion to my facility."

"And Laurie and Evan don't know about this?"

"I plan to tell them at dinner tonight. Hit my

recalcitrant kids with a double whammy. Since I have so much room here, and it's so isolated, Fred is moving his entire rehab unit to Eagle Crossing. We've already started building more enclosures. Once they're completed, I'll have four lions here on this mountaintop, along with two bobcats and an ocelot. But that's just the beginning. By the way, I hope you packed a nice outfit."

"Why?"

"Fred and I will take a short break next weekend to get married. You're my maid of honor. Let's go. Dinner should be about ready."

Chapter Two

Emily Ann's simple dining room, an extension of the den, also had a panoramic view of the mountains. The window arched upward and joined the ceiling, creating a solarium effect. A solid oak table and chairs took up much of the space. Despite its minimal furnishings, the room had a homey feeling.

Evan slid open the deck door and announced the hens were ready. A delicious aroma of garlic wafted in, filling the house. Kate brought the salad to the table while Emily Ann and Jack went outside for the rest of the food.

On her way upstairs to get Ben, Laurie called over her shoulder that it might be a good idea if Brian put down his wineglass and came along to help. Splotches of red appeared on his cheeks. He emptied in his glass in one gulp, steadied himself, and followed. Kate suspected that Laurie's request was a guise and that Brian was about to receive a wifely warning concerning his imbibing.

Jack walked in with the platter of grilled vegetables. He set them down in the middle of the table. "Dickhead's not so bad once you get to know him," he whispered. "He's really a pretty funny guy."

"If we don't start calling him by his real name, I'm going to slip and call him by his nom de plume."

"He's also a talker. I've learned more about him in

the last hour than I knew about my mother, but I was grateful for the conversation. Evan pretended to be busy grilling, but I have a strong feeling that he's not thrilled with us visiting."

"Don't feel bad. I'm not one of Evan's favorite people. I think he feels threatened by anyone who was part of his mom's life back in Austin—maybe even blames my father for the divorce."

"But your father and Emily Ann never saw one another after she left for California." He plucked a crouton from the salad and popped it into his mouth.

"They didn't, but I believe she regretted leaving Dad, and that regret found its way into her marriage. I'm sure Evan sensed that, even though he was very young at the time. I need to go upstairs and change."

"Dress for dinner here in the San Juans?" Jack asked.

"At least change out of my jeans into a pair of loose-fitting slacks. With all the food we've prepared, I'll need the extra room. Don't eat any more of those croutons."

On the way upstairs, Kate heard voices, angry voices. She tiptoed past Brian and Laurie's room as Brian barked, "Knock it off, Laurie." Curiosity got the best of Kate, and she stopped.

"Brian, let me talk to Mom. She'll understand," Laurie pleaded.

"No way. I just need a little more time. Honey, I'm sorry. I shouldn't have spoken to you like that. But don't confuse things, Laurie. I know you don't mean to, but please, let's not go over this now. Let's go downstairs and enjoy dinner. Besides, I wanted to come here to relax and think things through. I promise I'll think about what you said. Can't we talk about it in the morning?"

Kate regretted listening and chided herself to mind her own business, but feeling protective of her friend made Kate wish that Laurie and Brian's problems would not become Emily Ann's. She walked down the hall toward her room just as Brian jerked open the door and slammed it behind him. The sudden noise caused a large, dark mass to jump and dart between Kate's feet, almost knocking her over. She suppressed a cry and caught her breath just as Valentine, Emily Ann's gray cat, scampered down the steps.

****

Kate traded her jeans and T-shirt for her black pleated slacks and a white silk blouse—an outfit chosen for comfort. Little good that did. A knot formed in her stomach when she saw the family gathering around the table. She loved Emily Ann dearly, but Kate dreaded her friend's announcements. Maybe Emily Ann would wait until after the meal. People tended to be more reasonable on a full stomach. The wine might help, or it could make things much worse.

Laurie came in, carrying Ben on her hip. The little boy had chubby cheeks like his father. Dressed in olive-green corduroy overalls, a matching checkered shirt, and a tiny hiking boot on his left foot, he looked like a baby model for an outdoor clothing company When he saw the crowd at the table, he stuck his fist in his mouth and buried his face in his mother's neck.

"He wouldn't let me put on his other boot," Laurie said. A fresh layer of makeup covered up most of the evidence that she had been crying.

"Hand him over," Emily Ann said. "You should

have let him sleep, Laurie. Poor baby's had a long day."

"He's not the only one," Brian said through clenched jaws.

Laurie shot her husband a hateful look. "I couldn't do that, Mom. If I did, he'd be hungry and wide awake later tonight."

"You can sit with me, honey," Emily Ann said. "Say hi to my friends, Kate and Jack."

Ben squirmed and started to fuss.

"I have something I think you'll like." Emily Anne sat Ben in the high chair and placed a small bowl of tiny cheese crackers on the tray. He tentatively stuck his hand in the bowl, drew out a fistful, and turned away again.

"I'm starved," Brian said. He reached over and helped himself to two pieces of garlic bread.

Evan sighed and started passing the platters and bowls around the table. Brian tried to engage his brother-in-law with talk about their high-tech jobs in Seattle, but Evan did little more than roll his eyes and grunt. The conversation drifted to increased property taxes and how living in the city had become outrageously expensive. No matter what statement Brian made, Evan jumped to disagree.

Hoping to ease the growing tension at the table, Jack said, "What company do you work for, Evan?"

"A software company called EnviroTech. I've been with them since college. In the last ten years, it's grown from a small start-up to a multi-million-dollar company with almost three hundred employees. I head up the video division."

"EnviroTech? Don't you have a friend that works for them?" Jack turned to Kate.

"Jill Michaels. She lived in Chicago before moving here. I think she works in personnel."

"I've heard of her," Evan said. "But as I said, it's a big company now."

"I've tried to talk Evan into coming to work for me," Brian said, filling his plate a second time. "I could use someone with experience. And I keep telling him that he's wasting his time. I used to work for one of the big tech firms and got out two years ago to start my own business. Working for a huge company stifles you. Unless you get in on the ground floor, you're just there to put money in the bigwigs' pockets."

"I did get in on the ground floor," Evan said, his voice cold and hard. "You seem to have forgotten that. And that bull about being stifled is just an excuse unless you don't know what you're doing."

Evan's abruptness only added to Brian's antagonism. He refilled his glass, placing the bottle next to his plate. "Yeah, but you'll never get rich working for others."

"And you are?" Evan scoffed.

"Just a matter of time, buddy. Just a matter of time. Besides, making my own hours gives me time to focus on what's important, like my family."

Evan glared at Brian.

"Sounds like an enterprising business." Jack turned to Kate. "Brian was telling us about it earlier. He designs inventory software programs for new businesses."

"I opened my doors two years ago, and I have more contracts than I can handle." Brian emptied the wine bottle. Laurie looked as if she were about to come unglued but said nothing.

Kate glanced at Emily Ann, whose plate was barely touched. She hadn't spoken much during dinner. Ben squirmed, and Laurie lifted him out of his chair. He waddled off into the den. Emily Ann started after him.

"It's okay, Mom. He's eaten enough," Laurie said.

"Anyone for cheesecake and coffee?" Emily Ann asked.

"I'll make the coffee, Mom." Laurie rose from the table. Suddenly, Ben let out a loud wail and the Jack Russells flew out the doggie door.

"Laurie, could you do something about him? He's got to learn to leave the dogs alone," Brian said.

"He's just tired, honey. It's been a long day."

"I'll get Ben," Jack said. "Four dogs and one little boy. Doesn't seem like an even match to me."

Kate gathered up a stack of plates and followed Laurie into the kitchen.

"I hope you didn't take offense to my husband's earlier comments when we ran into you on the ferry." Laurie filled the coffee pot. "Brian's from a long line of hunters. He takes his sport seriously."

"I'm the one who should apologize. I have a big mouth." Kate began filling the dishwasher.

"Brian doesn't always act this way. He's a reasonable, open-minded person, except when he gets in the same room with my brother. I'm sorry for their childish behavior."

"Where did you and Brian meet?"

"In college. We hit it off immediately. We'd dated only two weeks before Brian brought me home to Idaho to meet his huge family. I still can't keep all their names straight."

Kate sliced the cheesecake and gathered a stack of

25

plates. "A large family can be fun."

"That's an understatement. The Fullers are a blast, but they took a while to get used to. Our family's so small." Laurie's cheeriness suddenly disappeared. "With just the two of us growing up with Mom. Dad was absent from the picture. He remarried soon after their divorce and started a *new* family." Laurie took a carton of cream from the refrigerator, filled a small pitcher, and set it on a tray. "Brian wants a large family." She forced a smile. "That's fine with me. He's a great father. He's so devoted to Ben."

"I'm happy for you, Laurie."

"Thanks. I guess, as an adult, you look for what you missed growing up. I'm being silly. But I'm glad you're here, Kate. I've been worried about Mom lately."

"In what way?"

Laurie took several mugs from the cabinet. "I'm not sure. It's just that she's been too quiet. I know something's bothering her. I've asked, but she always gives me some flimsy reason like she's overworked with the aviary, or she's overextended herself volunteering at the library. How does she seem to you?"

Kate was unsure how to answer, so she went with the most obvious. "Working with injured animals, wild animals especially, can not only be physically exhausting but can take a toll emotionally as well."

"What do you mean?"

"It's easy to get attached to the animals we care for. There's no nice ending. If the animal survives, we return it to the wild. And if we've raised it, that can be difficult." Kate's attempt to reassure Laurie did not do much good.

"But she's had this facility for years," Laurie responded. "Maybe it's too much work for her at her age. Maybe it's time she slowed down."

"Hey, are you two scarfing all that cheesecake, or what?" Brian called from the table.

"When it comes to dessert, my husband can be a pig." Laurie picked up the tray. "We're on our way. Honey, can you check on Ben?" she called to her husband.

Kate passed around the cheesecake and Laurie the coffee mugs. Brian called from the stairs. "Start without me. I'm going to put Ben to bed. Be down in a minute."

Emily Ann started to get up from the table. "I'll take care of Ben and let Brian enjoy dessert."

"No, Mom. Brian can do it. As soon as Ben lies down, he'll be asleep."

Brian returned a few minutes later, and Laurie went into the kitchen to get him a fresh cup of coffee.

"Asleep?" Emily Ann said.

"What?" Brian picked up his fork and then set it down. He reached for his wineglass but found it empty. "Oh, yeah. He was asleep before I got him undressed."

"You okay?" Laurie asked.

"I'm fine," he said. "I guess I've had a long day too."

Kate glanced at Emily Ann, curious about how her friend would bring the conversation around to her upcoming marriage and the facility's new addition. She needn't have worried. Brian provided the impetus.

"Kate, you and my mother-in-law are two peas in a pod," he said. "Is it that misplaced maternal instinct that makes you two want to work with orphaned animals?"

Kate detected a slight edge to his voice. Before she

could answer, Laurie piped up. "Brian, shut up and eat your cheesecake."

"Brian likes to tease me about my animal rescue work, but being an avid member of Ducks Unlimited, he understands the need for conservation." Emily Ann winked at her son-in-law. "He just likes to play the devil's advocate." She pushed aside her uneaten dessert and took a sip of coffee. She glanced at Kate. "Speaking of rehabbing animals, I will be making some changes around here."

Evan spoke for the first time since the conversation drifted away from business. "Mother, this is a family matter. Let's not discuss it now."

"We're all family. I've already spoken to Kate about it."

Wrong thing to say. Kate fought hard to keep from coming to her own defense.

Jack rose and started stacking the dessert plates to take to the kitchen.

"Leave those, Jack. I'll get them later," Emily Ann said.

"No problem. I'll take these to the kitchen and bring back the coffee pot," he said.

"Evan and Laurie, I understand your concerns about me handling the work." Emily Ann sighed. "But someday you'll be grateful that I decided not to sell the acreage along the ridge."

Evan threw his napkin on the table. "Mother, we've been through this several times. The property taxes are killing you. You don't need that land. Why keep it?"

"I do need it, honey. My financial situation isn't as bad as you make out. Besides, I'm expanding my facility. I've already started."

"Mom, you can barely keep up as it is," Laurie chimed in. "And that crazy Ray-guy you have working for you is scary. Where did you ever find him anyway? He looks like he lives in the county dump."

"Ray's harmless," Emily Ann responded.

"Besides," Laurie continued, "you should be relaxing, taking it easy, not adding more work for yourself."

"This work is my life," Emily Ann said.

"Maybe your family should be your life," Evan huffed. "How are you going to manage this? What's going on? Eagles are falling out of the sky, and you've appointed yourself their sole guardian? A hobby's one thing, but you've become obsessed with this crazy cause."

With Evan's last remark, Emily Ann's forbearance started to wane as a deep flush spread across her face.

"Evan!" Laurie shouted.

"Shall I break out another bottle of wine and top off your glass?" Brian said and pointed to his and Emily Ann's empty glasses.

The gesture made Emily Ann laugh. "Hear me out. You talk as if I have one foot in the grave. Bottom line, Evan, this is my property. I'm adding new cages to house other animals. Not many people do wildlife rehab work, and there's a great need for it. Anyway, I'll not be working alone. I'll have help." Emily Ann glanced at Kate. "A gentleman named Fred Marlow and I are partnering up. He's worked in rehab longer than I have."

"How are you going to afford more animals and pay hired help?" Evan asked.

"Fred isn't hired help, and finances won't be a problem." Emily Ann picked up her wine and took a gulp. "Fred and I are getting married next weekend."

"You're full of surprises, Emily Ann!" Brian chuckled. "This calls for a toast. Here's to my dear mother-in-law." He started to rise.

"Sit down!" Laurie swatted her husband on the shoulder. "Next weekend! Mom, have you lost your mind? How long have you known this guy? We haven't even met him."

"You will, honey. He's flying in on Sunday. We'll have brunch as soon as he gets here, before you head back to the city."

"This is unbelievable, Mother. Laurie's right. Next weekend?" Evan's words were barely audible through his pinched lips. "Why are you rushing into this? Have you considered what this might mean?"

"I'm not getting any younger, as you keep pointing out. I've known Fred for months. He's been here building the additional cages, and in a few days, he'll fly the rest of his animals over. There's nothing to consider. My mind's made up. Besides, we have a lot of work to do."

"I'm at your service while I'm here. Congratulations, Emily Ann," Jack said. "Kate and I are happy for you."

"Did you know about this?" Evan turned to Kate.

"I told her while we were up at the cages, Evan."

"Hey, I haven't even seen your facility yet," Jack said, trying once more to ease the tension. "We still have a little daylight. Kate can show me around."

Kate smiled. Her husband's ability to mediate had become a honed skill and a lifesaver on more than one

30

occasion. Tonight, however, his attempt failed.

"What do you mean, 'fly the animals over?' " Evan asked, ignoring Jack. "What's this guy bringing, an entire zoo?"

"I've always wanted to try my hand with mammal rehabilitation. So far, so good. My latest ward and I haven't killed one another."

"Mom, what are you talking about?" Laurie said. "What ward?"

"A mountain lion. She is healing nicely from buckshot wounds. If she continues at this rate, we'll transport her to Alaska for release in a few weeks."

"A mountain lion! Don't tell me you have a lion here on the property. Mom, did you even think about your grandson?"

"The lion isn't wandering around loose, and Ben isn't going to trot up the ridge to the cage."

"We're not staying here!"

"Laurie, you're overreacting."

"No, I'm not! Brian, call Windsong Inn, or Moon Glow, or whatever. We're leaving!"

"You're being ridiculous, young lady." Emily Ann's anger finally surfaced. "I've planned this weekend for—"

"For whom, Mom? For your family?" Laurie ran upstairs, and Brian followed.

"Laurie, come back here!" Emily Ann declared.

"I'm not staying in this house with that wild cat in the friggin' backyard!" Laurie called over her shoulder.

"Time for that tour. I'll get your jacket." Jack grabbed Kate's hand and led her from the table.

Evan's glare followed Kate to the back door.

****

Kate and Jack climbed the ridge to the eagles' cages. Filtering through the tall evergreens, the bright scarlet and golden afterglow of the sunset gave the illusion that the forest in the distance was on fire. The quiet was intoxicating.

"Sorry. I had no idea what we were getting into," Kate said.

"What? You imagined us having a relaxing vacation?" Jack chuckled. "We've yet to do that. We weren't in Wimberley, Texas, five minutes last summer when you found Jesús Flores' mangled pickup covered in blood. And we hadn't even finished our first meal with Max and Olga before the sheriff arrived announcing he'd found Flores' body."

Kate and Jack wandered around the cages and then over to Emily Ann's bench. She sat and hugged her jacket tight around her. The wind had picked up, turning the evening cool.

"I seem to go from one catastrophe to another," Kate said.

"Hey, forget it. Playing with the team all those years prepared me for it."

"Laurie and Evan have no right telling their mother what to do," Kate said. "Or how she should handle her finances."

"Is Evan always so edgy?"

"He's having marital problems."

"I figured that since he's here alone."

"This should be a happy occasion for Emily Ann. She's excited about her new venture. I hate to see her upset over this."

"They'll have to work this out themselves. Maybe once Laurie and Evan meet Fred, they'll take a liking to him."

"You think so?"

"No, but that's not our concern. Let's call it a day. I'm beat. I'll take Kenya for a short walk."

****

Kate helped Emily Ann clean the kitchen. She tried a few words of encouragement. When that didn't work, Kate changed the subject. An hour later, she went upstairs and fell into bed.

"How's Emily Ann?" Jack asked, setting down his novel.

"She's tired."

"Aren't we all?"

Kenya hopped onto the bed and wriggled between them, stretching out sideways.

"This will be nice and cozy," Jack said, sliding the greyhound around. Kenya responded by turning onto her back and extending all four legs into the air. Kate and Jack laughed.

"She's used to our king-size bed," Kate said.

"It didn't take long to spoil her. I'll throw the blanket over her legs, and we'll have a cozy tent to sleep under."

Minutes later, they had settled into a reasonable sleeping arrangement. Kate woke to the smell of coffee brewing and bright light shining from the window. She rolled over and curled up alone in the middle of the bed. Sleeping late was a rarity, and she was grateful that Jack and Kenya had crept out, allowing her to luxuriate in bed. But the aroma of fresh coffee was irresistible. Kate pulled on her robe, washed her face, and hurried downstairs to a quiet house.

A stainless travel mug sat on a note on the kitchen

table. "Jack has volunteered to walk the dogs, and I'm having my coffee on our bench. You can join me if you ever get out of bed. Emily Ann." Kate filled the mug with coffee and rushed upstairs to change.

Kate stepped outside to a glorious day. A few clouds drifted over, and a mild breeze blew from the south. Just as she reached the trail, a burly figure dressed in a flannel shirt and sweatpants rushed by, almost running into her. He nodded and mumbled something that sounded like "Good morning" and hurried by. Kate made her way to the bench and sat down next to Emily Ann.

"I think I just met your neighbor."

"Jacob. Yes, he just passed by on his morning walk. A man of few words." Emily Ann paused and then put her arm around Kate's shoulder. "Sorry about last night. I knew the news wouldn't be well received, but I was surprised at my children's rude reaction."

"Laurie and Brian haven't left the island, I hope?"

"No. They checked in at Windsong Inn. I called this morning and talked to Brian. He said Laurie was still asleep, but I suspect she was awake and just refused to talk to me. Evan closeted himself in his room. In a little while, I'm driving to the market to pick up some things. Want to come along?"

"Do I have time for a jog and a shower?"

"Certainly. I'll have some walnut and cream scones ready by the time you get back. Remember the road down to Watmough Bay Beach? If you run the beach road and back and then down to where Watmough Head Road dead ends, it's about three miles."

"Perfect."

Kate met Jack and his wards walking up from the

bay, all the dogs running harum-scarum down the road, happy to be off their leashes. Dotty and Speckle looked like two white rats next to the long, lanky Kenya, who had no clue as to her size.

"The bay's beautiful this morning. A sailboat anchored offshore, but you'll have the beach to yourself. I found a forest trail that leads up to the top of Chadwick Hill. Maybe we can hike it while we're here."

"It's a date. Thanks for letting me sleep in."

"Are you kidding? You were too cute to wake, hugging your pillow and snoring like an old man." Dotty started barking at something in the woods. Jack leashed her before she could take off. "I'll take these two mutts back before they disappear after a chipmunk. Why don't you take Kenya with you for the rest of your jog? She needs the exercise."

"Good idea. I'll see you back at the house. And I don't snore."

Kate took Kenya's leash and continued her jog. When she and Jack first adopted the greyhound from Molly Gibson's rescue kennel in Wimberley, Texas, the dog had been traumatized from a bad racing accident. It took weeks for her hip to heal enough that she quit whimpering every time she stood. Now, except for a slight limp, the greyhound was as good as new. After Kenya recovered enough to run again, Kate trained the greyhound to trot alongside her without pulling her down the road. At first, she kept Kenya on the leash, concerned that the dog would bolt as she'd been trained to do during her three years as a racer. But now, the greyhound pranced gracefully and stayed at heel position.

They trotted down the road to the trail that led to the beach. The sun was well over the Cascades, warming up the U-shaped bay. A dinghy rested on the shore. A bald eagle glided overhead, then swooped over the water. Kate watched as it soared up to the top of a Douglas fir on Chadwick Hill. She shaded her eyes against the sun and looked closer. Then she saw it, a massive nest about the size of a small boat. Any fledglings that had called the nest home in the summer were gone now, out fishing for their own food.

"A rescue dog?" someone shouted.

Kate turned to see a brown, wrinkled man standing on the bow of his sailboat moored just offshore.

He wore swimming trunks and a baseball cap and had a coffee mug in his hand.

"Yes, she is," Kate shouted back.

The man raised his mug in salute. "See my wife anywhere? She pulled ashore a little while ago to go bird watching. She loves greyhounds. She'll be sorry she missed seeing your dog."

"Maybe next time." Kate waved goodbye. She and Kenya left the beach to continue their run down the main road.

Emily Ann's place came into view as Evan coasted down the drive on his bike toward the village. If he'd seen her, he didn't let on.

Kate slowed as she approached the driveway. She reached down to remove the leash, but Kenya erupted, barking and lunging forward. Kate grabbed Kenya before she could charge. A man came around from the back of the garage. Startled, he dropped his armload of supplies. A bag of food pellets split, and pellets scattered across the pavement.

"Sorry," Kate said. "She never acts that way. I've got her." She jerked on Kenya's leash, and the dog reluctantly sat. "You must be Ray."

"I don't like dogs, ma'am." Laurie's assessment of Emily Ann's hired hand was right on the money. His flannel shirt looked like he'd used it as a cleaning rag. His hair needed shampooing, and his long scraggly beard hung down past the bib of his patched overalls.

"I'll put Kenya in the house, and then I'll help you with that."

"No, ma'am. I can manage. Thanks just the same," he said, his eyes on the greyhound.

Kenya stared, intent on Ray's every move. Kate had to drag her toward the house.

Kate opened the back door, and the pleasant smell of scones brought on hunger pangs. She hesitated when she saw Emily Ann pacing across the kitchen, gripping the cell phone in her hand.

"Okay. Fine, then!" Emily said. "But I don't understand what you have to think over. I know you're upset, but your feelings won't change anything, Laurie. So I suggest you come over right now, and we'll talk about this."

After a pause Emily Ann let out a deep sigh. "Fred will be here tomorrow. Think as much as you want today, but I want you, Brian, and Ben here in the morning. Understand? Fred's expecting to meet my family, and I'll not have him disappointed—Damn!"

"Sounds like Laurie's still upset."

"She hung up on me! She's angry because she had to board Mattie. The inn doesn't allow dogs. This is all such nonsense. Evan's upset too. He threatened to leave today, but I put my foot down. I told him that he'll stay

37

and meet Fred tomorrow, or else. He stormed out of here a few minutes ago without saying a word."

"I saw him on the way out. He looked as if he were competing in the Tour de France. It sounds like Laurie's not coming today?"

"No. I'll call later and talk to Brian. For all his faults, my son-in-law can be reasonable. It looks like it'll just be the three of us for most of today. Still want to go to the village with me?"

"Let me get cleaned up. I'm sure Jack will come, too. But I'm not leaving without sampling those scones. Be down in a sec. Oh, I just met Ray. I'm afraid Kenya scared the hell out of him."

"Ray's not a dog person. I'm not sure what his problem is. I even have to keep my little mongrels inside when he's here. When I advertised for help, Ray was the only islander who applied. Unfortunately, he doesn't always show up on time. We've had a few talks about that."

"I'm sure jobs on the island are scarce."

"I try to be sympathetic. Ray and his wife are scraping out a living and trying to get around with one unreliable car. I know times are tough, and I'm trying to be patient. He's responsible for the feedings, and I must be able to depend on him. We're working through it. He's great with the eagles, though."

"He's not scared of cats, is he?"

"No, thank goodness." She laughed. "He seems okay with cats, wild and domestic."

As Kate ran upstairs, the phone rang.

"Laurie, sweetheart, please stop crying. It's okay," Emily Ann said. "Maybe I shouldn't have dumped it on you that way. I know it was a lot to take in."

When they left for the village, Evan had still not returned. Yesterday Kate wished that she and Jack had Emily Ann to themselves and, now that the wish had come true, Kate felt guilty. But Emily Ann seemed happy this morning, and Kate decided not to worry.

"Hey, I have an idea," Emily Ann said. "Let's drive to Agate Beach before we head to the village. I'd love to show you and Jack Iceberg Point. It's a short hike from the road near the beach. I spotted a huge flock of common murres feeding off the rocks a couple of days ago, and today's too perfect for sitting around indoors. We can pick up what we need at the market later."

The trail to Iceberg Point opened up to blue water and the tip of San Juan Island. A few murres and several species of gulls floated on the waves just offshore. Black oystercatchers probed the rocks for mussels onshore. A colony of dozing harbor seals sunned themselves on the rock below the cliff. Using the binoculars, Kate spotted a bird she'd never seen before, a black turnstone living up to its name.

Back in the village, they stopped for coffee at Honey Bee's Bakery. Jack insisted on searching the liquor store for a good bottle of port. And after filling two shopping carts with groceries, they returned home and spent the afternoon lounging around, listening to Harry Connick Jr. Evan had returned, but sequestered himself in his room. He finally emerged as Emily Ann and Kate laid out cold cuts and bread for a simple dinner. Kate had made a blue-cheese potato salad, and Jack opened a bottle of anchovy-stuffed Kalamata olives. Evan apologized for staying away all day, blaming his absence on work that had to be done. He made a sandwich, sniffed the potato salad, and decided against it. He poured a glass of wine and took his dinner upstairs.

Time had a way of taking the edge off bad situations. Kate and Jack helped Emily Ann tend to her birds and her new feline. Before they knew it, the bright sky had turned a steel flat gray that seemed to hang heavy and compress the atmosphere.

Once they settled in for the evening, Jack built a fire in the fireplace, and Kate picked up the novel she'd been reading. Emily Ann went to her office to update her notes. When Emily Ann emerged, Kate could see her friend looked relaxed.

"Brian called and left a message," Emily Ann said, joining Kate on the sofa. "He said Laurie was feeling better, and he promised they'd be here to meet Fred in the morning. Brian took Ben to the Long Ranch Riding Stables and let him ride a pony. All in all, the day worked out well. The best part for me was spending time with the two of you. I really needed that. My children can be high drama."

"You think?"

Emily Ann laughed and tossed a pillow at Kate.

"Hey," Jack called from the kitchen. "Guess what I found?" He walked into the den carrying three plates of cheesecake. "The remains of last night's dessert. I made a pot of coffee. After we finish this off, I'll open the bottle of port."

Jack watched *The Shawshank Redemption* for the umpteenth time. Kate and Emily Ann finalized the menu for the next day's brunch. Emily Ann had perked up, and they spent the next hour chatting. Kate loved seeing the sparkle in her friend's eyes when she mentioned Fred Marlow. Emily Ann was clearly in love. By the time they drained the bottle of port, it was after eleven, and they called it a night. Not used to so much sweet alcohol, Kate swallowed two ibuprofens and drank a glass of water before crawling into bed. She fell asleep before her dog and husband joined her.

Kate's body jerked. Her eyes shot open, and she sprang up in bed. The tail end of a fading sound echoed in her head. She listened, then realized that it wasn't a sound that had awakened her. It was silence and a strange sense of things not being as they should.

Kate stared at the clock. Her mind, slow on the uptake, refused to believe it was ten minutes after seven. In Kenya, she would have been up well before dawn. Sunlight spilled in through the window. Uncertain of where she was, she looked around, recognizing Kenya's chew-toy on the floor near the love seat. Then she remembered getting up in the middle of the night and stepping on the hard piece of rawhide as she went to open a window. Lately, she'd been having night sweats, her skin clammy enough to dampen the sheets. Menopause at her age was unusual but not unheard of. Now the room was cold.

Reality slowly filtered in as the fog cleared from her mind. She was at Emily Ann's. Jack and Kenya must have risen early and gone for a walk. Oversleeping this morning did not have the same satisfying feeling it had yesterday. Old guilt, her unnecessary baggage, as Jack liked to call it, tended to surface at odd times, catching her off guard, reminding her of something she should have done, something she should have said, something she should have fixed. It weighed heavily like a huge slug crawling up her back and over her shoulder. Kate threw back the covers and stepped out of bed.

Last night, their planning sounded perfect. Emily Ann wanted comforting, nurturing food—food that would bring a reluctant family together. Food that would fill the house with delicious smells and soothe ill feelings. Today they'd all dine together—sort things out. By the time Kate's deep-dish apple pie got to the table, the situation wouldn't seem so bad, or so she hoped.

Kate pulled on her jeans and sweatshirt and went downstairs to an odd feeling and an empty kitchen. *Emily Ann must be sleeping late also. Good*, Kate thought. *Emily Ann needs her rest.*

Kate peered out the patio door. A light mist hung in the air. Still a bit groggy, she set the coffee to brew and decided to hike the ridge trail to get her blood flowing. At the opening of the door, Dotty and Speckle ran into the kitchen.

"Where were you two when Jack and Kenya left? Too lazy to get out of bed? I should talk." Kate grabbed their leashes. "Okay, girls. Let's go. We'll let Mom sleep a little longer. A morning walk will do us all some good." Not waiting to be leashed, the dogs darted ahead, and Kate scrambled to keep up with them. A light fog had moved over the mountain, shrouding the treetops. Speckle bolted up the trail and headed straight for Emily Ann's bench. She started digging, flinging dirt about her like a badger rooting out a meal. Her yelping caught her sister's attention, and Dotty ran over to investigate. The dogs scurried around, dancing a little too close to the edge. Kate called them away. Emily Ann's plan for putting up the rock barrier along this cliff was a good idea. Too much ground had eroded over the years, and if Emily Ann did not act quickly, her favorite spot, the bench, the garden, and all, would slide down the cliff.

Kate leashed the Jack Russells, Speckle whining in protest. She walked over for a closer look, and her breath caught. A good-sized chunk of earth had crumbled away since yesterday. Kate shivered, imagining one of the dogs falling to her death. Without warning, Dotty erupted into a frenzy, and Kate had a hard time keeping the dog from choking herself with the leash. Kate crept closer to the edge to see what all the fuss was about.

As her mind made sense of what she saw, an unseen force struck her chest, knocking the air out of her lungs and turning her insides to liquid. She jerked the dogs away, stumbled, and fell back onto the bench. Hallucinations. Of course. Too much wine the night before. Too much sleep. Then panic rose in her chest, and she rushed back for another look. *God, no!* Kate's words echoed in her head. She tied the leashes to the bench, then ran back to the ridge, looking frantically for a trail to the bottom. There was none. It was too late anyway. Emily Ann could not have survived the fall.

Chapter Three

Too stunned to speak, Kate and Jack listened to the sirens grow louder and sat on the back porch steps. Kate's mind drifted back to two days ago when she fretted about something as insignificant as arriving late for the ferry. And then last night, the fun they had, laughing and indulging themselves like teenagers. Now Emily Ann was gone. All of the questions she had for Emily Ann—why she suddenly left Austin, why she didn't attend Kate's father's funeral, why she shied away from certain topics—would remain unanswered. Kate laid her head on Jack's shoulder. He wrapped his arms around her. His warmth offered immediate comfort.

Within minutes of the first siren, the property was crawling with emergency personnel. EMS technicians, volunteer firefighters, and officers from the San Juan County Sheriff's Department made their way to the cliff's edge. Deputy Dave Fitzroy was in the house gathering information. Evan responded to the deputy's questions with a shout. Laurie was hysterical, and Ben was bawling. Brian, red-faced and growing impatient, couldn't handle both Laurie and his son. Jack offered to take Ben away from the melee, and Brian was only too happy to consent. Finally, a doctor, who arrived with the EMS team, tried to get Laurie to take a sedative.

A man Kate did not recognize drove up, rushed out

of the car and into the house. "What's going on here?"

Kate hurried over to him. "Mr. Marlow? I'm Emily Ann's friend, Kate Caraway."

"Where's Emily Ann?"

"There's been an accident. I'm sorry, but Emily Ann fell from the ridge this morning. I'm afraid she's dead."

The tragedy took hold. His knees buckled, and he grabbed the banister. Kate grasped his arm and helped him sit down on the stairs. Fred turned white and said nothing.

"Mr. Marlow?" Kate sat down beside him.

"Emily Ann's dead?" Fred whispered. "No, she's not. She's not."

Kate took him by the shoulders and forced him to stand. "Mr. Marlow, please come upstairs with me. Please." He offered no resistance. They went upstairs to the room where Kate and Jack were staying.

Fred Marlow sat on the edge of the bed and removed his well-worn felt hat. His close-cut hair and goatee, a subtle shade of blond-gray, blended with the color of his skin. The few extra pounds he carried only added to his healthy, robust appearance. His work with wildlife rehabilitation was evident from the scratches and scars that marred his big hands. Fred turned to Kate, his blue eyes glistening with tears. "We were going to be married in a few days."

Kate wanted to give him time to compose himself, to prepare him for the reception he was certain to receive from Emily Ann's children. She was considering what to say when Jack walked in holding Ben with one hand and carrying a glass of brandy in the other. The toddler was sucking on a Popsicle.

"Mr. Marlow, I'm Jack Ryder. I saw you drive up." He handed Fred the brandy.

Fred took a deep swallow, and the color began to return to his face, and for the first time, he seemed to notice Kate and Jack.

"You're Emily Ann's friends from Chicago," he said. "Emily Ann was so happy about you coming. I can't believe this."

"Mr. Marlow—" Kate said.

"Fred. Call me Fred. How could Emily Ann have fallen off that ridge? She's familiar with every inch of that trail."

"It looks like the ground crumbled from underneath her," Kate said.

"Emily Ann wouldn't stand that close to the edge. That's crazy." He drank some more brandy. "I flew in this morning looking forward to meeting everybody and…and to celebrate."

Kate looked at Jack.

"What? What is it? Something else has happened," Fred said.

"No. It's just that…Emily Ann's children weren't exactly overjoyed with the news of your engagement." Kate looked at Jack for help.

"Friday night during dinner, Emily Ann told us about your plans to marry and to expand the rehab facility," Jack added. "Then Laurie found out about the lion being here and became hysterical, afraid for the safety of her son." Jack paused to wipe the Popsicle melting down Ben's arm.

Fred sat in disbelief. And then, as if returning to reality, he noticed Ben. "Oh, heavens. Is this Emily Ann's grandson?"

"This is Ben," Jack said. "He's starting to get sticky, I'm afraid."

Fred stood and held out his hands. Ben raised his arms and went to Fred without hesitation. "Let's go meet the rest of the family."

"There's more," Kate said.

"I'm listening."

"Emily Ann's son, Evan became furious when he found out Emily Ann had decided not to sell the property," Kate said. "After that, things erupted into a family quarrel."

"Well, avoiding them will do no good."

Kate and Jack followed Fred downstairs. To Kate's surprise, Evan came over and introduced himself. "I suppose you're Fred Marlow. I'm Emily Ann's son, Evan Thurston. That's my sister, Laurie, and her husband, Brian. I see you've met Ben."

Laurie sat on the sofa with her head laid back and her eyes closed. She did not acknowledge the introduction.

"Will you look at that?" Brian said. "Ben never goes to strangers. You must have a way with kids, Mr. Marlow."

"Please, everyone call me Fred. Evan, what have you learned?"

Evan flinched when Fred called him by his first name. Evan shut his eyes. He rubbed the palms of his hands over his forehead. "What do you mean? Mother fell. What's there to learn?"

"What can I do to help?" Fred asked. He sat on the sofa next to Laurie, perching Ben on his knee.

"We can handle things," Evan retorted, his voice hard and cold. "Mother had everything pretty well laid out. She's to be cremated."

"If you don't mind, I'd like to stay here for the next few days. Someone will have to take care of the animals, and I'm familiar with Emily Ann's routine," Fred said.

"Jack and I will help," Kate offered.

Laurie's eyes shot open. "You will not stay in this house!" she said to Fred. "This is all your fault." She reached over and grabbed her son. The boy started crying.

"I understand you're upset, but we have to be—" Before Fred could make his plea, Deputy Fitzroy walked in.

"We've brought up the body. Mrs. Thurston will be taken to the medical clinic for a postmortem."

"Why?" Laurie shouted. "Why is that necessary?"

"It's routine," he explained, "whenever an unexpected death occurs. Detective Clover will be here shortly. He'll need to speak to everyone here." He twisted his hat in his hands.

He can't be more than twenty-five years old, Kate thought. She suspected he had not gotten used to retrieving dead bodies.

"Was Mrs. Thurston planning on releasing one of her birds this morning?" Deputy Fitzroy said.

"Not as far as I know," Kate said. "She has two that were to be released soon, but they're still recovering."

"That's right," Fred said. "What makes you ask, Sheriff?"

"Deputy. Deputy Dave Fitzroy. One of the cages is wide open."

Fred stood up. "Which cage?"

"It looks like a newer one. Large, but not as tall as the others."

Fred ran out the back door and disappeared up the trail.

"What was that all about?" Brian said.

"Everyone stay in the house!" Kate rushed after Fred. "That's the mountain lion's cage."

Chapter Four

Moments later, Fred returned with two dart guns. "The lion's out all right. Just keep everyone inside, including the dogs. She's got to be close by. She's injured and can't go far."

"I'll call for help," Deputy Fitzroy said. "But the sheriff's on San Juan Island. It will take him at least forty-five minutes to get here."

"We can't wait," Fred said. "Besides, the more people milling around, the worse it'll be. I don't want the animal frightened any more than she is."

"I can't deal with this," Laurie cried.

"Take Ben upstairs, honey. I'll check on the dogs and bring them in." Brian rushed out.

Fred handed Kate one of the guns. "I assume you know how to use this. It's loaded and ready to go. I've also got a trap net and tarp, which I'd rather use than the guns. I don't want to dart her unless necessary. She's not a big cat, and if I can throw the net over her, two or three of us should be able to wrap the tarp over her and carry her back to the cage."

Kate took the gun, checked the dart, and nodded.

"I'll send the guys back to the village with Mrs. Thurston's body," Deputy Fitzroy said. "Let's get this done. I don't want word to get out and have everyone on the island in a panic."

"I need everyone here to help. We'll split into two

groups," Fred said. "Evan, Deputy Fitzroy, and I will check around the cages and the shed where Emily Ann kept food and supplies. Kate, Jack, and Brian can head up along the ridge. Let's go."

"You must be out of your mind if you think I'm going to stalk a lion through these woods," Evan said. "What if it sees us first and attacks?"

"She's more frightened than you are," Fred responded. "If you see her, don't approach."

"Oh, yeah. Like I would walk up to a mountain lion and try to slip a leash around its neck," Evan said. "I'm staying right here. I'm no fool. That's what killed Mother. The lion got loose and attacked her while she stood there watching the sunrise. You guys can play the big white hunters. I've got funeral arrangements to make." Evan stormed off upstairs after Laurie.

"Let's get Brian," Kate said to Jack. "Fred's right. We can't waste any more time." They walked into the den and found all three dogs safely inside. Sitting on the window ledge was one of Emily Ann's house cats, a tortoiseshell with golden eyes whose name had escaped Kate. The shy Valentine was undoubtedly in one of her hiding places. With all pets accounted for, Kate locked the doggie door. Then she and Jack went outside to look for Brian, but he was nowhere in sight. Kate called his name. No response. "Damn! Looks like our resident hunter has taken off."

"Like Evan said, stalking lions isn't everyone's idea of fun."

"Yes, I know. You're right. Let's go. Emily Ann's neighbor lives along the ridge. We need to warn him." She turned toward the trail, and Jack followed.

Thick layers of fallen evergreen needles browned

the forest floor and silenced their steps. Dirty white mushrooms swollen with water grew over the dead foliage. Yesterday the woods were alive with nature sounds. Today, the quiet unsettled Kate's nerves. Throughout the woods, fallen trees the size that would make Paul Bunyan gasp lay rotting. Hollowed from decay and entangled with vines, they provided shelters large enough to conceal a grizzly. As Kate scanned the dark forest floor, the task of spotting a well-camouflaged lion was suddenly daunting. There were too many places for the animal to hide.

A twig snapped. Kate and Jack spun around. Kate gripped Jack's arm, and for several moments, they remained motionless—watching, listening. Across Africa's grassy plains, lions moved through tall grass as lithely as a breeze. No one with half a brain strolled in the open fields of the Serengeti, at least not without watching their backs. And when they found themselves in an acacia grove, they turned their attention upward for leopards lounging on the branches. Mountain lions, even injured mountain lions, were able to climb trees. Suddenly the scope of their search increased.

As if reading Kate's mind, Jack looked up. Unease spread across his face. In Kate's experience, capturing injured and frightened animals, especially large predators, was about as bad as it got in the wild animal rehab business. Unfortunately, Fred Marlow's assessment of the situation did not ring true. She chided herself for being drawn in by his foolhearted confidence in his ability to subdue the cat. Who was this man who understated the danger? Or was it his effort to avoid causing panic?

Seeing nothing, they continued in silence. Kate

scanned the undergrowth while Jack kept a sharp eye on the branches above.

"We should have brought a flashlight," Kate whispered. "This thick canopy makes it too dark to see well enough to spot anything."

"Too late now," Jack said.

Before they reached the top of the trail, someone shouted a protest. A shot rang out. Kate and Jack left the trail and scampered up through the woods. Among the building supplies, near the site of the new cages, Fred stood about twenty yards behind Brain, pointing the dart gun at his back.

"You fire that pistol again, son, and this dart ends up in your backside," Fred said.

Brian held a pistol with two hands, Dirty Harry style. Not ten yards away, the mountain lion stood on a felled fir, back hunched, spitting and screeching, ready to pounce.

Fred cocked his rifle. "No one move."

"Mr. Marlow," Deputy Fitzroy said. "Take it easy now."

Fred crept up closer. Brian raised the gun. Damp patches of sweat had formed on Brian's white dress shirt. His arms began to shake.

"Lower that pistol, Brian," Fred whispered.

"No fucking way!"

Suddenly the mountain lion stepped forward and lowered its head. Fred aimed and fired. *Sfit*! The dart lodged in the cat's hindquarters, but not before the animal leaped straight for Brian. Fred shoved Brian out of the way. Brian hit the ground, accidentally discharging the gun, the bullet ricocheting off a boulder. The cat went straight for Fred, swiped at his leg, darted into a clump of undergrowth, and then stumbled and fell.

Brian lay face down, and for a moment, Kate feared he was dead. Jack and Deputy Fitzroy ran over as Brian turned over and sat up. Unhurt, he rose to his feet with Jack's help.

"He tried to kill me!" Brian cried.

"He saved your life, you idiot," Kate shouted. She ran to Fred and knelt beside him. Above his left knee, a heavy stream of blood seeped through his khaki pants. "We need to get you to a hospital. You're bleeding pretty badly. We need something to stop the bleeding."

"I'll be fine. Please check on the lion. I-I didn't want to dart her."

Kate understood his concern. Nature programs made it look easy. The reality was that darting an injured animal often did more harm than good. At too close a range, the dart left a sizable hole. And even if they were fortunate to have calculated the correct dosage for the dart, the animal often died from shock.

"I'll take care of Mr. Marlow," Deputy Fitzroy said. "Do something with that animal before it wakes up."

From a safe distance, Kate watched the cat and once she was certain it was sedated, Jack pulled the tarp over.

"What do you think?" he asked.

"Looks like Fred hit the hindquarter. There's not much bleeding. She's out cold. Throw the tarp over her head, and I'll remove the dart." Kate felt a weak, but steady pulse near the groin. Lying there, entangled in the brush, the cat looked small and harmless. Kate had darted many animals and had hated it each time.

Suddenly, a deep hurt pressed hard on Kate's chest. For the first time that morning, the realization that Emily Ann was dead took hold. *Now is not the time to lose it*, Kate chided herself. Tears welled up, and her voice caught in her throat. "Let's wrap the tarp around the rest of her. I'll tend to her when we get her in the cage."

Once they got the cat settled in, Kate ran to the house for antibiotics Emily Ann kept in the refrigerator. Evan was standing just inside the kitchen door. "I heard shots. Is it dead?"

"The lion's back in its cage—alive. Fred's been clawed, thanks to your brother-in-law." Kate pushed past him. "Bring a blanket. We need some help."

"That animal should be destroyed," Evan said, staring out the window, the look in his eyes as hazy as the morning.

"Did you hear what I said?" Kate screamed. "Fred is badly injured. He's losing a lot of blood. Get a blanket!"

Evan hesitated, then ran inside. Kate gathered what she needed and ran back outside.

Fred was sitting on the ground, leaning against a tree, pale and shivering. Deputy Fitzroy found a towel from the storage shed and used it to put pressure over Fred's wound.

"Evan's bringing a blanket," Kate said. She bent down and placed a hand on Fred's wrist. His pulse raced. "How are you doing?"

"Okay." He took a deep breath. "I'll be fine."

But he didn't sound as if he believed his own words. A glassy stare at nothing alerted Kate that he was going into shock. The injury and Emily Ann's death now took hold. Kate needed to bring him back and quickly.

"Your shot was perfect. Very little damage." Kate smiled.

Evan tossed her the blanket, and Kate tucked it around Fred's shoulders.

"I didn't want to dart her." Fred leaned his head back and closed his eyes. "I really didn't. She's already too traumatized."

"Nonsense. The cat will be fine. So will you. I've got antibiotics, and I'll suture the cat's wound if necessary. She'll be fine."

"You better get busy." Fred swallowed hard. "That drug should be wearing off soon."

"Right. Anything else I should know about her condition?"

"She's got stitches in several places, right hindquarter, two places on her rump, and behind her right ear. They're about six days old and should've done their job by now."

"I'll check. Sit tight."

Kate finished suturing the cat's wound, and by the time she checked the other stitches, the mountain lion was whimpering and trying to raise its head. Kate backed out of the cage just as her patient rose on her front legs. The cat wobbled and flopped back onto her side. Then she rose again and steadied herself. Good sign. Kate wanted to watch for a few more minutes, but she needed to return to Fred before the ambulance took him to the hospital.

By the time Kate gathered her equipment and locked the cage, four EMS personnel were tramping up the trail for the second time that morning. Following them was a man in a three-piece suite. Kate marked him as out-of-place on this laid-back island. Slightly out of shape from carrying about twenty extra pounds, the guy paused to catch his breath. Deputy Fitzroy walked over. The two men spoke briefly to Fred as the medical technicians loaded him onto the stretcher. Minutes later, Fred was on his way to Lopez Island's medical clinic.

"This is Detective Randy Kraus," Fitzroy said to Kate and Jack.

Kraus ignored the introduction. "Sheriff Montego is at the clinic waiting to talk to Marlow," Detective Kraus said. "I'll look around here, and then I want to talk to everyone at the house."

"Things seem under control," Deputy Fitzroy said. "It was pretty hairy for a while."

****

Evan was alone in the den when Kate and Jack walked in. But the house was far from quiet. Brian and Laurie were going at it upstairs, and Ben was crying.

"My sister deserves better," Evan said. "I never understood what she saw in Brian Fuller. The guy's nothing but a bag of hot air."

Kate went upstairs and knocked on the door. Brian flung it open. Red splotches covered his face. A bruise was forming over his left eye. "That guy's crazy. He almost killed me." Kate pushed past him and went over to Laurie, curled up in a rocking chair, holding Ben.

"Let me take him," Kate said. "I'll make him some breakfast. Detective Kraus will be here in a few minutes to speak to everyone about what happened."

"And I have a lot to tell him," Brian shouted. "Marlow threatened to shoot me with the goddamn dart gun."

"Brian, would you please lower your voice for

Ben's sake," Laurie whispered. "Ben likes cheese toast," she said to Kate.

Ben went willingly with Kate. Once in the kitchen, she sat him in his high chair and poured some Cheerios on the tray. Then she dampened a paper towel and wiped his face.

"Granny," he said.

"Granny's not here, Ben." Kate's voice caught in her throat. *How do you explain death to a two-year-old?* "Would you like me to make you some cheese toast?"

He shoved a few pieces of cereal into his mouth and nodded. Then said, "Milk."

Kate filled a plastic cup halfway and set it on his tray. The Cheerios were almost gone, so she gave him some more. By the time she had Ben's toast ready, Detective Kraus had returned from the facility to start his interviews.

"I'd like to talk to you first, Ms. Caraway, since you found Mrs. Thurston's body." He sat down at the kitchen table and flipped open a spiral notebook.

"Would you like some coffee?" Kate asked.

"Please."

"I'll make a fresh pot." She poured the coffee she had made earlier down the drain.

"Who's this?" Detective Kraus looked at Ben and offered to shake his hand.

Ben handed him a Cheerio. Then he picked up a piece of toast and held it out.

"This is Ben," Kate said.

"No, thanks, Ben. Coffee's enough for me."

Brian stormed into the kitchen. "There you are! I want you to arrest that man." His outburst caused Ben to cry, but Brian barely noticed. He filled a cup with ice cubes from the freezer. Then he searched through several drawers, opening and slamming them shut until he found a washcloth. Wrapping the cloth around a handful of ice cubes, he pressed it to his eye. "See what he did?"

"You must be Brian Fuller. I'll get your statement in a moment. Maybe you could take your son while I ask Ms. Caraway a few questions."

"It better be fast." Brian yanked Ben from the high chair and left the kitchen.

Detective Kraus' gaze followed Brian out of the room and then turned to Kate. "What time did you find Mrs. Thurston?"

Kate went over the morning's events from the moment she awoke to when she saw Emily Ann lying on the rock at the bottom of the cliff. Detective Kraus seemed satisfied and shifted to the subject of the lion.

"At the bottom of the cage is a small gate-like opening. I assume that's for feeding."

"That's right. The idea in wildlife rehab is to have as little contact with the animals as possible. In the case of a predator such as a mountain lion, to protect yourself as well."

"Any reason why Mrs. Thurston would open the cage?"

"Only to tend to the lion's wounds. But Emily Ann would never go in without drugging the cat first."

"Well, the cage was opened, and we found her keys near her body. Where are the keys to the cages kept?"

"Here in her pantry." Kate opened the door and showed him a wooden plank with several hooks, all holding various keys.

"When you walked up there this morning, did you

notice anything out of the ordinary?"

"Everything seemed normal. Except for everyone sleeping later than usual."

For the next two hours, Kraus took everyone's statements. He wrapped things up, and on his way out the door Emily Ann's phone rang. Deputy Fitzroy was calling from Bellingham. Fred had been flown by helicopter to Bellingham General Hospital where he had received eighty-two stitches. Kate called and spoke to Fred briefly. He still felt the effects of the drugs but was adamant about returning to Lopez for Emily Ann's funeral.

****

Once the authorities left, Kate and Jack tended to the eagles, while Evan and Laurie dealt with the tragedy of losing their mother. Working with animals side by side with her husband was the best therapy for Kate. Until five years ago, when she'd established her research camp in Kenya, Jack had no experience tending to injured or orphaned wildlife. But once he learned the ropes, he proved to be a natural. Soon he was mixing formula and feeding wild babies like a pro.

When they finished the last feeding and cleaned up, Jack said, "Feel like talking about Emily Ann?"

"I'm having trouble making sense of all this," she said, locking the last eagle cage.

"I was wondering when you'd start questioning the circumstances." Jack gathered equipment—feeding syringes, plastic bowls containing a frozen concoction of blended rodent remains, and several vials of medication—and placed everything into a tub to carry back to the house. "I can't make sense of it either. Things aren't right."

60

"I keep asking myself what brought Emily Ann up to the ridge in the first place. She wasn't here enjoying her coffee."

"She rushed up here for some reason. Maybe Evan was right. Maybe Emily Ann saw the lion was loose. I mean, it didn't exactly turn out to be a joyous evening. Emily Ann was upset. Maybe she forgot to lock the cage."

"That's possible but unlikely. Emily Ann was very careful. If she saw the lion loose from its cage, she wouldn't have run out after it. She would've awakened us for help."

They started back down the trail to the house. It was only just past noon, but Kate felt as if she had been working for hours. Her stomach thundered loud enough to echo, but the idea of food brought on a feeling of nausea.

Long before they reached the house, they heard Evan's voice. "I'll take care of it when I get back. There's been some sort of communication breakdown, that's all. I've got my hands full here right now." Evan paced on the deck, his cell phone held tight against his ear. He ignored Kate and Jack when they walked up.

"Listen. I said I'd take care of it. Right now, I have to bury my mother!" He listened for a few more seconds, then shoved his phone into his pocket.

"Can we help with anything, Evan?" Kate asked.

"No. This is something I need to finish myself. Laurie was making things worse, so I sent her and Brian back to the inn. I wanted the funeral to be tomorrow, but two people from the nursing home passed away, so Mother's service is scheduled for Tuesday. I just want to get this behind me."

Kate thought about how some people handled grief or didn't handle it. She wanted to stop time. She didn't want the funeral ever to take place or to hear about cremations and services. She just wanted her friend back.

"An extra day will be better for Fred," Kate said. "He wants to attend the funeral."

"Fred! Is that all you're concerned about? I can't stop the son of a bitch from being there, but as soon as this is all over, I don't ever want to see or hear his name! Or yours, for that matter. I don't know why Mother ever maintained a friendship with you. You were a constant reminder of what she left in Austin. She dragged that life into her marriage with Dad, making it impossible for it to work. Laurie and I talked, and we're going to sell this place as soon as possible."

"What about the facility? What about your mother's animals?"

"I don't give a shit about those animals. Marlow can take them. They're his problem now. I want those cages cleared by the end of the week, or I'll open them and let nature take its course. I'm going for a ride." He stormed off.

Chapter Five

Kate and Jack had the house to themselves for the afternoon. After Evan had returned from his bike ride, he packed his things for his return to Seattle and announced that he'd be back the next day for the funeral. Jack made a plate of sandwiches and leftovers and insisted Kate eat. Despite her hunger, she managed only a few bites, just enough to take the edge off the numbness. The emotions followed—denial, anger, sadness—one after another like falling dominoes. Acceptance, however, was another matter, one that Kate could not grasp. When her father died, letting go took a long time. Clinging to her grief meant clinging to him. If she accepted his death, he'd become only a memory.

Kate sat on the sofa staring out the window. She kept expecting Emily Ann to walk in from the kitchen. Dotty and Speckle seemed to expect the same thing. Every time someone walked into the den, the two dogs raised up as if hoping to see their mom. Now they competed for Kate's lap. Kenya slept on the rug in front of the fireplace. Emily Ann's tortoiseshell, whose name Kate just remembered was Tortuga, was crouched on the window ledge, watching the birds on the deck. Valentine, as usual, had found a hiding place and had not made an appearance.

Jack handed Kate a cup of coffee and sat next to

her. She told him about Evan's flare-up and about the accusations he made against her father, about never wanting to see Fred again, about his plan to sell the property. "I can't understand Evan's heartlessness."

"He's hurting too, sweetheart. Did you think that Evan would just let Fred continue with his and Emily Ann's plans? He believes the lion frightened Emily Ann and caused her to fall. And he might be right."

"It doesn't make sense. Emily Ann would not open that cage."

"Well, someone did."

****

The phone continued to ring, one call after another. Kate did her best to answer questions and comfort Emily Ann's friends. Laurie called to talk to her brother. Evidently, Evan had not told his sister about his plan to return to the city. Laurie directed her anger at Kate by shouting that she, Brian, and Ben were leaving the island too. Kate's patience with Emily Ann's dysfunctional children had torn thin, but before she could respond, Laurie slammed down the phone.

Kate and Jack fed the animals again in the early evening. The lion was up and around. Although she limped to her food pan, she tore into her meal like a healthy, ravenous cat.

After dinner, they tried to watch TV. Their choices were the national news or *American Idol*—neither was appealing. Kate found an Elizabeth Peters mystery on the bookshelf, but even the entertaining Amelia Peabody couldn't shake Kate from her stupor. Finally, Jack scrolled the HBO channel and found Eddie Murphy's *Doctor Dolittle*. The laughter felt good. Kate's tension began to subside. Before the movie ended, she had fallen asleep on Jack's shoulder.

****

The morning had brought with it a Texas-style rain, not a slow, steady drizzle typical to the Pacific Northwest, but a gusher where swollen clouds spilled their contents as if slit down the middle with a machete. Ray showed up for the morning feeding and went about his business. Kate considered speaking to him about what had happened but felt it wasn't necessary. After all, what could she say? She'd talk to him later about his wages. Emily Ann was gone, but the eagles still needed tending to.

Evan had called to say he'd be returning to the island after lunch. He had an appointment to see Emily Ann's attorney in Seattle to review her will and start the ball rolling to put the property up for sale. Kate slammed down the phone. Before she could remove her hand, it rang again. She let the call go to voice mail. Just as she settled down with a cup of coffee, the doorbell rang. Kate considered ignoring that too, but she saw Deputy Fitzroy and Detective Kraus standing on the porch through the front door window

"Afternoon. May we come in for a moment?" Deputy Fitzroy sounded hesitant when Kate jerked open the door.

"Sure. I just made some coffee. Would you like some?"

"No coffee for us, thanks." Detective Kraus had no problem answering for both.

"I'm afraid Laurie and Evan are not here at the moment."

"That's fine," Detective Kraus said. "They don't have to be here. We have a warrant."

"A what?"

"The sheriff got the postmortem results. Did you know that Mrs. Thurston had been ill?"

"What are you talking about?"

"She had cancer, bone cancer. It was in the advanced stages. She wasn't expected to live for very long, a few months at the most."

"What?" Kate whispered, feeling a chill rush through her body.

"There's a possibility that Mrs. Thurston's death wasn't an accident. She may have killed herself. Deputy Fitzroy and I need to see if she left some indication."

"A suicide note? I think we would have found one by now, Detective Kraus."

"You might be right, but let's make sure."

"But was a warrant really necessary?"

"Just in case," Kraus said. "Her son Evan is unwilling to accept what was happening, and I didn't want to delay this any further."

While Kraus and Fitzroy searched the house, Kate stood at the patio door, staring at the mist rising off the fir trees. Ray, now soaked with rain, wearing that same filthy flannel shirt, came around the corner. He stopped when he saw Kate. His shoulders tightened, and he looked away.

Before the two officers arrived, the downpour had stopped, and Jack had taken all three dogs for a walk. They had just returned. The dogs looked as if they had scampered through every mud puddle on the road. Jack, attempting to clean and dry all twelve paws, was on his second towel before Dotty and Speckle's white coats became visible. He looked up and smiled at Kate. Then he let the dogs in and rushed to Kate's side.

"What's happened? Honey, are you okay?"

"Deputy Fitzroy and Detective Kraus are here. They think Emily Ann may have killed herself. They're looking for a suicide note."

Jack took Kate by the arm. "Let's sit down. Why on earth do they think that?"

"The autopsy showed Emily Ann had bone cancer. Seems no one knew, not even Evan and Laurie. She had only a few weeks, six months at the most. Jack, why would she not tell me?" Kate slumped back into the armchair. "Do you think that was why she was in a hurry to marry Fred?"

"You think he knew?"

"He must have. That's why Emily Ann was in such a hurry to finish the new cages and have Fred move in the rest of the cats. Why else would she move so quickly with the wedding plans? She wanted everything taken care of before she died. It was so like her to squeeze every last moment out of life. But she would never kill herself, Jack. That idea's absurd."

"Slow down. I agree. But let's not jump to conclusions. We should talk to Fred and find out how much he knew."

Detective Kraus came downstairs. "I just searched her bedroom as well as her office. I didn't find anything," he said. "But we had to check. I still need to talk to her children."

"They've returned to Seattle," Kate said. "Evan should be back this afternoon. I'm not sure about the others."

"We'll be in touch," Kraus advised her. "Don't get up. We'll let ourselves out."

The sound of the front door closing triggered

Kate's anger. "What the hell does that mean? 'Be in touch.' They come in here, go through Emily Ann's things, ask a few questions, search the place, and leave. Are they finished? What's the official cause of death? Accident? Are they satisfied she didn't kill herself?"

Kate ran upstairs to their room, planning to close the door on all the madness of the last two days. She found the door to Emily Ann's bedroom ajar and stepped inside. The bedspread was thrown back. Emily Ann's nightshirt hung over the bedpost. A book lay on the floor by the bed. The door to the walk-in closet stood open. Shoeboxes were neatly stacked, except for one box lying in the middle of the closet floor.

Kate could almost visualize that morning. Emily Ann wakes up, looks out the window, and notices the cat is loose, or maybe she remembers she forgot to lock the cage the night before. She throws on her clothes and hiking boots and rushes outside. This was not the room of a woman who had planned to kill herself. Emily Ann planned to return, take a shower, get dressed, and start her day.

Kate sat on the bed. She recalled a few weeks ago when Emily Ann had called, asking her and Jack to visit. Kate remembered hearing the strain in Emily Ann's voice. Could she have wanted to see her friends for the last time? No. Emily Ann arranged for the visit as a celebration. She would never gather her family and friends around and have them present while she took her life. In fact, she probably would have eventually told Kate about the illness. She wouldn't have done that over the phone. Kate picked up the book: *Living with Cancer*. This was the friend Kate knew. Emily Ann would learn as much as she could about her illness. She would tackle the disease, not run from it.

Kate went downstairs. On the coffee table, Jack had set up a chessboard.

"Sit down," he said. "How are you doing?"

"I just came from Emily Ann's room."

"Find anything?"

"A room that awaits her return. Nothing points to suicide. That idea is ludicrous." Kate walked over to the table. "I should have known something was wrong. Now that I think back, the first thing I noticed when I saw Emily Ann was that she had lost weight. And when we hiked up the trail, she was easily winded."

"Those aren't necessarily signs of illness. Just aging."

"Are you suggesting we play?" Kate nodded at the board.

"Why not?"

"It's been years. I don't remember how. You'll most likely win."

"I'd win anyway. Sit down. Ray's cleaning cages now, and we have nothing to do until the evening feeding."

An hour later, they were in a stalemate. "Not bad," Jack said.

"You went easy on me." Kate picked up the phone. "I should give Fred a call at the hospital." Before she could punch in the number, a loud popping sounded from outside. Kate and Jack rushed to the kitchen door. Pulled up in the driveway was an old wreck of a Cadillac. The passenger door was held shut with several layers of duct tape wrapped around the doorframe. Burnt-smelling fumes belched from the tailpipe, an engine screaming for oil. A chunky woman standing barefoot next to the car screeched like a banshee. Most of her strawberry-blonde hair had come loose from her stringy ponytail. Orange leggings rode high above her ankles. Her short brown T-shirt did little to cover the rolls of fat spilling over the lip of her pants. A faded denim shirt acted as a shield against the chill.

"What the hell are you doing here, Ray? The woman's dead! I told you to go see about that job at the Petersons' farm."

"What are *you* doing here? You know I put in a full day here every Monday. Mrs. Thurston's paid me until the end of the month. I'll call the Petersons tonight. Now go home, Paula. I got work to do." He turned and started to walk up to the cages. Paula followed.

"You were supposed to wake me and the kids up before you left this morning," she yelled. "We overslept, and the kids missed the school bus. Know what happened then? I tried to start this piece of shit you call a car. But you let the tank run dry. I had to call Lisa to come get *our* kids and take them to school and deliver me some damn gas."

"If you weren't up all night, you wouldn't have overslept," he called over his shoulder.

"If you'd been at home, I wouldn't have been up. How do you do it, Ray—stay out all night drinking with that scumbag Louie Fister? Where do you get the money to do that?"

"Don't badmouth Louie. If it wasn't for him, I wouldn't have a ride to work. Now, if you ain't gonna leave, then grab a shovel from the shed. There's plenty of shit to shovel around up in them cages."

Paula's shriek sounded like a wild animal. She reached down and grabbed several pinecones and flung them at Ray. Two hit him square in the back. He kept walking. When Paula didn't get a reaction, she turned on her heel and headed back to the car, screaming obscenities. Paula hopped in and gunned the motor to make the most of what life the battery had left. She turned the car around and threw the transmission into drive. Before speeding away, she hung her head out the window and yelled, "You're a loser, Ray. A goddamn loser." Then she flipped him off.

"Well, now," Jack said. "Seems like the Steiners are having a lovers' spat."

"Sounds like a well-practiced lovers' spat."

"I'd better help him finish up and then give him a ride home." Jack stepped out on the back porch.

"Good idea. I'll call Fred. If he didn't know about Emily Ann's cancer, he should. I hate to have this conversation over the phone, but I want to talk to him before I tell Evan."

"You're too late," Jack said, looking toward the road. "Evan just drove up, and he doesn't look happy. Why don't you go upstairs and call Fred? I'll deal with Evan."

Kate smiled at her husband and turned to leave just as the door flew open and Emily Ann's son stormed into the house. "You knew about this! Just like you knew about the wedding! Get out of this house! Get out now!" Evan made a move as if to shove Kate.

Jack grabbed Evan by the shoulders. "Watch it, young man, or the only one leaving this house will be you."

Evan tried to pull away, but Jack held tight. "Listen, son, you have about two seconds to grow up. Your mother has died, and your little sister's falling apart. Calm down and tell us what this is all about." Evan deflated somewhat, and Jack let go of the young man's shoulders.

Evan's tough-guy façade crumbled, and he buried his face in his hands. Kate suspected that these were the first tears he'd shed over his mother's death. Finally, Evan caught his breath and opened his eyes. The anger had not entirely faded from his face, but for the first time since Kate spotted him preparing the grill on the patio three days ago, he appeared almost human.

"Let's all sit down and talk about this," Jack said. They went into the kitchen, but no one bothered to sit.

Evan folded his arms across his chest and paced around the kitchen. Finally, he said, "Things haven't been going well lately. Susan called the night before Mom died to tell me that she was seeking sole custody of the girls. And I find out Mother left her house and property to this Fred Marlow. Oh, and in her generosity, she left a little cash for Laurie and me, but this place is now his. I don't even know who this guy is." Evan's anger was returning. "He's some kind of con artist. I plan to find out. If he thinks he's getting this property, he's got another thing coming. I know he's still in the hospital, but I'm calling him anyway." He reached for the phone.

"Evan, wait. There's something you need to know. I'm sorry to bring this up now. Has Detective Kraus contacted you?"

"About what?"

"Your mother was ill, Evan."

"Ill? Mother wasn't ill."

"She had cancer. It was fairly advanced." Kate prepared herself for another explosion. None came.

After a few moments, he spoke. "Mother had breast cancer a couple of years ago, but she'd recovered fully. Who told you?"

"The autopsy report came in. Detective Kraus brought the news a little while ago."

"Detective Kraus? Here again?"

"Under the circumstances, Evan, the sheriff felt that your mother may have killed herself," Jack said.

****

Center Church, a small wooden building perched on a hillside in the middle of the island, stood alone in a grove of Douglas firs. On a clear day, from the grounds in back, blue water shone in the distance. The Catholic parish used the nondenominational church for Sunday Mass and, like today, for funerals.

Father Bill, pastor of St. Francis Parish and Emily Ann's close friend, came over from San Juan Island to say Mass. He stepped to the podium and smiled, then began speaking of Emily Ann's early departure. Kate's gaze drifted toward the window, and she watched a small flock of sheep meandering through the nearby pasture. Then a flock of white cattle egrets landed and began picking through the grasses, reaping their own harvest. Earlier, when Kate had walked in, something about the church felt different from any place of worship she'd ever visited. She hadn't been able to put her finger on the difference until now.

The church had clear glass windows, not the usual stained or crazed glass that only allowed in muted light. Looking out at Lopez Island's pastoral views, Kate felt a sense of peace. She liked the effect. *Why hadn't other churches opted for clear glass?* Maybe for concern that the congregation wouldn't be able to pay attention to the service inside. *How ironic*, Kate thought. She'd always found it impossible to focus under the daunting gazes of martyrs venerated in stained glass and statuary. She often felt oppressed and guilty for not being spiritually moved from being surrounded by religious grandeur. Here, in this small unpretentious church, with Father Bill's voice softly droning in the background and sheep grazing in the pasture, Kate felt closer to God than she had in a very long time.

A movement out of the corner of her eye caused Kate to turn toward the window again. An elderly couple strolled through the cemetery where the interred had lain peacefully since the late 1800s. They stopped at one grave adorned with a sculpture of a lamb curled up at the base of the gravestone. On a small plot of land beyond the cemetery, a farmer on an ancient tractor plowed a small field. A feeling of peace washed over Kate, and for a moment, she wished for time to stand still.

"Emily Ann and I loved this church," Fred leaned over and whispered. Kate's serenity evaporated as she realized that this was where Emily Ann and Fred had planned to marry. She patted Fred's hand. He felt warm, too warm. He was on antibiotics and pain medication but could wind up back in the hospital if he wasn't careful.

Emily Ann's children and grandchildren sat in the front pew. Ben fussed and squirmed on Brian's lap. Because of the sedatives Laurie had been taking, she looked as if she were about to topple over. She seemed shrunken and withdrawn inside her black, tailored suit. Also in the front pew were Evan and his soon-to-be ex-wife, Susan. She sat a few inches away, not so apparent as to announce their estrangement but far enough to make a personal statement. Their two daughters sat on Susan's other side, away from their father. The younger girl leaned over to try and get her father's attention, but Susan gently pushed her back. Evan turned his head away as if he hadn't noticed the gesture.

Sitting next to Fred was his son, Zach, who'd picked up his father from the hospital in Bellingham that morning. Zach was about Evan's age but had a sense of old soul about him. Like his father, Zach seemed free of life's trivialities, something that Evan had yet to achieve.

Susan was the only family member crying. Kate had met her when she and her daughters arrived at the house as everyone piled into their cars for church. The other family members had little to say to her, so Jack invited Susan and the girls to ride with him and Kate. Kate drove, and Susan sat in the passenger seat. In the short drive to the church, Kate gained more information about the Thurston family than in the previous three days, adding to her suspicions surrounding Emily Ann's sudden death.

"I suspected that Emily Ann's cancer had returned," Susan had said. "I asked her about it many times, but you know how she was—a master of evasion. I confronted her, and she finally admitted to seeing a doctor in Seattle. She made it sound like everything was routine, just some tests because she had been so tired lately. But I knew it was more serious than she let on because she made me promise not to tell Evan or Laurie. Did you know that she had a mastectomy about two years ago?"

"Not until Evan mentioned it yesterday," Kate said.

"Don't feel bad," Susan responded. "I don't think she would have told anyone, but I insisted, and she finally told Laurie and Evan. My mother had breast cancer, so I knew the signs."

They sat in silence for a few minutes, then Susan spoke again. "Evan said that the detective suspected Emily Ann may have…" Susan stopped and looked at her two daughters in the back seat. Jack was trying his best to engage them in conversation, but even he was having a difficult time. The older girl, Angie, buried her nose in a picture book, and her sister, Melissa, stared at Jack as if he would bite. Once Susan saw that her children were distracted, she continued, "Well, that's crazy. Emily Ann was too comfortable with life, no matter what complications came with it." Susan reached in her purse and pulled out a tissue. "She was also too careful to have fallen off that ledge."

They had arrived at the church before Kate had a chance to voice agreement with that opinion. "Let's talk later."

Father Bill, asking everyone to stand for a final prayer, brought Kate out of her ruminations. He then announced a memorial luncheon at one o'clock at the community center. People filed out of the church. Kate and Jack waited with Fred and his son for the church to empty. Shuffling out among a bunch of people was not something Fred could do on his crutches. "I'd like to join everyone at the luncheon, but I'm afraid I've overdone it," Fred said. "My leg's bothering me. So Zach's going to take me back to Emily Ann's."

"Good idea," Kate said. "You don't look so good. Just rest and take it easy. I made up the sleeper sofa in the den so you wouldn't have to deal with the stairs.

76

You and Zach make yourselves at home." Then she remembered that, according to the will, the house now belonged to Fred. Kate wasn't sure if Fred even knew that yet. After Evan's abrupt announcement yesterday afternoon, Kate hadn't had a chance to call Fred and talk to him about Emily Ann's illness or about the will. That conversation would have to wait until later.

On the way to the car, Susan walked up. "Kate, there's been a change of plans. The girls and I are riding with Laurie and Brian out to Iceberg Point."

At first, Kate didn't understand, and then it became clear. Emily Ann had wanted her ashes scattered from her favorite spot on the ridge.

"I'm sorry." Susan blushed. "Evan insists that only the family should be there. Laurie agreed. I wanted to wait until after the luncheon, but he wants to get this 'over with' as he put it. He's anxious to return to Seattle as soon as possible." She turned to her daughters. "Girls, put on your sneakers. They're in my bag. You're not walking out to the Point in those good shoes." Then to Kate, "We'll try to get back before the event at the community center ends. Hopefully, I'll see you there. How does that sound?"

"Great," Kate said, and hoped the look on her face didn't betray the disappointment she felt.

Chapter Six

By the time Kate and Jack reached the community center, all the parking spaces were taken, so they parked on the side of the road. Emily Ann's friends at the library had organized the event. Every Lopez resident seemed to be there.

The venue housed a community theater as well as a small banquet room. Every table was occupied, and people were standing around chatting. Two easels stood next to the reception table. One announced the event as a celebration of Emily Ann Thurston's life. On the other stood a huge collage with pictures of Emily Ann—at community picnics, working with her birds, having dinner with friends. Kate and Jack signed in and were enjoying the photo display when a tall, wispy woman walked up.

"Hi, I'm Jeannie Shuttleford." She held out her hand.

"Jack Ryder and Kate Caraway," Jack said. "We're Emily Ann's friends from Chicago."

"I know. Emily Ann had been telling me about your visit for weeks. Y'all knew each other from Austin, Texas."

"Do I hear a Texas accent?" Kate said.

Jeannie laughed. "I grew up in East Texas, a small town called Big Sandy."

"A place known for its Victorian B&Bs," Jack

said. "We know Big Sandy well. We used to drive through on our trips from Chicago to Austin."

"How did you end up in the San Juans?" Kate asked.

"Like a lot of people. Looking for a greener pasture, one that's less humid and cooler in the summer. Several of us uprooted Texans live around here. Just keep your ears open. You'll hear us."

"You're the librarian," Kate said. "Emily Ann mentioned you."

"Emily Ann and I moved to the island about the same time and just kind of found each other. Two magnets drawn together. We became friends immediately." Her voice turned to a whisper as if speaking the words aloud was too painful. "None of this seems real." Her eyes teared, and she drew a calming breath. "I need to check on the food. Please find a place to sit. We'll be serving soon."

Kate and Jack met more of Emily Ann's friends—everyone anxious to trade stories that lessened the pain of grief. The seats at the tables slowly filled up. They found two places near Jacob Bower, who sat alone at the end of the table.

"Mind if we join you?" Kate asked.

The look on his face told Kate he clearly did mind, but he managed a polite smile. Kate introduced Jack, but Bower ignored the introduction. Instead, he said, "What's going to happen now?"

"We'll be eating soon, and then there will be program." Kate said.

"No, I mean, what's going to happen to Emily Ann's wildlife?"

"I'm not exactly sure, but Fred, Emily Ann's

fiancé, and his son will be taking care of things for now. Jack and I will help while we're here."

"Emily Ann's what?" He looked directly at Kate.

"Emily Ann was to be married in a few days—to Fred Marlow, the man who plans to relocate his mountain lions."

"Oh, yes, I've seen that guy around. I had no idea that he and Emily Ann were engaged. Well, that is a surprise. I heard that the lion attacked him. How did that happen?"

Kate and Jack never had a chance to tell him Sunday morning that the animal had gotten loose. Kate avoided the question. The fewer people who knew about the incident, the better. "A hazard of working with wild animals," Kate said. "You let your guard down for a moment, and that's all it takes."

"Is he hurt bad?"

"He spent one night in the hospital. I think he should have stayed a couple more days, but he wanted to attend the funeral. He's at Emily Ann's right now resting."

"Poor guy," Mr. Bower said.

Kate quickly turned her attention from Emily Ann's neighbor to a woman who'd just walked in. Her heels clumped loudly on the hardwood floor. Several people in the room turned to look. Her expensive clothes and gold jewelry could finance a small house. Murmurs drifted across the room as the woman stopped for a moment at the photo display and glowered. Then she walked over to a table and took a seat.

Jeannie Shuttleford stepped up to the podium. "Excuse me, everyone. Thank you so much for coming. It's wonderful to be here with so many people who loved Emily Ann. As a community, we'll feel the loss for a long time, and, as her friends, for the rest of our days. A few people would like to speak. We won't take long, and then we can start the buffet line. And for those of you who would like to stay later, we have a special treat in store."

Kate's mouth fell open when Jacob Bower stood and walked up to the podium. Kate had not realized he and Emily Ann were good friends. She had barely mentioned him, only describing him as a recluse. He adjusted the microphone and shuffled through some index cards. Bower cleared his throat and kept his eyes lowered. After an uncomfortable amount of time, he finally began reading a poem. Kate recognized it as Emily Dickinson's "If I Can Stop." Not quite what one would expect to hear at a funeral but touching nonetheless. Jeannie spoke next. She told a few moving but humorous anecdotes about Emily Ann, how she kept her priorities clear and unwavering, how integrity had ruled her life.

After Jeannie, several more friends spoke. Kate waited, and once sure that no one else would take the podium, she walked up and read from one of Emily Ann's favorite books, *A Prayer for Owen Meany*. Emily Ann and Kate had always been great fans of John Irving. One night years ago, when Jack was on the road with the team, the phone rang long after midnight waking Kate from a deep asleep. Grasping the phone, afraid that something had happened to Jack, she heard Emily Ann's voice.

"I know it's late, but you have to listen to this," Emily Ann said. "This is how I feel about us, about our friendship. I know we don't see each other as much as we used to, but I love you as if you were my daughter. Make that my little sister." She laughed. Kate listened to the passage, and the next day she went out and bought the book.

This morning she'd found the book in Emily Ann's bookcase. She had no trouble finding the passage. Emily Ann had marked it with a photograph of them taken years ago in Austin, swinging in a hammock in Emily Ann's backyard. Ted, Kate's father, had taken the picture the day before Emily Ann moved to San Diego. All her possessions had been packed in a U-Haul in the driveway. The hammock was the last thing to be taken down. Kate managed a wide grin but couldn't hide the hurt she felt. Then she looked closer and saw the anger in her eyes. Back then, she could not understand Emily Ann's decision to leave.

Kate finished her reading. Jeannie invited everyone to the buffet table. For the next hour, Kate and Jack met more of Emily Ann's friends. Tears were shed, but, for the most part, the humorous stories shared gave rise to comfortable laughter. Emily Ann touched so many people, and being with them was the best medicine for Kate.

After the meal, Jeannie announced that she and a few others had created a slide show—photos of the 4th of July parade, showing Emily Ann driving a golf cart pulling a small float with an Eagle Crossing display, photos of her teaching students at the elementary school about bald eagles, more photos of community picnics and festivals Emily Ann had attended. Words were not necessary, instead music accompanied the show, not the typical say goodbye-to-a-friend music, but light nature sounds of water and waves.

When the show ended, Kate looked around, surprised to see that Laurie, Evan, and their families had arrived from Iceberg Point. "They must have hurried to the point, tossed the ashes, and rushed back to the car," Kate said to Jack. "I'm surprised they even bothered to attend the memorial."

"This must be hard for them, Kate."

"I know, but Laurie and Evan had little to do with Emily Ann's life here. Her friends seemed more like her family."

"Maybe they were. Evan and Laurie have their hands full with work and their own families."

"And divorce. I understand that, but there's more to it. I don't know. Family dynamics, I guess. Who can explain or understand what goes on?"

"Don't even try. Shall we go check on Fred?"

Kate and Jack rose to leave when Kate noticed the woman who had arrived late standing in front of the photo display again. Jeannie Shuttleford scowled and hurried over. After an exchange of angry words, Jeannie spun around and came over to Kate and Jack.

"Thanks again for coming." Jeannie said. "Emily Ann would have been pleased with the turnout."

Kate glancing at the strange woman.

"That's Eleanor Grommer," Jeannie said. "I hoped she wouldn't show up, but I knew she couldn't resist."

"Who is she?" Kate asked.

"A rich, nosy old woman."

"She didn't seem too happy about the photos."

"She's not happy about anything. Her husband died about ten years ago and left her with more money than she knows what to do with. Instead of giving any of it to charity, she spends it on suing anyone over anything.

She subscribes to the philosophy that you can sue anyone for any reason."

"Does she win?" Jack asked.

"Luckily, no. I don't think she cares whether she wins or loses. It's just a way to draw attention to herself about whatever beef she has. Most people do that by ranting on social media. Eleanor drags them to court. She and Emily Ann had gone a few rounds in the past."

"About what?" Kate asked.

"You name it. The trouble started in church, I think."

"In church?" Kate said.

"I don't know what it was all about. Eleanor's a bit of a contradiction, if you ask me. From what Emily Ann told me, Eleanor sits on every church committee the parish has. She tried several times to get Emily Ann involved but couldn't. Eleanor doesn't like to be told 'no' and took Emily Ann's refusal as a personal affront. Oh, please excuse me, I must speak to the caterer before she leaves. Thanks again for coming. Perhaps we can visit before you leave the island."

Kate and Jack walked out to their car in time to see Laurie, Evan, and Brian head-to-head in a heated discussion. Susan shook her head in frustration. When she saw Kate and Jack, she came over.

"Do you mind giving the girls and me a ride back to the house?" Susan inclined her head toward the others. "They've been out here for the last half hour bitching about Emily Ann's will. Evan wants to contest it. Brian agrees with him. Laurie doesn't seem to care much either way. But once she comes back to reality, I'm sure she'll agree. Evan can't talk about Emily Ann's property without dollar signs in his eyes. I'm going to stay out of this."

****

When they arrived at Emily Ann's house, Susan and her daughters said a quick goodbye and left to get in the ferry line for their return to Seattle. The rest of the family left the island directly from the community center. The house held an eerie, unsettling quiet. Kate stepped out onto the deck. Jack followed. "Fred must be upstairs resting," he said.

"He needs it. I know it sounds bad, but I'm glad they are gone," Kate said. A cloud drifted overhead. She hugged her sweater close. "The sun can't decide whether to stay hidden. One moment it's warm, and then chilly." Just then Dotty yelped from the yard, bringing Kate out of her maudlin mood. Kenya held a chew toy in her mouth high over the heads of the smaller dogs. Speckle jumped and tried to snatch the toy but couldn't reach it.

"I think for the first time Kenya realizes how big she is," Jack laughed.

"And how playing unfairly can be fun," Kate said.

"They've been in and out all day." Fred slid open the door and hobbled out to join them.

"I hope they weren't too much trouble. I know you need your rest." Kate tugged the toy from Kenya and tossed it to Speckle.

"Actually, they've kept my mind off things. There's no way I could rest."

Fred looked much worse. His complexion had turned pasty and his skin was drawn. Kate suspected that most of his pain medication had remained untouched. She wanted to place her hand on his forehead to check for fever but stopped herself. Fred might not appreciate her motherly gesture.

Zach came out of the kitchen with two cups. He handed one to his father. "I just made coffee. You guys want some?"

"I had my share at the luncheon," Kate said.

"Me too. I'll be up all night," Jack said.

"Have you told them?" Zach said.

"Not yet," Fred said. "Let's go inside."

"Told us what?" Kate asked as she and Jack walked into the den. Had Evan already called with the news about contesting the will? *Typical of Emily Ann's son not to waste any time*, Kate thought. Fred sat on the sofa and picked up what looked like a scrapbook. "This was what we were using to plan the wedding. Emily Ann had collected designs for wedding invitations, recipes for what we'd serve at the reception, and all that stuff. I went through it to select a few things and then throw the rest away. I'm sure Laurie wouldn't want any of this since she was so upset over us getting married." The angry tone in Fred's voice was slight but unmistakable.

"I didn't come across that when I looked through Emily Ann's things yesterday," Kate said.

"She kept it in the kitchen drawer." Fred slammed the book shut and shoved it off his lap. He closed his eyes. His shoulders shook with silent sobs.

"Dad, it's okay." Zach draped his arm over his father's shoulder. "He found this," Zach said. "It was in the scrapbook." He handed a sheet of paper to Jack. "It's addressed to Dad."

Jack read it and looked up at Kate. She knew immediately what it was.

Fred opened his mouth to speak, then just shook

his head.

"Fred, there was no time to tell you earlier. Detective Kraus was here yesterday," Kate said. "He'd just gotten the autopsy report."

Fred gathered himself for a moment. "Emily Ann's cancer…I've been with her every step of the way. She never once seemed suicidal. Was I so blind?"

Kate read through the note again. Only a couple of lines and Emily Ann's familiar EA signature underneath. "Couldn't go through what again? Was she referring to the cancer treatment?"

"No, that couldn't have been it. Emily Ann had stopped the treatments a few weeks ago. She had been seeing a nutritionist instead. The natural remedies seemed to be working. At least she felt better. We were both optimistic. And I don't know what she could've meant by letting me down. Emily Ann never spoke of death. She never doubted that she would lick this thing."

"She must have been really stressed," Zach said. "She may have been putting up a front for your sake. I mean, with Evan pushing her to sell part of the land, and with the other stuff we found."

"What other stuff?" Kate said.

"Show them." Fred nodded toward the kitchen. Zach came back with a large brown envelope.

"I found those in the drawer where she kept the scrapbook," Fred said. "They were underneath it."

Kate opened the envelope. Four letters, all the same. Hate mail from someone who did not want mountain lions on the island, along with a newspaper article about mountain lion attacks near urban areas— places where development had encroached on the lions' habitat. The article told of a toddler who had been taken from her backyard. When the authorities finally found the child, her neck had been snapped. Kate handed Jack the letters and article.

"These are pretty threatening," Jack said. "Burn the place down if she continued with her plans?"

"I've been rehabbing these cats for fifteen years, and up until two days ago, I've never had one get loose and harm anyone," Fred said.

"If Emily Ann didn't forget to snap the lock shut," Kate said, "then someone unlocked that cage and opened the door."

"She might have forgotten," Jack said. "It was hectic around here. Several people to contend with, several angry people after her announcements the night before."

"Emily Ann was cautious when it came to her animals," Fred said.

"Could that have been the reason Emily Ann left the house the morning she died?" Kate said. "It wasn't her usual morning walk. Evan thinks that the lion frightened her, and that's why she fell. He may be right."

"Well, we know now that that didn't happen," Zach said. "If Emily Ann had planned her suicide, she might have been confused and accidentally left the cage unlocked the night before. We can't be sure, but we now know the cat's not what caused her death."

"I'm not sure about that, Zach," Jack said. "From what I know, people who plan their demise make sure all loose ends are tied up. You know…straighten up the house, leave everything in order, that sort of thing."

"And from the look of Emily Ann's bedroom,"

Kate added, "she had planned to return. It appeared as if she'd left the house suddenly."

"I don't think it matters now," Fred said. "Emily Ann's gone, and whatever happened will not bring her back."

It damn well does matter, Kate thought. *Emily Ann would never kill herself.*

She studied the note again. Two short lines:

"Fred, please forgive me. It's all been too much. I can't deal with this anymore. And I won't let you down again.

Forever,

EA"

The note was typed except for Emily Ann's initials—her familiar floral script, written without lifting the pen from the paper.

"Emily Ann hadn't told you about this hate mail," Kate said.

"No," Fred whispered. "I guess she didn't want to worry me. We were so intent on getting the facility ready."

"We have to call Detective Kraus and tell him about the note," Jack said.

"And the letters," Kate added.

"I'll take care of it tomorrow," Fred said. "I'm not up for another round of questions. I just need some air." He grabbed his crutches, stood up too fast, knocking the coffee table askew. The sudden noise startled Tortuga, who'd apparently been hiding underneath. She leaped and darted between Fred's legs. Zach caught Fred before he tripped.

"That's one crazy cat," Zach said.

"She's jumpy like the rest of us." Fred adjusted his

crutches and hobbled out onto the deck.

****

During the next two days, Kate, Jack, Fred, and Zach settled into a routine. Since Kate and Jack were earlier risers, they started the mornings. Jack walked the dogs while Kate made the coffee and a simple breakfast.

Fred still used the den as his bedroom, and Zach had moved into the second guest room upstairs. He had taken vacation time from his job as a forest ranger in Tahoe to stay with his dad until he could get around unassisted.

Feeding the animals took a couple of hours each morning and afternoon, even with Ray coming in part-time. Having Zach as an extra hand was a godsend. Jack and Zach tended to the injured lion while Ray cleaned cages and did any odd jobs. Kate fed the birds and ministered to the injured bald eagles. The one with the broken wing strutted back and forth along the branch, eager to take flight from her enclosure. To exercise the bird, Kate donned the protective leather glove, grasped the bird's talons, and let it flap away while she held it. With a wingspan of almost six feet, this majestic bird needed a larger cage. By the look in her eye, the desire for freedom was overpowering. The other eagle did little more than emit piping noises when anyone got close. Scars covered its head and breast where a discarded fishing line had cut deep. Despite its appearance, after a couple more weeks of rehab, this bird would have its freedom.

When they weren't tending animals, they worked on the new cages. Fred couldn't help with the building, so he went online and searched for a local construction crew to lay the foundation for the new structures. Ray wanted more hours, so Fred hired him to help with the building as well. Kate suspected that Ray's reason for wanting more work was to avoid his carping wife.

Despite Evan's threats to contest the will, Fred continued with his plans of expansion. Zach would fly several more animals in on Monday. If Fred could acquire a crew, his entire menagerie would be situated by the end of the month, and Emily Ann's wish to have large mammals in the facility would come true.

On Thursday, when Kate and Jack walked back to the house after the final feeding of the day, they saw Detective Kraus' car pull out onto the main road and drive away.

"Looks like Fred turned over the letters," Jack said.

"I was beginning to wonder when he'd get around to that."

****

That night at dinner, Fred brought up the very topic on Kate's mind. "Kraus was a bit sore that I hadn't called sooner, but I needed some time for it to sink in. As soon as Evan finds out, he'll be all over this like a fly on honey. I expect his lawyer will contact me. I can hear it now: 'His mother was unstable, and the charmer coerced her into changing her will.' " Fred pushed his food around on his plate but didn't eat much.

"What did Kraus think about the letters?" Jack said.

"He didn't say much. Said he'd check for fingerprints but didn't expect to get any help there."

"I don't like not knowing what's happening with the investigation," Kate said. "What did Kraus say about the suicide note?"

"What could he say?" Fred asked. "Things are still uncertain. Can we talk about something else? I'm still trying to process everything. I know it will take a while. I keep expecting to see Emily Ann walking down from the cages, her arms loaded with sacks of food pellets, looking like someone who'd had spent the day mucking out a barn. No matter how tired or dirty she was, her face always radiated happiness. Anyway, Ray seems to be picking up a lot of the slack."

"He is," Jack said. "I think he'll work out fine as a permanent addition. He's pleased with the extra hours."

Kate struggled to focus on the conversation. Her mind raced with too many unanswered questions and too many loose ends left dangling. Five days had passed since Emily Ann's death. To Kate, it seemed like a month. She wished she could share Fred's joyful image of Emily Ann, but all Kate saw was the image of Emily Ann lying at the bottom of the cliff.

****

The next morning, Kate rose to the sound of Jack and Zach talking in the driveway. She wanted to roll over for a few more winks, but with all the work that needed doing, she couldn't afford herself the luxury. Kenya pranced in, bounded up on the bed, and stuck her cold nose in Kate's ear. "Okay, I'm up. I'm up." Kate climbed out of bed and followed her dog downstairs.

"Sorry we woke you," Jack said. "Zach wanted to get an early start. He just left to return to California and arrange transportation for the cats."

At the sound of Jack's voice, Speckle and Dotty jumped from under the covers and flew to the door.

"I can take a hint," Jack said. "You do coffee, and I'll do dogs."

"Looks like some bonding is going on in the den," Kate said.

"Those two mutts have been sleeping with Fred every night he's been here." Jack laughed.

"They do make a happy little family." Kate sighed. "I'd hate to think of them being disrupted. Do you think Evan was serious about contesting the will?"

"Absolutely."

"Fred hasn't mentioned it all week. He must feel confident that he'll get to keep the house and property even if Evan makes good on his threat." The coffee started dripping. "Want to wait until it's ready and take a cup with you?"

"I'll wait until I get back." Jack grabbed the three leashes. "We haven't seen the will, so we don't know the specifics. I heard Fred talking to his lawyer on the phone, and evidently, he believes that Evan doesn't have a case."

"Surely, he must be concerned. But he's moving ahead quickly with the expansion."

"Does that bother you?" Jack asked.

"I guess it does. Fred's going to a lot of trouble and expense to relocate the mountain lions."

"And you think he's jumping the gun? I thought you didn't want this nice little family displaced."

"I don't, and, yes, things are happening too fast. Maybe it's because I still can't believe Emily Ann's gone. And I refuse to believe that she killed herself. She could have fallen. A large chunk of ground had crumbled right where she stood. And the more I think about it, the more I think that note could have meant anything."

"First of all, the ledge could have crumbled as

Emily Ann jumped if that were the case."

"She did not jump off that cliff, and she did not accidentally fall!"

"Kate, do you know what you're implying?"

"That someone pushed her. I know. But that doesn't make sense either. I haven't brought up the subject with Fred, but I think I should. We need to get this out into the open."

"Get what out into the open?" Fred rubbed the sleep from his eyes and limped to the counter for his coffee mug.

"You're walking better," Jack said.

"That's because you've got the dogs. It's kind of hard to walk with one on each foot."

It was the first time Kate had heard Fred laugh—it sounded warm and sincere. She could understand Emily Ann's attraction. Fred had a genuine charm that made liking him easy.

"Did I interrupt something?" Fred asked.

Neither Kate nor Jack responded.

"I did. Sorry, I'll just—"

"No," Kate said. "We wanted to talk to you about Emily Ann. About what could have happened. Despite the note, I don't believe she killed herself."

"I have a lot of questions, too," Fred said. "But do you mind if we wait until dinner tonight? I need some time to think things through."

"This evening's fine," Kate said.

"I certainly don't mind treating us to dinner in the village. You've been slaving in this kitchen all week," Fred said.

"Unless you're tired of my cooking, I'd rather stay in. Cooking is great therapy for me."

"How could anyone be tired of your cooking?" Fred said. "Let's see, artichoke lasagna, cream of garlic soup, rice and bean casserole, not to mention the baked goods every morning. You stay here a little longer, and you might just turn me into a vegetarian." Fred looked at Jack. "She must not cook like this all the time, or you'd weigh a ton."

"She does cook like this all the time, but I couldn't put on a pound if I tried," Jack said.

"He's disgusting," Kate said. "Today, you two will have to fend for yourselves for lunch. I'd like to make that hike to Iceberg Point. I didn't get to tell Emily Ann goodbye. None of us did, for that matter. But since her ashes were spread there, I want to pay her a visit."

"Do you want company?" Jack said.

"Thanks, honey. I need to do this myself."

Dotty scratched at the door. "I'd better go," Jack said. "Duty calls."

Chapter Seven

The road to Iceberg Point led past MacKaye Harbor to the small community of Agate Beach, where a scattering of modest homes overlooked the water. Kate pulled off the road onto a small parking lot at the end of the pavement. Few people lived here year-round, so many of the beachfront homes stood vacant. With no landmasses to catch the wind, Agate Beach was one of the few places on the island where waves could be heard lapping the shore. Small, well-polished pebbles rattled as the strong undertow pulled them back toward the ocean. The sound reminded Kate of chips of glass tumbling in a kaleidoscope.

Kate put her cell phone in the console, locked the car, and hiked out to Bat and Ball Lane. She would never have found the place if Emily Ann hadn't brought her here. The road ended at a fence partially hidden by overgrown weeds and vines. From there, a path led into the woods. About fifty yards down, the trail forked. The path to the right led to the McGeary property. If anyone was uncertain which trail to take, the numerous *No Trespassing* signs would remove all doubt. A quarter-mile down the trail, nailed to a tree trunk, a single laminated sheet of paper announced Iceberg Point up ahead and reminded people to pack out their trash. An old, wooden bike rack stood just off the trail. The thick growth of vegetation formed a canopy, blocking out the sun and making the forest damp and cold. Kate zipped her jacket and quickened her pace to warm up. The trail took a sharp left, and like magic, the forest opened up to a sunny meadow with golden grasses growing across the hillside.

Kate veered off toward a mound topped by a stone reference marker. From the top of the mound, Kate had a panoramic view of the island's southern tip. Emily Ann had chosen a perfect resting place. When Kate reached the marker, she sat down on a concrete step and leaned back against the base. The structure, also made of concrete, felt warm on her back. The bright sky, combined with the reflection off the water, almost blinded her. Kate shielded her eyes and watched the fishing boats trawling off the point. Grateful to have the place to herself, Kate closed her eyes and let the sun toast her face.

"Emily Ann, what happened? Why didn't you call me and talk to me? Why didn't you ask for my help?" Kate spoke aloud, her words carried swiftly away by the wind. Then it struck her. She, of all people, should understand how difficult it could be to talk about painful subjects. Her sadness deepened as she realized that she'd never had a chance to discuss with Emily Ann what happened in Africa. She turned her thoughts back to that Sunday morning, waking up late and not knowing where she was, and finding Jack and Kenya gone. She remembered shaking off an odd sensation as she walked downstairs to an empty kitchen. Reasoning had said she'd drank too much the night before and slept too soundly. Perhaps her own demons were haunting her again. Perhaps that self-doubt she strove so hard to keep buried had raised its ugly head. Perhaps she'd become too involved in her own life and blind to people whom she cherished. Perhaps Emily Ann knew this.

Despite her confusion, some piece of logic tapped at the back of her brain like a Morse Code spitting out a message. Some bit of reason spoke up, only to lose its voice amidst the clatter filling Kate's mind. A bald eagle flew by and shrieked a long hollow cry. Its eerie overture trailed on the wind and faded. But another sound resonated in Kate's head, a familiar sound—one that sent shivers through her body. Then all the noises in her head dissipated.

Suddenly she knew.

The reason for her uneasiness that morning after she'd awakened—the reason she'd awakened in the first place—it all made sense. The room had become too warm during the night, and she had gotten up to open the window. She returned to bed and fell back into a deep sleep. Then in the early hours of that morning, in her unconsciousness, she had heard the sound.

A scream that had jolted her awake—Emily Ann's scream as she fell from the ledge.

Kate had been pushing the idea away for the last several days. Now, here alone, Kate had to face the ugly reality that Emily Ann had been murdered.

"Someone wants us to believe you killed yourself, Emily Ann, but why?" Kate said as if her friend were seated beside her. Several people had a motive and opportunity. And except for Ray, they were family, those she had loved, those she trusted.

Calculating schedules, locations, and motives, Kate tried several different scenarios, and each one fit. Everyone knew Emily Ann's routine. It would be easy.

Evan could have followed his mother that morning or have been waiting up by the cages. Brian or Laurie could easily have driven back from the Windsong Inn to Eagle Crossing early that morning. But Fred had not flown in yet. He'd arrived on the island only moments before Kate had discovered Emily Ann's body on the rocks below the cliff. Ray knew Emily Ann's schedule better than anyone. An overwhelming feeling of sadness washed over her, and Kate pressed her palms over her eyes. She did not want to think about the task facing her. She had no right to question people, but she had an obligation to Emily Ann.

Kate opened her eyes and looked across the gray water. She needed to walk, to breathe, and to let her brain absorb this dreadful new reality and come to grips with what she needed to do. The eagle soared above her again, then banked and dipped in her direction. It seemed to hang in the air, defying gravity, defying the wind, defying Kate's intrusion into its domain. Kate's melancholy disappeared. She channeled her grief into action—to hell with worrying about stepping on anyone's feelings.

Someone killed Emily Ann. Kate planned to find out who. And quickly.

She sprinted down the rock and picked up the trail along the ridge. A fisherman out on his boat waved, and Kate waved back. But here, where the narrow trail skirted close to the ledge, she had to watch where she stepped. The steep cliffs along Iceberg Point weren't bad enough to bring on her acrophobia, but Kate didn't want to risk the onslaught of vertigo. As the trail turned west, the deafening howl of the wind blew strong in her face. She stopped to tie her hair back and glanced back at the fishing boat. This time the fisherman waved his arms in air and pointed. Kate looked out over into the water for the telltale signs of orcas breaking the surface. The peak whale watching season had passed, but the three resident pods could often be seen feeding in these familiar waters into early fall. Only white caps, however, disrupted the ocean surface. No whales.

Then Kate heard an annoying buzz and turned just in time to see a small remote-control plane swoop over her head, missing her by a few feet. She ducked as the plane flew out over the water. This was no child's toy; the apparatus's wingspan was almost eight feet. Kate looked around to see the careless operator of the plane, when suddenly it flew back and headed straight for her. This time it dipped directly over her head and came close enough for Kate to read the insignia on the plane's body. Someone was about to become a focus of a week's worth of Kate Caraway's wrath as soon as she could find the idiot. She jogged down the trail and up to a higher perch for a better look but saw no one. The plane continued to circle overhead, then banked steeply, glided back toward the trees, and disappeared. *Right*, Kate thought, *take your toy and go home*.

Before she headed back to the car, Kate wanted to hike down to the southwesternmost tip of the island where the volcanic rocks met the water, forming tide pools where only the toughest of sea life could handle the pounding waves. Brightly colored orange algae grew over sharp rocks. Dried barnacles crunched underfoot, and a few aggregating sea anemones waved their tentacles, tasting the water. Just off the rocks, a sea lion poked its dome-shaped head out of the water and watched Kate until it lost interest and swam away.

In the distance, across the strait, the light of the Cattle Point Lighthouse on San Juan Island blinked.

Kate smiled. She liked to believe that when people died, they had the freedom to visit those left behind by taking the form of any of God's creatures. Once, soon after her father's death, a fat raccoon began making nightly invasions onto Kate's patio. It methodically inspected every nook and cranny, looking for treats and tidbits fallen from the bird feeders. One night, the animal removed a compass Kate had affixed to the bow of her canoe. The compass had been a gift she had given to her father. Kate jumped up and switched on the patio light. Instead of scurrying away, the raccoon scowled at Kate, its facial expression startlingly familiar. Then he slowly waddled off with the compass in his paw. Kate let him go. Ted Caraway never questioned his direction in life, but maybe he needed a little help in his new world. Kate never saw the raccoon again.

Kate drew comfort knowing Emily Ann would always be near. Being here restored Kate's energy and affirmed her vow to find out what really happened to Emily Ann.

The wind shifted from the southwest, forming angry whitecaps across the water's surface. Waves slammed against the rocks, spraying Kate with cold, salty water. She shimmied up to the trail as it ascended along the cliffs. With the wind now at her back, Kate jogged along the trail back to the reference marker for a final wave to Emily Ann. As she crested the ridge, a shadow flitted across her vision. Before Kate could duck, something struck hard on her shoulder, knocking her to her knees. She heard the buzz of the remote-control plane and turned in time to see it change course and head back in her direction. Kate flattened herself on the ground, covering her head with her arms. She felt the swish of the plane inches away as it flew over her again. After a few seconds, she looked around but saw nothing.

Whoever was flying the plane was no idiot. The person was aiming for Kate and had chosen the right place to attack. Behind her, a mound of earth rose up, and she could not see beyond it. In front, the cliff dropped straight down. Kate's blood pounded in her head. She stayed close to the ground, fairly certain she was hidden from view. Visions of the crop-duster scene from Alfred Hitchcock's *North by Northwest* flashed in Kate's mind. Cary Grant had a cornfield to hide in. Kate should be so lucky.

Finally, unwilling to wait for his next move, Kate crawled to the edge and braved another look over. The ninety-degree drop-off dashed all hope of finding a path to the rocks below. Before she could formulate a plan, rocks crumbled down from above. Then the sudden movement of earth startled her. Kate turned in time to see a basketball-size rock rolling in her direction. She jerked to the side, lost her balance, and fell backward, tumbling down the face of the cliff and coming to rest on a precarious overhang no wider than a foot. She landed, twisted and tangled, but dared not move.

Fifty feet directly below, the rocks spiked out of the water like exposed stalagmites. Shearing pain shot through her limbs. Kate tried to slowly untangle herself, but the slight movement threw her off-balance, and she slipped. She grabbed the rock above, holding on by her fingertips, her feet scrabbling against the rock face, trying to find a toehold. She managed to slip her foot into a crack in the rock and shifted her weight to the side.

A Madrona tree, tenaciously growing from the cliff face, hung within her reach. When the muscles in her shoulders and arms began to burn and her fingers grew numb, Kate lunged and grabbed for the branch. She slowly pulled herself up enough to slide her knee and hip between the rocks. That's when she noticed that the opening in the rock angled upward. No more than three feet from where she hung, the crack widened, forming a crevice deep into the earth. Kate inched her way over and, letting go of the branch, she wedged her body into the wall of the cliff.

She was safe for the moment. Taking a few deep breaths to let her pulse slow, Kate took stock of her situation. She began to doubt her earlier suspicion of being attacked. Suddenly she felt silly. *There's no reason anyone would want to kill me*, Kate thought. *It was only a careless accident.* Surely whoever had operated the plane was bound to come investigate.

Kate planted her feet on the rock wall and tried to settle into a more comfortable position. She peeked over the edge and saw that the remote-control plane had crashed on the rocks below and split into several pieces. Some had washed up into a small cove; others swirled in an eddy and looked like toothpicks in a gigantic blender. Within minutes nothing would be left. She looked up from where she had fallen. The precipice that had broken her fall jutted out, hiding her from the trail above.

Kate cursed herself for leaving her cell phone in the Land Rover. Then she heard someone walking back and forth on the trail. She was about to shout for help when loose scree tumbled down from above and stopped her. No one called down to her. After a couple of minutes, a small white object came sailing down from above followed by another spray of pebbles. She watched as the object floated by, trailing a fine tail of smoke. She listened as the crunch of boots on gravel faded, and a sick feeling set in. The person had finished a cigarette, flicked the butt, and walked away.

Any doubt in Kate's mind disappeared. Her first instinct was correct. Her tumble down the cliff had been no accident. Whoever had operated the plane had to have seen its wreck on the rocks. They had to have seen her tumble over the cliff, but they didn't call out to see if she needed help.

If the person had intended to kill her and had not seen her body sprawled on the rocks below, he must know he hadn't succeeded. That realization didn't alleviate Kate's fear. All the guy had to do now was to come back with rappelling gear and finish the job. All Kate could do was wait and hope Jack could get to her first.

The western sky darkened with heavy rain clouds. Soon the fishermen in the next cove would head back into Fisherman's Bay. Kate needed to act fast. She listened intently for the engines of the fishing boats, but all she heard was the stiff wind whistling through the rocks. Caught in the narrow cove, it seemed to blow from several directions at once. Aches and pains emerged as the shock of falling subsided. She was sure no bones were broken, but her palms, bloody and tender, stung where the skin had been scraped. Although painful, she could move her knee. If she came out of this, she'd have only minor bruises and abrasions. That was a big if, however.

The smell of rain saturated the air. With the clouds rolling in, the temperature began to drop rapidly. Kate's mind drifted to the rock climbers in the Imax film she had seen years ago in Chicago. Those daredevils seemed unaffected by gravity as they hung under slabs of rock hundreds of feet high. Knowing a mere fifty-foot cliff would be a piece of cake for experienced climbers made Kate feel like a weak, helpless female, something she'd worked hard her entire life not to be. No matter how brave she willed herself to be, climbing back up was impossible. She considered ripping every stitch of her clothing and tying the pieces together to form a rope to lower herself down. But the rope wouldn't be long enough to reach the rock below.

As the wind whipped by, Kate heard the sound of a trawler motoring across the water. Kate tilted her head and listened. The puttering grew louder. Fearing that no one could see her tucked inside the rock, she quickly slipped off her jacket and removed her white T-shirt to use as a flag. She tied it to the branch of the Madrona and watched it flap in the breeze—a small white flag anyone could easily mistake for a seagull. If only she had dressed in brighter colors.

Just then, Kate caught sight of a fishing boat rounding the cove, fighting the rough water. It rode high on the crests and then disappeared as it fell deep into the troughs. Even though it was futile, Kate started waving her arms and shouting. Rain pelted down. The boat steadily battled the waves and disappeared around the bend. Kate slumped down.

Her only choice was to wait. The Land Rover was

parked on Agate Beach. Jack knew where she was, and he'd come looking for her eventually, but that could be hours. Maybe she'd be here all night. She could neither stand nor sit comfortably now, and hanging out here in this V-shaped crack in the earth for any length of time seemed an impossibility. Less than two hours had passed since she left Emily Ann's house. Jack would not begin to worry for a while.

Kate watched as the rain clouds blew across the sky. The weather in the San Juans changed rapidly, and already the rain had turned to a mist. With the storm passing, the sky to the west started to clear. Insects now flurried about, pursued by cliff swallows darting back and forth on sickle-shaped wings. Their blue- and rust-colored feathers glittered in the sun as the birds swept through the air, feeding on the wing and twittering with excitement.

Kate tried to focus on the nature show right before her eyes, but she could only think of the approaching sunset and being out here in the dark. She leaned back to take some pressure off her knee. A stab of pain ran up her back. Then, out of the corner of her eye, she spotted a sailboat drifting in the distance, but it was too far away for anyone to notice her, and if they did, they'd surely question their sanity seeing a woman stuck in the rocks below the trail. Useless as a warning flag, her white T-shirt, now wet and limp, hung lifeless from the Madrona branch. Except for ants crawling up and down on the rock wall and the bald eagle that drifted back and forth on the wind, Kate was alone. The eagle flew past again, this time so close Kate swore she saw an angry glare in its yellow eye.

Great, Kate thought, *not only am I stuck in a crack*

on the side of this cliff face, I'm being intimidated by an eagle whose prime perch I've stolen. The bird landed not thirty feet away, folded its majestic wings, and seemed to settle in and wait out its intruder. After losing the staring contest, Kate raised up a bit to ease the numbness on her tailbone. That's when she saw the sailboat tacking sharply to the right and sailing straight for the cove. She started waving her arms. And then just as quickly, she pulled back. What if her assailant had returned via the water? She ducked back and remained still.

The boat slowed as it neared the cove. Kate watched as a man bustled across the deck and lowered the anchor. Using binoculars, he looked directly at Kate, then cupped his hands around his mouth, and shouted. He seemed harmless and vaguely familiar, but Kate remained within the shadows of her hole. At first, she couldn't make out what he was shouting—something about "frog," or "fog." Then the wind carried his voice in her direction, and this time his shout was loud and clear. Relief washed over her. She began to laugh.

"My wife wants to see your greyhound," he chortled. "Is she in there with you?"

"I'm afraid I'm by myself today."

"Not for long. I spotted you while watching that eagle. I called the county sheriff. Help should be arriving shortly. I'll stay anchored here, so they'll be able to locate you when they come down the trail. Are you hurt?"

"Only my ego."

"Don't go away."

Kate waved her thanks and managed to laugh at his

joke. It was the man she had seen anchored in Watmough Bay when she and Kenya had jogged down to the beach. Suddenly Kate felt stupid. She wanted out of here so badly, she was ready to jump. But what she didn't want was a huge rescue party, complete with TV cameras, helicopters, and the works. Appearing on the nightly news was not Kate's idea of fun. She'd be labeled another careless adventurer who would cost the county a bundle.

The man on the boat started pointing, and moments later, Jack's voice called from above. "Kate, where are you?"

"Jack! I'm right below you. Wedged in a crack. Inside the wall."

"Are you okay?"

"Physically, yes. I feel silly, though. Are there any news cameras up there?"

"No. Do you want me to alert the media?"

"Not funny. Just get me out."

"Hang tight. A couple of rescue guys are getting ready to rappel down. We'll have you up in a few minutes."

Chapter Eight

"Most baseball players' wives are soccer moms whose only trouble is cleaning the fast-food wrappers and empty plastic bottles from their SUV," Jack said. "My wife is constantly the target of a mad person's deadly revenge."

"Most baseball players' wives are not me, for which I'm sure you are overjoyed, Jack Ryder. And may I add that you sound chauvinistic, which is unlike you."

"Correct on both points. My apology, but you'll have to forgive me if I'm not myself. I just watched my wife being rescued off the face of a cliff, all the while listening to the EMTs tell me how lucky you were not to have landed on the rocks and been washed out to sea. What would you rather have first, an icepack or a glass of wine?"

"Silly question. Pour and bring the damn bottle."

"You should have told Deputy Fitzroy before he left," Jack said, handing Kate a glass of wine.

"Told him what? That someone tried to kill me? How would that sound? I could just hear him now. 'Why do you think that, Ms. Caraway? Did you see the person flying the plane? Did you see him aiming for you? Is there any reason why someone would want to kill you?' "

"I understand, but with the possibility that Emily

Ann was murder—"

"They have the suicide note and have most certainly closed the case." Frustrated, she set her wine on the end table. "If I went to Kraus with my suspicions, he'd accuse me of being paranoid. I need time to—"

"Gather more evidence? Kate, we don't have a lot of time. If what happened today was intentional, the authorities need to get on it and quickly."

"Damn it, Jack! I know that, but—" Kate jumped up, and the pain in her knee sent her stumbling back down. "Shit!"

Kenya, who had been asleep in her basket, yelped when Kate shouted.

"Are you okay?" Jack rushed over.

"Yes. I just keep doing one stupid thing after another." Kate looked at her greyhound. "Do you think she is dreaming about her racing days?"

"That would be more like a nightmare. Speaking of which, if that guy and his wife hadn't been sailing around that cove scoping out eagles, you might still be there."

Kate smiled. "I knew you'd find me sooner or later."

"I was relieved when Fred and I saw the Land Rover parked across the road from the beach. But relief didn't last long. The fire department and rescue services pulled in right behind us. That meant trouble, and where there's trouble, there's Kate Caraway." Jack went over and scratched Kenya's belly. She groaned in ecstasy. "I understand your reluctance to go to the authorities, but if someone's trying to kill you, they could try again. And once Detective Kraus hears about your little episode, he'll come knocking with more questions."

"You're right. I should stop analyzing things to death and trust the sheriff's department to do its job. Who could it have been, Jack? Several people could have pushed Emily Ann off the cliff. But who knew that I drove out to Iceberg Point?"

"Maybe someone followed you."

"Like the person who sent those threatening letters? This has to be connected. But the question remains, why kill me? My death wouldn't stop Fred from rehabbing lions here on Lopez."

"Maybe their intention was to disrupt operations at Eagle Crossing."

"That's obvious. The lion was let out of its cage, and Emily Ann and I were pushed off cliffs, but we still don't have any hard evidence to point to murder and attempted murder. And there's something else."

"What?"

"Something came to me out on the point while I was thinking about Emily Ann before I tumbled off the cliff. I realized what had awakened me that morning Emily Ann died. Jack, she screamed. If she had jumped, she wouldn't have screamed."

"Are you sure about what you heard?"

"No doubt in my mind. I had gotten up in the middle of the night and opened the window. I'm surprised you didn't hear anything when you were out with the dogs that morning."

"I must have been off the property and down the road already." Jack ran his hands over his short hair. "That means we can pinpoint the time it happened. I'd been gone only about half an hour, forty-five minutes at the most. But the authorities won't put a lot of stock in what you just told me, especially after remembering several days later."

"That's what I was trying to tell you earlier! It's all mere speculation!" Kate slammed her fist down on the pillow.

"But not what happened today, Kate. That doesn't sound like speculation to me. However, you can't rule out the possibility that Emily could have fallen."

"No she couldn't have. She was too careful," Kate shouted. "Are we fighting?"

"Us? Never. Besides, you fight with yourself enough. There's no need for me to join in." He sat down next to Kate, gently lifted her leg, and draped it over his. "Sometimes you're too stubborn and headstrong for your own good."

"Makes life interesting."

"No shit."

"Something smells good."

"Garlic bread. Fred's cooking. You may have to fend for yourself this meal. I saw him take steaks out of the freezer."

"No problem. I'll find something. While we're eating, let's talk to Fred about this. Three heads are better than one."

"Come on, gimpy. I'll give you a piggyback ride downstairs unless you want to go another round with yourself. I'll referee."

"Don't be silly."

Kate and Jack walked into the den just as Fred hobbled in on one crutch, carrying two steaks from the outside grill. He had already set the kitchen table. "Sorry, Kate, I couldn't help myself. Watching people get rescued gives me an appetite. I made you a spinach salad and heated up the lentil soup. I hope that's okay."

"Sounds wonderful. You're down to one crutch, I see. Hope you're not overdoing it."

"Gotta stay busy," Fred said. "This morning you wanted to talk about Emily Ann's death. If I hadn't suggested we wait until this evening, you wouldn't have been at the wrong place at the wrong time and ended up falling over that cliff."

Jack glanced at Kate, then turned to Fred. "I think it's more complicated than that."

"What do you mean?" Fred asked.

"Kate doesn't believe her fall was an accident."

Fred set the steaks down on the table. "You'd better tell me what happened."

"I think someone deliberately flew that plane at me, knocking me off the trail."

"Two falls from a cliff in less than a week," Fred whispered.

"You up for talking about this?" Jack asked.

"I've had nothing much else to do for the past several days but think about Emily Ann's death. You don't believe she killed herself, and neither do I. And if what you're telling me is true, we have a bad situation here." He turned to the stove.

"Here, let me do that," Jack said. "Sit down."

"I don't believe that she accidentally fell either," Kate said, dipping into her bowl of soup. "Not after what happened to me today. It's all so confusing. It still may have been an accident. Whoever operated the plane could have become frightened when he realized what he had done, and rather than help me, he bolted."

"But he stood right over you, smoked a cigarette,

kicked the dirt, and then left," Jack said. "That doesn't sound like a frightened person."

"I agree with Jack," Fred said. "Innocent people have caused accidents, panicked, and left the scene. But it doesn't sound like that's what happened."

"When I finally faced the reality that Emily Ann was murdered, I naturally thought of her family," Kate said. "Evan was counting on Emily Ann selling the property. With the divorce hanging over Evan, and his financial problems…well, that gives him a motive."

"But the profit of that sale wouldn't be his," Jack said.

"That's true," Kate agreed. "But if Emily Ann sold the property, he'd have a resource available to him. I don't believe he'd hesitate to ask his mother for money if he needed it. But with her out of the way, he'd assume the property would be his."

"What about Brian?" Fred asked. "He's got that new business. Maybe he's having cash flow problems."

"I overheard Brian and Laurie arguing the day before Emily Ann died. It didn't sound good," Kate said.

"From talking to Brian that first night, I gathered his business is booming," Jack said. "His only problem seemed to be keeping up with it. Of course, he could have been bragging in front of Evan. What about Laurie?"

"As a suspect?" Fred said.

"Laurie *was* a bundle of nerves, even when she and Brian first arrived. However, I can't imagine her killing her mother," Kate said.

"I'll never understand why some kids feel that their parents owe them financial assistance throughout their entire lives," Fred said. "I told Zach once he turned eighteen, he was on his own. I'd be there to support him, but not financially. Some people may think that attitude is a bit heartless, even archaic, but my son turned out just fine. Anyway, financial trouble or not, I can't believe Emily Ann's kids would kill their mother."

"If Emily Ann's death is linked to my so-called accident, it couldn't have been her kids; they were all in Seattle today. Being at the mercy of the ferry schedule, it takes several hours to get to Lopez Island from the city," Kate said.

"Kenmore Air leaves Lake Union and arrives on the islands in just under forty-five minutes," Jack reminded them.

"True, but once you get here, you need a car. Renting one is possible, but that leaves a trail," Kate said. "No, the more I think about it, the more I believe it was someone here on the island."

"The same person who wrote those threatening letters," Fred added. "Let's have another look at them."

"You didn't turn them over to Detective Kraus?" Kate said.

"I did, but I made copies first. I'll make coffee, and we can go into the den. How was your salad? I looked in the refrigerator and anything that didn't once have a face, I chopped it up and threw it in the bowl."

"It was wonderful." Kate smiled. "Although anchovies have a face, but I'll forgive you this time."

Fred opened the drawer containing the letters and handed them to Jack. "Here they are. Oh, I almost forgot." He turned to Kate. "Brian called this afternoon."

"You mean he no longer believes you tried to kill him?" Kate asked.

"I think he was hoping you'd answer the phone. He wasn't exactly glad to hear my voice."

"What did he want?" Jack said.

"Sounds like he's got his hands full. He said Laurie's seeing a therapist. He'll be out of town for the next few days, checking on clients. He's worried about her. I left their phone number on Emily Ann's desk. I got the impression he wanted you to check on Laurie while he was gone."

"Me?" Kate said.

"I don't think he has anyone else to turn to."

"I'll call her tomorrow," Kate said. "I am going to Seattle to visit with my friend, Jill Michaels, and I'll get the scoop on Evan. Then I'll drop by and check on Laurie. I know you'll need all the help you can get when those cats arrive. I hope you can spare me."

"Got it covered. Zach is bringing several guys from the forestry department to help. And with Jack here, we'll manage fine."

They spread the letters out on the coffee table and arranged them according to date. There were four in all, typed and in a large, block font.

"Do you have the envelopes they came in?" Kate asked.

"No. Emily Ann must have thrown them away. I found all four letters in this brown envelope," Fred said.

"That's strange," Kate said. "If Emily Ann kept these, surely she'd have kept the envelopes to show when they were sent."

"Each letter is dated," Fred pointed out.

"That's even stranger," Jack said. "Who dates their

threatening letters?"

"Maybe they weren't delivered through the mail. Maybe they were hand-delivered. The first one was dated just two weeks ago. The day after the lion arrived," Kate pointed out. "The last one came the day before Jack and I got here. Has Emily Ann ever had any trouble before concerning Eagle Crossing—people objecting to her keeping the eagles here?"

"None that I know of, except for Eleanor Grommer. I never met her, but Emily Ann told me about all the trouble she causes. My guess is that she's an old woman with nothing better to do. Otherwise, the community seemed supportive. Emily Ann spent a lot of time with the school kids, teaching them about eagles and injured wildlife."

"News travels fast. The lion was here only one day before she got this first letter." Jack turned to Fred. "You said she kept mum about this."

"She did. We both did," Fred said. "But we weren't exactly stealthy about the lion's arrival. I had to report in at the airport. And what you said is true, Jack—news does travel fast on this small island. I wouldn't be surprised if half the locals knew what we were up to even before we left the airport."

Kate picked up the letters. "The message in each one is very personal. I mean, whoever sent them seemed to believe that Emily Ann's decision to include mountain lions in her rehab facility was a direct affront. This one, for instance. 'You've had your warning. The cat—' "

"That's the first letter?" Jack said. "It mentions 'cat.' The others refer to 'cats.' This person knew that more cats were coming."

"Could it have been someone delivering the building materials for the cages?" Kate said.

"I doubt it. Emily Ann and I only said that we were expanding. We never said why."

"She could have confided in one of her friends who leaked the news," Kate speculated.

"Emily Ann was the one who insisted we keep everything quiet. I seriously doubt that she would have told a soul."

Fred was right. Kate knew firsthand how well Emily Ann could keep a secret.

"It sounds like she knew from the start that she'd run up against opposition," Kate said. "But Emily Ann didn't scare easily. These letters all refer to an earlier warning. "Did she have any trouble before?"

"Nothing that gave her any concern," Fred said.

"How about Ray Steiner?" Kate said. "Surely he knew about the lions."

"He did, but not until the last minute. And it didn't seem to matter to him one way or another. He just shows up a few days a week, does his work, and leaves. He seems to have his hands full with that wife of his. I doubt the presence of mountain lions could be as troublesome as living with her."

"Jacob Bower?" Jack said. "He's the closest neighbor. Since he hikes around the property, he would have seen the cat immediately. If the letters were hand delivered, who better than the neighbor? He's familiar with the rehab facility and Emily Ann's routine."

"He's an odd fellow," Kate said. "I don't remember exactly what Emily Ann told me about him, but I got the feeling that their friendship had recently cooled. But that poem he read at her memorial luncheon sounded too odd, and he seemed strangely affected by her death."

"What poem?" Fred asked.

"One by Emily Dickinson," Kate said. "She wrote beautifully about death. The one he read was more about easing one's pain, maybe in a regretful way."

"You think his interest in Emily Ann was romantic. If that were the case, he would have pushed me off that cliff, not her," Fred said. "I don't think the guy is playing with a full deck."

"Easing his own pain? Regretful he killed her?" Jack asked. "Where's Bower from?"

"California. Emily Ann told me he's a retired engineer," Kate said.

"It might be worth finding out more about him," Jack said.

"How?" Fred questioned.

"Maybe we *should* go to the sheriff with our suspicions," Jack said.

"Not just yet," Kate said. "I'd like to have something solid to give him. Let's see what more we can find out. I know we're on a tight deadline this weekend to get the cages finished. But first thing Monday morning, I'll do some serious nosing around. I'll go see Jeannie Shuttleford at the library before I leave for Seattle. I can understand Emily Ann keeping the lion a secret, but if she was troubled by the letters, she might have talked to Jeannie."

Kate put the letters back into the envelope. "I don't know about you two, but I've had enough for one day."

"What, spending the afternoon on a cliff face with the eagles isn't your idea of fun?" Jack teased.

"No, actually that was fun. It's the way I got there

that bothers me."

****

The Lopez Public Library resembled a little red schoolhouse but larger and newer. Kate was surprised to see the parking lot was almost full on such a glorious morning. She pulled into one of the few spaces left. Inside she found Jeannie Shuttleford instructing an elderly man how to log on to the Internet and research a topic.

"All you have to do, Grady, is type in a few words about what information you need. Then hit search and see what comes up."

"You mean I can find out about anything?" Grady said.

"Just about." Jeannie looked up, saw Kate waiting at the front desk, and smiled. The librarian patted the old man's shoulder. "Let me know if you need more help."

"How about Viagra? Can I find out how that works? Damn!" He didn't wait for Jeannie's answer. He started typing.

"Kate, how nice to see you," Jeannie said. "I'm glad you're still here. How are Emily Ann's children?"

"Not good, I'm afraid. I was hoping you'd have a few minutes to spare."

"Wow!" Grady said. "I'll be damned."

"Let's go into my office." Jeannie inclined her head at Grady and lowered her voice. "He comes in every day. And every day for at least five years, I've had to show him how to find something on the Internet. I used to chalk it up to dementia, but I think he's lonely and needs the attention since his wife passed away. One day he's researching some medication, and the next day, he's looking for information about some conspiracy theory. And people think the life of a librarian is boring." Jeannie closed her office door behind them. "But you're not here to chat, are you?"

"I'm not sure where to turn, Jeannie. You and Emily Ann were good friends. I'm hoping you can help clear up a few things."

Jeannie's brow furrowed. "What things?"

"Was Emily Ann troubled about something lately?"

Jeannie leaned back in her chair and took a deep breath. "You mean her cancer? Yes, she told me."

"Did she say anything about her plans over the upcoming weeks?"

"It had been several weeks since we visited. In fact, Emily Ann didn't tell me about the cancer until after her treatment. I had to pry it out of her. She used to come to the library two or three times a week, and then she stopped coming. Whenever I called, she just told me how busy she was with her eagles."

"We were shocked to hear about the cancer. Seems like the only ones who knew were you, Emily Ann's daughter-in-law, and Fred Marlow."

"Fred Marlow? Who's that?"

"A close friend. Lately, he's been helping Emily Ann with her eagles."

Jeannie looked doubtful but said nothing.

Now Kate questioned how close the women really were if Jeannie knew nothing about the engagement. Kate had begun feeling this visit was a mistake when Jeannie spoke up.

"What's this all about, Kate?"

Kate decided to go ahead with her other questions.

"Emily Ann had received several anonymous threatening letters concerning Eagle Crossing. Did she mention them to you?"

"No. She hadn't said a word."

"Could it have been that woman, Eleanor Grommer?"

"Eleanor was opposed to almost everything Emily Ann did, for no other reason than to give her a hard time. I can see Eleanor sending threatening letters, but believe me, she would have signed her name."

Word would be out soon enough, so Kate leveled with Jeannie. "Emily Ann and her friend, Fred Marlow, were expanding Eagle Crossing to include mammals, specifically injured mountain lions and other wild cats. The first one arrived a few days ago, and several more are scheduled to arrive today. Evidently, someone was not pleased with the idea."

"Emily Ann never mentioned any mountain lions." Jeannie paused. "You know, I just remembered something Eleanor said at the luncheon. She said there were rumors about Eagle Crossing. I didn't want to engage her, so I refused to listen. She must have heard about the mountain lions. That's just the sort of thing she'd get riled up over. I told her that we were here celebrating Emily Ann's life, and if all she came to do was spread gossip, she could just leave."

"Can you think of anyone else who would send her those letters?"

"People who live on Lopez are fairly tolerant of one another. Emily Ann wasn't the only one doing her own thing. I can't imagine anyone sending those letters. You mentioned Emily Ann's friend who was helping her with the expansion. Who is this guy?"

"Fred Marlow. He and Emily Ann were to be married soon."

"No way." Jeannie's shoulders slumped. "Maybe I wasn't such a good friend after all. Maybe I was the one who was too busy." Jeannie teared up, and her breath caught.

Kate hated to bring up the topic, but she needed to hear Jeannie's opinion on the matter of Emily Ann's apparent suicide, which sounded more and more absurd.

"I'm sorry, Jeannie, but there's something else. I shouldn't have hit you with all of this. But other things have happened, and I need all the information I can get."

Jeannie removed her tissue from her face. "What things? Please tell me."

"Fred found a suicide note written to him and placed in a scrapbook where only he would find it. I cannot believe Emily Ann would kill herself. But I hadn't seen her in years, and so much has happened to her since then. I need to hear from someone else who knew her, someone on the island.

Jeannie rose from her desk, pulled a paper cup from a dispenser, and availed herself of the water cooler in the corner. She looked out of her window at the apple trees behind the library. They were heavy with fruit; some already littered the ground. Jeannie seemed to think carefully before she answered. "Never! Emily Ann would never do that. Ever." She turned around and faced Kate. Jeannie swallowed her tears, then looked at her watch. "I have a board meeting in a few minutes, but I want to find out more about what's going on. How long will you be here?"

"A few more days," Kate said. "You're welcome to stop by. We can talk some more. You can meet Fred."

"I'll be there tonight. I close the library at eight. I hope that won't be too late."

"Not at all. I'm on my way to Seattle to see Emily Ann's daughter. I'll be back before then."

"Good." Jeannie crumbled her paper cup and tossed it into the wastebasket.

"I'll let you get back to work. Oh, do you know anything about Jacob Bower, Emily Ann's neighbor?"

"That's an odd one for you. Rumor has it he moved to the island after some tragedy that occurred, in California, I think. He pretty much keeps to himself. We have a few of those on the island. They move here to get away from something. Silly, you know. Whatever they are running from or trying to avoid follows them no matter what."

"Thanks, Jeannie. See you later this evening."

Chapter Nine

Kate pulled into the Green Lake neighborhood a few minutes before noon. Just a few miles north of downtown Seattle, Green Lake was one of the city's quaint neighborhoods. Brian and Laurie's home sat on a hillside overlooking the small lake itself. Built in the forties and newly remodeled, the two-story English Tudor must have cost them a fortune.

As Kate drove up, she noticed a woman standing on the front porch with Ben on her hip. At first, she didn't recognize Laurie. The impeccably dressed and groomed woman Kate had seen at Eagle Crossing a few days ago looked as if she hadn't washed her hair or changed her clothes in days. A wrinkled dress hung limply over her small frame. Her hair, loose and uncombed, separated into listless strands. Mattie bounced up and greeted Kate with slobber and a grin.

"Just push her down," Laurie said. "I'm sorry. She's a bundle of energy. I just haven't felt like walking her lately."

"Where's her leash? I'll do that while you brew some coffee."

"I usually walk her around the lake. It's about three miles, but you don't have to go around the entire thing."

"No problem. I haven't had my exercise today. We'll be back in about forty-five minutes. I haven't had lunch either. Does the Urban Bakery across the street make sandwiches?"

Laurie started to cry. "I'm sorry. I just can't seem to get it together." She pushed her hair out of her face. "I know I look like shit. I should've had something ready for you."

"It's okay, Laurie. Just make the coffee."

"Mommy," Ben said.

Laurie turned and walked inside. Kate suspected that Mattie wasn't the only one who had been ignored these last few days.

As soon as they reached the path surrounding Green Lake, Mattie bolted, almost jerking Kate's arm from its socket. With her sore and swollen knee, Kate couldn't jog. She had to tug hard to keep the golden retriever at heel.

The beautiful weather brought out hordes of people. Picnickers, sunbathers, and Frisbee throwers covered the lawn. Along the trail, people were pushing baby strollers, walking dogs, jogging, and rollerblading. A guy on a unicycle wove in and out of the pedestrians. Halfway around the lake, Mattie had burned enough energy to walk next to Kate. Finally, not having to struggle with the dog, Kate could concentrate on what she'd tell Laurie. She doubted that Laurie would be much help in discovering what had happened to Emily Ann. Kate found it strange that Laurie knew so little of her mother's life in those last few months. Emily Ann had chosen to withhold so much from her children: the recurring cancer, moving predators to the island, marrying Fred. Was their relationship so strained that Emily Ann couldn't confide in her? When Kate was a teenager, and Emily Ann was dating Kate's father, she could talk to Emily Ann about anything. But family dynamics were hard to understand.

Completing the loop, Kate crossed the street to the deli's take-out window. She ordered two Swiss cheese and artichoke sandwiches and a hot dog for Ben, then walked back up the hill to the Fuller house. She knocked on the screen door and heard Ben crying. She knocked a second time and finally let herself in. She unleashed Mattie, and the dog bolted inside.

"Laurie, it's me," Kate said. She followed Mattie into the kitchen, where she found Ben sobbing on the floor amid a pile of toys. Kate knelt beside him. He gave no resistance when she picked him up. "It's okay, sweetheart. Where's your mommy?" Kate grabbed a paper towel and cleaned the tears off the child's face. She found a jug of apple juice in the refrigerator. Sitting in the sink was a child's drinking cup. Kate rinsed it out, filled it with juice, and handed it to Ben. He drank it right down. Kate looked around. The coffee pot was also in the sink.

"Laurie," Kate called. The TV blared from the living room. Kate found the remote and turned it off. That's when she noticed Laurie on the sofa. Kate sat Ben down on the rug.

"Mommy sick," he said.

"Laurie!" Kate took the young woman by the shoulders and sat her up. "Laurie! Wake up. Can you hear me? It's Kate."

Laurie's eyes fluttered, and she raised her head. She looked around the room. "Ben?"

"He's okay. But I'm not sure about you. When was the last time you ate?"

Laurie didn't answer. She picked up a throw pillow and hugged it to her chest. Silent tears slid down her cheeks. "I can't deal with this," she finally said.

"I know it's hard, Laurie. A shower will make you feel better. I brought us some lunch."

"Ben hasn't had his lunch either."

"I'll feed him. I hope he likes hot dogs."

"You'll have to cut it up for him."

Kate smiled. "I will, Laurie. Just get cleaned up."

Laurie stood, steadied herself, and disappeared into the bedroom.

Fifteen minutes later, Ben had finished his hot dog, a second glass of juice, and begun crumbling an oatmeal cookie on his high chair tray. Laurie walked into the kitchen and slumped into a chair. Kate placed a sandwich and a cup of coffee down in front of her.

"I can't eat," she said.

"You must eat something, Laurie. Are you still taking those tranquilizers?" Kate asked.

Laurie nodded.

"Where are they?"

"In that cabinet where I keep the spices.

Kate opened the cabinet.

"What are you going to do? I need those," she sobbed.

"Laurie, this vial of antianxiety meds is almost empty." Why had Brian left on a business trip with his wife in such a fragile state? "If I hadn't walked in when I did, something horrible could have happened to Ben. How long have you been like this?"

Laurie pinched a piece of bread crust from her sandwich. "I don't know what's happened over the last several months. Brian's business suddenly took off, and things became so hectic. Mom came over several weeks ago. I knew she was upset about something. But Brian was trying to close this big deal, we were in the middle of remodeling this monster of a house, and Ben had come down with a nasty virus. I was angry that Mom didn't seem to care about…my stupid problems. I realize now that she was trying to tell me about her cancer. If I'd only known." Laurie dropped her head in her hands.

"It's okay, Laurie. How long will Brian be gone? I don't want you to stay by yourself."

"For two more nights."

"I wish you'd come back to Lopez with me."

"I won't! Not with the lion there."

"Can someone come to stay with you? How about Susan?"

"Susan? Evan's such a fool. I can't believe she put up with him for so long. But Susan's teaching, and she has her hands full with the girls."

"It won't hurt to ask. Do you have her phone number?"

Laurie scrolled her contact list and handed her cell phone to Kate. "She'll be teaching now. That's the school number."

An hour later, Laurie had at least eaten half her sandwich and Ben was down for a nap when Susan knocked on the back door.

Kate let her in. "Thanks for coming."

"No problem. I called for a sub and was able to take the afternoon off." She walked over to where Laurie sat curled up on the sofa. "Laurie, why didn't you call me? You look like you haven't slept in days."

"I just can't deal with this."

"It's okay. I can come and stay the night. But I'll have to teach tomorrow. I'll pick up the girls and come over after school." She looked at her watch. "How long will you be here?" she said to Kate. "I have to pick Melissa and Angie up at two o'clock."

"I have another errand to run. I wanted to make the six-thirty ferry," Kate said. "But I can stay until you get back."

"Mommy," a little voice from the back bedroom called out.

"I'm coming, honey." Laurie rose to attend to Ben.

"Stay put," Susan said. "I'll get him."

Color had returned to Laurie's face. "Thanks for coming, Kate. I feel like such a fool."

"You've been through a lot. It'll take a while."

"I wish I could believe that," Laurie said.

Susan came back carrying Ben. "Laurie, what happened to Ben's room?"

Laurie turned around, giving Susan a questioning look.

"That lovely wallpaper. You worked so hard putting it up," Susan said.

"Oh, that. I decided I didn't like it. Last night when I couldn't sleep, I moved Ben into our room and started peeling it off the wall. I want something more lasting."

"But his room was so cute." Susan turned to Kate. "Ben's room was the first one Laurie remodeled after they moved in. She dragged me all over Seattle looking for just the right wallpaper."

"Ben will outgrow the design in no time."

"He's only two, Laurie," Susan said.

Laurie started to cry. "I just felt like making some changes. I can't seem to do anything right. Brian will kill me when he finds out."

"I'm sorry," Susan said. "I shouldn't have opened

my mouth. We'll go shopping this weekend. I'll help you pick out something else. Don't worry about Brian. He'll get over it."

"I'm going to lie down for a while." Laurie took Ben from Susan and went to her bedroom and closed the door.

After Laurie left, Kate leveled with Susan. "A lot has happened the last few days. I was hoping Laurie could give me some answers, maybe clear up some things, but when I saw the shape she was in, I knew that was impossible. Also, after talking to her, I realized that she couldn't help me."

"What do you mean?" Susan said. "What's happened?"

"There are questions about how Emily Ann died. Evan hasn't told you."

"Told me what?"

"At first we thought it might have been suicide."

"What! He hasn't said a word, and neither has Laurie. So, how do you know?"

"Emily Ann had started a scrapbook for her wedding. A few days ago, Fred went through it and found what could be a suicide note."

"That's crazy! Emily Ann would never kill herself!" Susan said, lowering her voice.

"Jack, Fred, and I don't believe it either, especially after we found a stack of threatening letters."

"What threatening letters?"

"Someone was not happy with Emily Ann's plans to expand her facility. The letters warned her not to move the lions onto the island."

"You can't take those seriously," Susan said. "I'm sure it was just some jerk spouting off. Emily Ann has

131

lived on Lopez for years. Wait, what are you implying?"

"After what happened yesterday, there's a good chance someone pushed Emily Ann off that cliff."

"You mean it was deliberate? What happened yesterday?"

"I hiked out to Iceberg Point and tumbled off the cliff. If it weren't for a scrawny Madrona tree, I could have been killed. It wasn't an accident." Kate explained her ordeal. Susan listened without taking her eyes off Kate.

"I don't understand. Why would someone want to kill you? It doesn't make sense."

"I can't figure it out either, but it's too much of a coincidence—two people in one week falling off cliffs on Lopez Island."

"Oh, my God!"

"And it wasn't suicide. According to Fred, her cancer was in remission. She had every reason to hope things were looking up."

Susan hugged her sweater around her as if to ward off a sudden chill. "It couldn't have been an accident?"

"Had it been a normal morning and had she been standing on that ridge, drinking her coffee when the ground underneath her crumbled, no one would have questioned it. But that wasn't the case. I wouldn't say anything to Laurie just yet. Let her recover a bit more."

"She'll never be able to handle this."

"The important thing right now is to make sure she stops medicating herself."

"I'll do what I can. Since Evan and I have been having trouble, I've been reluctant to call Laurie. I'm not sure how she feels about the separation."

"She knows how difficult her brother can be. And I believe she values your friendship. For now, the best thing you can do is just be here for her."

"I can't believe this. Someone murdered Emily Ann. Please call if you find out anything else."

Susan left to pick up her daughters. Kate went to the kitchen and started cleaning up. Except for granite countertops and modern appliances, the kitchen had been restored to its original state. The cabinet doors were made of glass and framed by newly painted white pine. It was apparent the Fullers had spared no expense in restoring their home. After finishing the dishes, Kate stuffed the trash into a bag and took it out to the backyard. She removed the lid from one of the garbage cans to find it crammed full. So was the next one. Kate was about to try the third one when she heard someone walking up the driveway.

"Mrs. Fuller?"

Kate turned around to see a man dressed in an olive-green jumpsuit walking up, holding a clipboard in his hand. Another man stood by a large white van parked in the street.

"Mrs. Laurie Fuller?" he asked again.

"No," Kate said. "Mrs. Fuller is inside. Can I help you?"

"We're from Goodwill. We're here to pick up some boxes."

Kate looked around.

"Says here, they're supposed to be in the garage."

Kate raised the garage door. Inside were several large boxes marked Goodwill. "Here they are," Kate called.

The man walked in and called to his partner. "Up

here, Derek." Then he said to Kate, "We came by earlier, but no one was here. Someone has to be here so we get the right stuff. Looks like someone's been doing some housecleaning." He lifted one box and walked down the driveway. A few minutes later, Derek walked in. Just as he was about to grab the second box, he stopped. "Hey, look at this. It looks brand new."

Kate looked down to see a toy helicopter about the size of a shoebox. Derek picked it up. A small piece of the tail had broken off. He flipped a switch on the side, and the blades started rotating. He turned it off and sighed. "It still works," he said to Kate. "Kids. One little thing breaks, and they don't want it anymore." He looked at Kate and frowned as if she were the one guilty of discarding the toy. "Sorry," he said. "Like they say, 'One man's trash…' " He left the adage incomplete as he returned the toy to the box and hefted it up onto his shoulder. "I could fix it, you know. I have a grandson who would enjoy it."

"Derek, you know that's not allowed." The other man came back to the garage. "We're not supposed to take things for ourselves," he told Kate. "Against the rules."

Kate looked at Derek. "My lips are sealed. I hope your grandson enjoys the toy."

Derek smiled. Fifteen minutes later, Laurie's garage was cleared of boxes.

Kate went back to the garbage can rack and lifted the lid of the last can. This one was filled as well, stuffed with wads of stiff blue paper. Kate lifted a piece from the can and unfolded it. It was covered with pictures of brightly colored birds with human faces. Cartoon figures darted through fluffy white clouds.

Kate had to agree with Laurie. The wallpaper was a bit too cute.

Chapter Ten

Kate sat in the reception area of EnvironTech. The slick offices were on the eleventh floor of the Bank One building in downtown Seattle. The view took in the Cascade Mountains to the south. Kate was trying to identify the different peaks when the receptionist said, "Today is a bit hazy, but when it's clear, I can see Mount Rainier through those windows. Those mountains put me in a good mood. My last job kept me in the basement of the public library. I never knew what the weather was like until I got off work." The phone buzzed. "Ms. Michaels is on her way. Her office is on the thirteenth floor. She'll be right down."

While Kate waited, she prayed that Evan wouldn't come through the reception area. He wouldn't be happy to see her, and she was in no mood for a confrontation. The elevator dinged, startling Kate out of her ruminations. Jill Michaels and another woman stepped out. "She sounds good to me too, Lisa. Call her in the morning and give her the good news. That department could use a levelheaded woman at the helm for a change."

Years ago, when Kate first met Jill Michaels, she found her annoying. The woman felt not one ounce of compunction about voicing her opinions—loudly—as if she needed everyone to know her business. She was impossible to ignore, although Kate had tried. Kate and

Jack were at a team Christmas party. Jill was dating someone in the team's front office. She had been telling a funny story, and the more attention she got, the louder she became. Kate heard enough and left the room. Later that evening, they had run into one another at the bar by the pool. Kate still remembered that encounter and Jill's first words.

"So, you think I'm a loudmouth. It's okay. You're not the first person who's given me that look. I'm really not that irritating once you get to know me."

"Kate Caraway." Kate put out her hand.

"Jack Ryder's wife. I know. I'm Jill Michaels. I think this is my first and last team Christmas party."

"Why do you say that?"

"The guy I'm dating is passed out drunk in the back bedroom."

"Maybe you should throw some cold water on his face."

"The woman next to him might not like that." Jill laughed, but Kate could see the disappointment in her eyes. "I've only been in Chicago six months, and I'm moving to Seattle next week. Want to go out for coffee sometime before I leave?"

"Sure." Kate realized she really meant it.

Jill didn't miss a beat. "Let's make it lunch. How about tomorrow? We'll meet at Zorba's. Know where that is? It might be the last really good Greek food I'll have for a while." That night they became instant friends.

Jill walked over and kissed Kate's cheek. Then all in one breath, she said, "Have you eaten lunch? If so, let's go out for coffee. It's been a tough morning. I've had to rearrange some employee assignments in the video department. Sometimes I feel like Bobby Fisher, even though I've never played chess. Rumor has it that you've been back from Africa for almost a year. I should be mad that you didn't call sooner, but I'm not. Let's go."

After a short wait, they found a table at VeeVee's coffee shop. Over a concoction of melted chocolate with a double shot of espresso that Jill insisted Kate try, they caught up on the last few years, Kate avoiding the reason she left Africa.

"So, what's this about you being interested in Evan Thurston?"

"His mother is, was, a close friend of mine. She died a few days ago. Jack and I are staying at her house on Lopez Island for a while."

"I know about Evan's mother. I sent company flowers to the funeral."

"How well do you know Evan?" Kate asked.

"Too well, I'm afraid. He's one of those pawns I had to move around in the video department."

"Evan's not the easiest person to get along with."

"That's an understatement. He's been with the company since the beginning, and he has the attitude that he can do no wrong, coupled with the idea that the company owes him something for his loyalty."

"Loyalty's a good thing."

"True loyalty, yes. But Evan has been making mistakes lately. He's not what you'd call a team player. For the first few years, his team consisted of only him. Now that the company has grown, he's had to work with others. When his ideas are voted down, and they often are, he finagles his way around and gets what he wants. Until recently, that childish behavior has been ignored."

"What's happened recently?"

"Bad decisions, decisions that have cost the company money. Evan's been called on the carpet more than once."

"Can he make such costly decisions on his own?"

"I know what you're getting at. Designers have always been encouraged to explore on their own even if the company has reservations about their ideas. We have what's called an individual creative fund. It's sort of like internal grant money. If their ideas pan out, the company finances the projects, and the creator is rewarded financially. This was how the company was built, with a lot of think-outside-the-box people whose ideas worked. To be honest, Evan's hit the wall with creative ideas, but he refuses to admit that. If he'd just learn to work with people, he'd get back on track. But how do you convince someone like Evan to take a dose of humility? We all know he's been having a difficult time lately, so we've cut him some slack, but no more. He's been given his walking papers."

"Evan's been fired?"

"He's been Plutoed."

"Excuse me?"

"Demoted. We gave him the option of taking another position or leaving. He opted to leave. He'll be gone by the end of October."

"Damn. Any idea what he's going to do?"

"Evan plays his cards close to his chest. We'll give him a reference, but no one's called inquiring about Evan Thurston."

"Was Evan at work yesterday?"

"What's going on, Kate?"

Without going into the details, Kate told Jill about the trouble at Emily Ann's place. She tried to keep from sounding accusatory, but Jill was too perceptive.

"You think Evan's having money problems and pushed his mother off the cliff for his inheritance?"

Kate couldn't help but laugh. "Actually, putting it that bluntly makes it sound ridiculous. I knew Evan was having a hard time. I just wanted to see what I could find out."

"I see. Evan was at work yesterday. Why?"

"Because whoever pushed Emily Ann did the same to me yesterday."

"And you suspect Evan?"

"I'm just eliminating possibilities."

"Are you okay?"

"It was just a tumble. I was lucky. I'm fine."

"You don't sound fine, and neither does that situation. So, does Evan inherit?"

"A little bit from what I understand. But as far as the land and house, no." Kate told Jill about Emily Ann changing her will and leaving her place to Fred Marlow.

"And Evan didn't even know about this guy until his mother had everybody seated around the dinner table? That's cold."

"Emily Ann and her children haven't been that close."

"Poor Evan. I don't like the guy, but life doesn't always seem fair, does it?"

"One more thing. Emily Ann said that Evan was having an affair with a coworker. Hear anything about that?"

"Oh, there were rumors. But Mary doesn't work

here any longer. She took a job with a large aircraft company. I don't know if she's still seeing Evan."

****

Traffic slowed to almost a stop as Kate approached Everett. Hopping on Interstate 5 outside of Seattle felt like entering the Indy Speedway, and inching along was a welcome change. Now with her mind off the traffic, Kate pondered Evan's situation. She could understand his desperation. For a young man who had risen rapidly, facing termination certainly could have caused him to react and kill his mother. If Kate's episode at Iceberg Point was related to Emily Ann's death, Kate couldn't add Evan's name to the murder-suspect list since he was at work yesterday. Then her thoughts turned to Brian and Laurie. Things weren't right at the Fuller household. Brian was on the island the day Emily Ann died. But he was on the road yesterday, making business calls. The key to unlocking this mystery meant connecting all three incidents: Emily Ann's death, the attempt on Kate's life, and the threatening letters—a task she was unable to do. Trying to make sense of all this was like swimming through mud.

Arriving in Anacortes, Kate pulled into the ferry lane with no trepidation about making the six-thirty boat. It was a weekday, and the line was much shorter than when she and Jack arrived on that busy Friday. Despite the high-octane coffee drink, fatigue hit Kate like a hammer. She wished she hadn't agreed to Jeannie's visit. Kate wanted nothing more than to walk into the house, take off her shoes, and spend a quiet evening with Jack. But Fred was there and several others who'd been transporting animals all day. The house might well be full of people.

What Kate hadn't expected was to find a string of patrol cars in the driveway.

Chapter Eleven

Kate reached the front door as Jack stepped out. "Everybody's fine," he said. "We had a break-in while we were out working. The sheriff's department got here a little while ago."

"Was anything stolen?" Kate asked.

"Don't know yet. Emily Ann's office was the target. Fred's upstairs looking around."

Jack introduced Kate to Sheriff Bob Montego. He stood well over six feet, and his complexion spoke of Latin origins. Until now, the local authorities stationed on Lopez had handled events at Eagle Crossing since the sheriff's office was located in the county courthouse annex on San Juan Island.

"Ms. Caraway, let me express my condolences for Mrs. Thurston's death."

"Thank you, Sheriff."

"Mind if we have a seat? I have some questions. My guys here have filled me in on what's been going on."

Kate led them into the den. Fred joined them.

"Nothing missing from upstairs as far as I can tell," Fred said.

"Any idea of what they were after?" the sheriff asked.

"Not a clue. Listen, Sheriff, this is the third time the authorities have beaten a path to Eagle Crossing in a little more than a week. First Emily Ann dies, and someone lets the lion out of its cage, and I end up in the hospital with eighty stitches, and now this. *And* Kate's fall at Iceberg Point."

"Heard about that. Those cliffs can be tricky. Sounds like you had quite a day at the Point yesterday, Ms. Caraway. Glad you're all right."

"Actually," Kate said. "I don't think it was an accident."

"Oh? Maybe you should tell me about that, too."

Kate explained her suspicions. Sheriff Montego listened, wrote in his notebook, and snapped it shut. "There's not much we can do now," he said. "I can have a deputy ask around at Agate Beach. Maybe someone noticed a guy flying a remote-controlled plane. We get a lot of vacationers here on the islands. People come and go by the hundreds. Deputy Fitzroy said you were pretty shaken up, which is understandable. And sometimes an amateur trying to fly one of those things can quickly lose control."

"Sheriff, whoever saw my wife fall from the cliff trail tossed a cigarette over the cliff and walked away, leaving her hanging on that rock," Jack said. "I agree with Fred. Too many so-called accidents are happening here at Eagle Crossing. I want some answers."

"We're working on it, Mr. Ryder." He turned to Kate. "You didn't express these concerns yesterday when Deputy Fitzroy was here?"

"No," she said. "I was afraid that the entire thing sounded ridiculous. Who would want to kill me? But it was just too much of a coincidence. I'm sure the incident was deliberate."

"We've got fingerprints," Deputy Fitzroy said,

coming from Emily Ann's office. "And we'll need to print everyone here. I'll set everything up in the kitchen."

Sheriff Montego stood. "If nothing was stolen, there's not much we can do here either. It may be connected to the letters." He turned his attention to Fred. "You're not going to have an easy time, Mr. Marlow. If there's someone or a group that doesn't want these lions here, you're going to have more trouble. We'll assist any way we can, but if that's the case, it'll take a while for things to die down."

"Sheriff, what about Emily Ann's death?" Kate asked. "It's been over a week, and we haven't heard any official ruling. I know the situation points to suicide, but after what happened to me yesterday and knowing Emily Ann, I can't accept that as the cause of her death."

"We're still investigating, Ms. Caraway. With the threatening letters Mr. Marlow found, we're looking into the situation further. Suicide's still a strong possibility, especially with her having cancer, but without a note, we can't easily rule it as such."

"Without a note?"

Deputy Fitzroy walked in. "We're ready."

"I'll go first." Fred hurriedly followed the deputy to the kitchen.

Kate sat dumbstruck. She stood to go after Fred to confront him immediately. Jack stopped her with a slight shake of his head. If Sheriff Montego had noticed the exchange, he said nothing. And neither would Kate for now.

After Fred had been fingerprinted, he announced that he was calling it a day. Able to maneuver the stairs now, he'd moved into Emily Ann's bedroom.

Kate and Jack were also fingerprinted, and shortly after, the sheriff and his crew left.

"What was that all about?" Kate asked. "Fred didn't give them the note along with the letters?"

"I was as surprised as you," Jack said.

"Surely, Fred doesn't expect us to deny Emily Ann's note exists. I've already told Susan, and I'm sure she'll tell Evan and Laurie. We should talk to him now." Kate rose. "Find out what's going on."

"Let's wait until the morning. Give him a chance to bring it up, which I'm sure he will."

Kate sat back down. "I don't know. I don't like this—not one bit." Kenya crept over and laid her head on Kate's knee. "Tell me what happened here today."

"We were at the facility for much of the afternoon. The move went smoothly, and the five new arrivals are in their homes. It didn't take as much time as we had thought. We wrapped things up around five and sent Zach and his friends on their way. Fred went back to the house around two-thirty to rest. He came back after about an hour and helped us clean up. They must have broken in between three-thirty and five. We heard the dogs barking. But with all the commotion around here, we didn't pay attention to them."

"Dotty and Speckle might not seem too threatening," Kate said. "But what about Kenya?" At the mention of her name, the greyhound raised her paw for a shake. "We know she'd welcome anyone into the house, friend or foe, but if a huge greyhound glared at me from the inside, I'd think twice about breaking in."

"Well, breaking in isn't what exactly happened," Jack said. "The door was unlocked. So they just walked right in from the deck. Did you learn anything in Seattle?"

"Some. Laurie's been overdoing the sedatives, but Susan's staying there until Brian gets back. Evan's been fired. If Emily Ann was murdered, he's the most likely suspect. Then again, if my little *accident* was connected to her death, he has an alibi for yesterday. He couldn't have been at Iceberg Point. He was at work."

"Evan's life certainly seems in an upheaval."

"Desperate enough to kill his mother?"

"Maybe Emily Ann's announcement about not selling her property was the last straw. Maybe he snapped. It happens. Sorry," Jack said. He moved closer and brushed a stray hair from her face. "How's Jill?"

"As loud and crazy as ever. She sends her best. Did you have a chance to check on Jacob Bower?"

"I went to see him right before Zach and his friends arrived. Bower is one strange man. I rang the doorbell several times, but he didn't answer. I heard someone inside. I was about to leave when he finally came to the door. I told him I came to let him know about the arrival of the lions."

"What did he say?"

"He just stood on the front porch and stared as if I had green skin and horns. At first I thought he'd been asleep, but then I figured he'd been drinking. I reminded him who I was and finally got a reaction. He said that he was sorry to hear that the lions were on this mountain. Then he walked back inside and closed the door."

"That's all he said?"

"That's it."

"If he's afraid of the mountain lions, he won't be

hiking around here anymore. Do you really think the letters could be from him?"

"He's the most obvious."

"You think he's crazy enough to push Emily Ann to her death?"

"Jeannie Shuttleford said Bower moved here trying to get away from something that happened in his past."

The doorbell rang.

"Oh, I forgot," Kate said. "That's her now. Jeannie Shuttleford said she wanted to stop by."

"I'll let her in. You look beat. Relax."

Summer days in the San Juans were long. It was after eight, but sunset still shone like a weak lantern, casting a yellow haze over the evening. In the distance, toward the Olympic Mountains, the sky had deepened with shades of lavender and goldenrod. She'd been awake and on the move for more than seventeen hours. Her body was calling her to bed, and her mind spun with nervous exhaustion. Too many odd things had occurred. She wanted to find a connection between them, but everything she'd discovered thus far had made the situation more confusing. She hoped Jeannie could help.

The delicious aroma of pizza wafted across the room, and suddenly Kate's stomach rumbled.

"Dominick's Deli makes the best pizza on the island," Jeannie said. "I hope you're hungry." She placed the box on the coffee table.

"Cooking wasn't part of this evening's agenda," Jack said. "We're starved. I'll get some plates. Anyone want a beer?"

"Not me," Jeannie said. "I have to drive. I live way on the other side of the island."

"I'll have one," Kate said. "After today, I need one. How about iced tea or a soft drink?"

"Water's fine." Jeannie sat and looked around. "I can't believe she's gone. It's going to take a while for it to take hold." She sighed. "So, after what you told me this morning, Fred's going to continue with Emily Ann's work? I'm glad. Ned Hornsby from Windsong Inn stopped in the library today. He reported a caravan of cages leaving the airport and heading to Emily Ann's. I guess more animals are here."

"Three more lions, a bobcat, and a mangy coyote. We've spent all week getting the confines ready," Jack called from the kitchen. "The animals are settling in as we speak."

"I guess it's none of my business, but I'm curious how's everything been arranged? I mean the house and Emily Ann's property."

"No secrets there," Kate said. "Emily Ann turned her foundation into a nonprofit organization. She left the facility and house to Fred."

"How did the kids react to Fred? More importantly, how did they react to Emily Ann leaving this place to him?"

"About how you'd expect," Jack said, walking in carrying three plates, a stack of napkins, and a glass of ice water. "Evan's contesting the will, but Fred feels that Evan doesn't have a case." He lifted a slice of pizza onto each plate and passed them around. "I'll get that beer."

Jeannie set her plate down. She looked at Kate, as if coming to a conclusion, and finally spoke. "You think Emily Ann was murdered, don't you? I can assure you she would never have killed herself nor been careless enough to have fallen off the damned cliff! This is a small island, and word travels fast. I heard about what happened to you at Iceberg Point yesterday and about the break-in this afternoon. Level with me. What's going on here?"

"That's what we're trying to find out, Jeannie," Kate said.

"It's always a member of the family," Jeannie said. "That's what they say when someone's been murdered, isn't it?"

"We're not pointing any fingers," Jack said, handing Kate her beer. "We're just trying to piece things together. Whoever attacked Kate at Iceberg Point couldn't have been one of the family. Everyone had gone back to Seattle."

"Still, it's hard not to suspect her children. You said Evan was contesting the will. He and Laurie must be furious. Emily Ann never dwelled on it, but I know that there was contention between her and her kids."

"Evan had been trying to talk his mother into selling some of the land," Kate said. "And until last Saturday night, I think he believed that his mother was going to. It also seems that he's having financial problems."

"They weren't happy about her getting married either, I suspect."

"That was another surprise that Emily Ann announced on Saturday night."

"You mean they didn't know until then? Where's this Fred anyway?"

"He's upstairs. He's still recovering from a tangle with a lion on the morning of Emily Ann's death. Sorry he couldn't join us."

"Is he that nice-looking man who was sitting next to you at the funeral?"

"That's him."

"And Emily Ann didn't tell her kids until Saturday evening?"

"That's true. She told me right before we set the food on the table. Fred flew in on Sunday morning to meet the family for a celebratory brunch. Instead, he drove up to emergency vehicles in the driveway and a hysterical family in the house."

A shadow settled over Jeannie's face. "You mean he drove up right after the accident?" She looked toward the stairs as if she expected Emily Ann's ghost to float down any second. It was a few moments before Jeannie could speak. "I have to go. I...I'm not ready to talk about this. I'm sorry. I feel so stupid." She stood up to leave.

"Please don't feel that way," Kate said. "It sneaks up on me too."

Before she could say more, Jeannie grabbed her purse and rushed out.

Chapter Twelve

Kate crawled into bed fully expecting her unease to bring on nightmares, but the moment her head hit the pillow, she drifted off and didn't stir for the next six hours. At six in the morning, Kenya claimed the pillow, and Kate gave up on sleep. Jack was in a deep sleep, and he seemed likely to stay that way for a while. Following Kate out of the bedroom, Kenya loped downstairs as gracefully as a ballerina. At the bottom, she placed her head between her front paws and arched her lithe body into a long stretch. She let out a loud squeak-yawn, and Kate laughed. "Is that your way of telling me you're ready for another day? If I could stretch like that as soon as I got out of bed in the morning, I wouldn't need yoga."

Kate let her dog out in the backyard, then went into the kitchen to make coffee. Grateful for the night of uninterrupted sleep, she felt ready to conquer the world. As she sipped her first cup, she studied the copy of the article Jack had found in the envelope with the threatening letters. Published in the *Los Angeles Times*, it was a story about how urban sprawl had devastated the habitat of wild animals, in this case, the mountain lions in Southern California. Rarely seen, the shy and elusive mountain lion had recently been making appearances, leaving evidence of its presence—not necessarily evidence such as tracks or scat, but evidence of a more serious nature—family pets snatched up as a quick meal. The story was not a new one. Since man began civilizing the earth, wildlife habitat loss had led to repercussions for humans.

It was the same everywhere. Soon after Kate had moved to Kenya, she had witnessed a Grant's gazelle sprinting for its life from a cheetah only to run head-on into a barbed-wire fence. The wire sliced through the animal like a knife through butter, blood and bone flying in all directions. The cheetah skidded to a stop, turned tail, and fled in the other direction, too frightened to claim its prey, most likely leaving its first meal in days for the hyenas and vultures. This was not how things were supposed to work. Even the cheetah knew that.

Kate turned her attention back to the article. The reporter mentioned an incident north of Los Angeles near Santa Clarita, the last vestiges of wildlife habitat. The city flows into Santa Clarita Valley, where canyons and river valleys replace strip malls. Three-year-old Macie Stevens went missing on her birthday. The police, looking for signs of a human perpetrator, at first didn't notice the enormous paw print in the child's sandbox. Hours later, they picked up the mountain lion's trail, but by then it was too late.

Engrossed in her reading, Kate didn't hear Fred come into the kitchen.

"What, no homemade goodies this morning?"

Startled, Kate spilled her coffee as she set it down. "Sorry, I didn't hear you come downstairs."

"Whatever you're reading must be good," Fred said, pouring himself a cup and handing her a wad of paper towels.

"I was reading about the little girl in California who was killed by the mountain lion."

"Sad," Fred said. "I hate to say this, but situations like that will continue. We do what we can to relocate them, but unfortunately, we don't usually hear about mountain lion sightings until a tragedy occurs."

"You're right," Kate said. In no mood to discuss the subject, she replaced the copies of the letters and the article into the envelope. "How about I make a full breakfast today? Omelets, toast, hash browns, you know, the usual boring fare."

"I think I can rise to the occasion. Sorry I pooped out early last night. We had guests? I heard someone drive up."

"Jeannie Shuttleford, Emily Ann's friend from the library, stopped by. I spoke to her yesterday morning. She wanted to come over and talk about what happened to Emily Ann, but it was too soon for her. She became upset and had to leave." Kate cleaned up the coffee spill and poured herself another cup. "Jack said the move went smoothly yesterday. I planned to hike up there and see the new arrivals. What are your plans?"

"There's so much to do, I don't know where to begin. Eventually, I'm going to need some help running this place." He sat at the kitchen table. "You and Jack have been a godsend, but you won't be here forever. I need to get my butt in gear and hire someone. But Emily Ann's death is the important thing. We need to get to the bottom of it." He glanced at Kate over the top of his glasses. "I guess you're wondering why I didn't give that note to the sheriff when I gave him the letters."

"I was, but I'm sure you had a good reason."

"I did at the time. I felt that if I gave the sheriff what might be a suicide note, then when we finally told them about our suspicions about her being murdered, they wouldn't listen. I saw how they handled the break-in yesterday. To them, it was just one of those things that happen. They didn't say it, but I'm sure they figured it was just some kids looking for something to pawn for some fast drug money but were scared away before they could get their paws on anything."

"If Emily Ann's note wasn't a suicide note, then what was it?"

"I don't know what it meant," he said. "It didn't sound like my Emily Ann. She was the most upbeat person I ever knew. I remember when I first saw her at the International Wildlife Rehabbers Conference. She was standing at her bald eagle booth laughing with some friends. I walked over pretending to peruse her photo display, and within seconds, she'd drawn me in. She was in several of the photos, always smiling. I looked at each one, and my heart swelled. As I stood there studying them, she came up behind me. Her voice was warm and liquid. She sounded strong, a woman of real conviction, free of the anger and hostility that often comes when one fights for a cause that, at times, seems hopeless. She said, 'You're the man who works with the mountain lions.' I was flattered that she recognized me, and I did something I hadn't done since high school. I blushed. We made a date for lunch, and my life changed immediately. Well, enough of that.

"I've been thinking about what Zach said. About Emily Ann hiding her stress for my sake, about her dealing or not dealing with her problems, and then suddenly snapping. I keep trying to remember if I had overlooked or refused to see a side of Emily Ann that indicated denial."

Denial. That word set off alarms. *Was Fred right? Emily Ann had always been a master of evasion, but maybe it was denial instead?* The questions settled in Kate's mind and refused to leave. When Kate was growing up, she felt closer to Emily Ann than any woman. But when Emily Ann abruptly left Austin, Kate felt her unanswered questions would crush her. Her father had said little, and Kate assumed that her dad and Emily Ann Thurston realized that they wouldn't be able to make it work. Was denial an aspect of her friend's behavior that Kate failed to notice? Running away from difficult situations. Is that what Emily Ann had done last Sunday? Run away from her cancer and from the potential problems with the community and her family?

"Maybe I'm the one in denial now," Kate said under her breath.

"What?" Fred said.

"Never mind. I'll take the dogs for a walk and then start breakfast. Can you wait a little while to eat?"

"For your cooking, most certainly." He winked and went over to the kitchen counter to refill his coffee cup.

****

After breakfast, Fred left to tend the animals. Kate had a chance to tell Jack about Fred's reason for withholding the note from the sheriff.

"That's one way of looking at it," Jack said. "But if Emily Ann was murdered, the killer's trail is getting colder by the day. Several people have been traipsing around on that hill and around this house. So even if the sheriff is convinced of our theory, he'll have his work cut out trying to find any evidence of foul play."

Kate smiled.

"What?" Jack said.

"I was just recalling the Neslund case. Remember reading about it at the San Juan Historical Museum on our last visit? Ruth Neslund, a local Lopezean, murdered her husband back in the early eighties."

"You mean that crazy woman who killed her husband, chopped up his body, and burned it in a burn barrel? What made you think of that?"

"The authorities continued to investigate years after the murder and gathered enough evidence to arrest Ruth Neslund, which eventually led to her conviction even though the body was never found. A TV special about the Neslund incident aired not long after. It reminded me not to underestimate the Lopez law enforcement."

Before they could get back to the subject of the note, Fred came in. "It's a gorgeous day. Things are nice and quiet up at Eagle Crossing. Emily Ann and I talked about renaming the place when we decided to expand, but we never had a chance. Maybe I should leave it. Cougar Crossing, I'm sure, would scare the hell out of a lot of people." Fred washed his hands. "Okay, let's talk."

"Wait. I want to get a notepad from the office."

"She makes two lists," Jack said. "Facts and speculations."

"Good idea. We have a lot that needs sorting out."

"Okay, I'm ready," Kate said, seating herself next to Jack.

"All right," Fred said. "We know that Emily Ann had received those four threatening letters and that article about mountain lion attacks. That's a fact. We know someone attacked you at Iceberg Point and started a rockslide that knocked you over a cliff. Another fact."

"That's still speculation," Kate said. "As far as suspects who could have pushed Emily Ann, I'll put Evan first on the list followed by Jacob Bower. Evan, because of his financial crisis and his unsuccessful attempt to convince his mother to sell several acres of her property. Bower, because of his unusual behavior and his proximity to the crime scene."

"How about Brian and Laurie?" Fred said.

"They're next. Something is definitely wrong between those two," Kate said. "Laurie's falling apart, and not just because of her mother's death. That was evident the first night we were here. And one more thing: I found out yesterday that Evan lost his job."

"Damn," Fred said.

"This is a pretty short list," Jack said. "I think we should add Ray Steiner. He has no apparent motive, but he was familiar with the goings-on around here. Did he know where Emily Ann kept the keys to the cages?"

"Ray has his own set of keys to the cages," Fred said. "It's not like anyone would want to steal these animals. Ray having his own keys wasn't a problem."

"The killer may be someone else on the island," Jack added. "Someone who's a stranger to us. And then there's the break-in yesterday. It's got to be connected. What could Emily Ann have here that someone would want?"

"The letters?" Fred speculated.

"The person who sent them wanted them back?" Kate scribbled notes under *Speculation*.

"Right," Fred said. "The threatening letters don't

work. Emily Ann moves the lion here anyway. So the writer takes more drastic action and kills Emily Ann. Then he or she, let's say he, figures that the letters may leave a trail, so he steals them. Not a very smart person."

"Or maybe someone who knows who the killer is and steals the letters to keep him from getting caught," Kate said.

"Or," Jack said, "someone who knows, as you said, who the killer is and plans to use the letters as blackmail. Too many speculations."

"Well, if that's true," Kate added, "someone trying to protect the killer eliminates Emily Ann's kids. They couldn't have broken into the office. They were all in Seattle yesterday. Maybe we should look closer at Ray and Paula Steiner. Their relationship wasn't exactly harmonious, but that doesn't mean she wouldn't try to cover for her husband if she knew what he had done." She turned to Fred. "What reason would Ray have for killing Emily Ann?"

"They had an argument a while back," Fred said. "But it wasn't all that serious. When he started working for Emily Ann earlier this summer, he was unreliable. He'd call and say he was running late and then wouldn't show up for several hours. The last time it happened, Emily Ann called me. She was furious and was ready to fire him. He was supposed to show up around ten in the morning. She had planned to go off island that day and had to cancel her plans. At one p.m., he still hadn't arrived. Emily Ann drove out to his trailer and found him passed out in his car, alcohol fumes thick. Paula was in the trailer. Emily Ann tried to get the crazy woman to come outside and help with

Ray. We finally figured out that the Steiners had had one of their drunken brawls that turned physical, and she must have locked him out. She told Emily Ann to fuck off. Excuse me, but those were her words. Emily Ann doused him with a bottle of water. She got in his face and laid down the law. If he wanted to work for her, this would never happen again. And it hasn't."

"Doesn't sound like a motive for murder," Kate said. "I'll talk to Jeannie and see if she knows anything about the Steiners." She looked at the list. "You're right. More speculations than facts. We're not doing so well. I'll go to talk to Bower before he gets too soused to stand."

"You want me to come along?" Jack asked.

"Better not. Bower might be willing to talk if he doesn't feel like he was outnumbered. He may also be embarrassed after slamming the door on you yesterday."

"Just be careful," Jack said. "If he's drunk, I'm not sure I want you going in there."

****

Kate rang the doorbell again, then turned to walk around to see if Bower's car was parked under the carport when she heard footsteps coming toward the door. A few seconds later, the deadbolt slid back, and the door opened. The man looked as if he'd been on a yearlong drinking binge. The dark rings sagging under his eyes looked as if he had matching shiners.

"Sorry to bother you, Mr. Bower. And for my husband disturbing you yesterday afternoon."

"Your husband?"

"Yes. He came by to tell you that more lions had been moved in. He was afraid he woke you up."

Jacob Bower swallowed hard. He rubbed his hands through his hair. He cleared his throat. "I…I don't remember your husband coming over. You say more lions are here?"

"Yes, Mr. Bower. Three arrived yesterday. A few other animals as well. Do you mind if I come in? I'd like to talk to you if I may."

He looked down at his clothes and seemed to notice his disheveled appearance for the first time. He hesitated and then stepped aside for Kate to enter.

Jacob Bower spared no expense in building the place. The main room had a huge picture window, with the view of a thick evergreen forest. Although the sun was out in full force, the deep shadows of the surrounding trees cast a dark curtain over the room. Kate felt like she'd stepped into a meat locker. A floor-to-ceiling fireplace made up one entire wall but looked as if it had never been used. What looked to be a genuine Navajo rug covered the hardwood floor. Old newsletters and magazines piled high on the end tables. Mugs cluttered the coffee table, each cultivating a nice healthy crop of fungus. The room opened up to a small kitchen, where dirty plates were stacked high on the counter.

Bower removed some clothes from an armchair and motioned Kate to sit down. "I should find someone to come in and clean. I just haven't felt up to it lately. I don't have visitors."

"Have you been ill, Mr. Bower?" Kate asked. Now seated across from him, the strong smell of alcohol hit her so hard it brought on nausea. Not the slight smell of someone's breath after a drink or two, but the odor seeping from Bower's pores, and it was so pervasive

Kate doubted even a good shower would remove it. He didn't look like the type who rose early every morning to take a healthy hike before breakfast. Bower's need for isolation might be due to his personality, but Kate suspected the man had another reason for the drinking binge.

"Ill? Perhaps. Would you like coffee? I could make some coffee." He glanced toward the kitchen. A look of horror spread across his face as if going in there was more than he could handle.

"No, thank you. I'm fine. The animals shouldn't be a problem for you. Fred hopes that you'll continue your morning walks through Eagle Crossing. He wants you to know you're welcome just like before...before Emily Ann died."

"Yes, well...it's nice he should think about me." He slumped back in a lounge chair.

"Your house is beautiful. Is it pine?"

"Redwood from Canada. I had a contractor from Idaho build it. I told him to make it small and simple. It took him six months to build, and I moved in sight unseen." He paused, and Kate let the silence linger. He continued as if he were alone. "A long time ago I used to bring my family to Lopez Island for summer vacations. A colleague owned this small piece of land. When he was ready to sell, I snatched it up, thinking...well, anyway. Things changed."

Kate suspected those changes were the reason he lived alone. He looked to be in his sixties. He wore no wedding ring, and as Kate looked around, she saw no family pictures. Several bird identification books lined a bookshelf near the fireplace.

"Are you a birder?" Kate walked over and picked

up a book. "David Sibley—I have several of his guides."

"I still prefer the Peterson's." He picked up a well-worn book from the floor and handed it to her—*Peterson's Guide to Birds West of the Rockies*. The binding had come loose. Kate flipped through it and saw dates and notes scribbled in the margins. "Why try something new when the old works just fine, I always say." Bower coughed to clear his throat.

"I agree," Kate said. "I still prefer the Peterson's books myself. But what's nice about Sibley's is that the maps are on each page rather than in the back. So you don't have to flip back and forth."

"Really?" He looked mildly interested.

Kate set the Peterson's down and opened the Sibley's. On the inside margin was a note. "Enjoy the book. Jo."

"A gift from a friend?"

Bower look puzzled.

Kate showed him the message.

"Oh, my ex-wife. To tell you the truth, I've never even used that book. Jo was always nudging me to change things. Never was satisfied with the status quo."

"Emily Ann said that you enjoyed her birds."

"I did. She did good things. She had a way with those injured birds."

"You know, Mr. Bower, Fred needs some help at the facility. Have you considered offering some assistance? I mean, since you know so much about birds."

"I don't know how much longer I'll be here," he said. His hands trembled slightly. He clasped them together, kneading them in his lap.

"Are you concerned with the lions being here?"

"No, no. Not at all." The words rushed from his lips so quickly Kate was taken aback. He went over to a cabinet, pulled out a bottle of Scotch, and filled a small juice glass. He downed half of it in one swallow. "Emily Ann's accident was a real shock."

"Mr. Bower, I'll be honest with you. My husband and I, and Fred, don't believe Emily Ann fell. We're trying to figure out what really happened."

"No, she wouldn't have fallen," he whispered to himself. "She was much too careful."

"Did you go on your walk that morning?"

Kate ignored his warning glare. "You probably read about it in the paper, but I wanted to reassure you that the lion getting loose is unlikely to happen again. There's some speculation that the lion startled Emily Ann, causing her to fall. But things just don't add up. Are you sure you didn't notice anything usual that morning?"

"You mean that cat was loose?!" He downed the rest of his drink. "I...I had no idea. I don't read the paper. Thank God I wasn't out that morning. Is that what happened? The lion frightened her, and she fell?"

Surprisingly, the alcohol brought Jacob Bower out of his stupor.

"That certainly seems possible, but Emily Ann would never have gone after that lion alone. She'd have come to us for help. Jack and I have worked with wild animals for years. At least she would have retrieved her dart gun before dashing out. I don't think Emily Ann knew the lion was loose."

"That's all the more reason she could have been startled."

"That's true. But what made Emily Ann go out there in the first place? It was not her usual greet-the-morning outing. So, you didn't notice anyone else around that morning?"

"I told you I didn't go out." His voice rose. "I was not well that morning. You seriously think Emily Ann's death was because of foul play?"

"There's reason to believe so."

"I see. I can't help you." He poured himself another drink and seemed to forget Kate was in the room. With nothing to gain by staying, Kate let herself out.

On her way back, she stopped to check on the new arrivals. A few were asleep; the others seemed uninterested in her presence. Of the four lions now in residence at Eagle Crossing, only one was a non-releasable. The others were in rehab and would be set free in Alaska where they would be less likely to encounter humans again. The permanent resident, a large male, dozed on a hay bale, occasionally flipping his tail to keep away a bothersome fly. At first glance, he looked healthy enough, but the white glassy eyes indicated blindness. A park ranger in Yellowstone found him abandoned when he was only a few days old. Left alone, he wouldn't have survived another day. He'd been in Fred's care ever since.

Kate walked past the cages. The yellow tape was gone from the place where Emily Ann had fallen almost a week ago. She hesitated as she approached the small garden around the bench. She had not been back since the morning Emily Ann died. Suddenly Kate's legs seemed unable to carry her. She hurried to the bench and sat. Tears cascaded down her cheeks. Knowing it was useless to fight, Kate let the feelings come. After a few minutes, she composed herself, drew in a calming breath, and gingerly stepped toward the cliff.

The chunk of earth that had crumbled away was about the size of a doormat. It had cleaved off in a straight line as if the ground had split in half. Kate squatted for a closer look. The newly exposed earth looked like a small road cut. A thin layer of topsoil covered a solid rock. To keep from getting vertigo, Kate lay on her stomach and studied the ground around the section that had crumbled. Then she realized that *crumbled* was the wrong word. It had been sliced or chipped away. The ground underneath Emily Ann's feet, where she stood before she fell, was solid, not a mound of eroding dirt.

Kate peered over the edge. The cliff's face cut downward at a ninety-degree angle for about fifty feet. It then jutted out slightly before sloping straight down again. If Emily Ann slipped and fell, she would have hit the outcropping before falling the rest of the way. Kate stared at the rock below where Emily Ann had landed. Something didn't seem right. It was too far out. The rock was a good twenty feet out toward the water. If Emily Ann had accidentally fallen, her body would have been much closer in. Even if she had jumped, she still wouldn't have landed that far out.

For Emily Ann to have landed where she did, she *must* have been pushed.

Pushed hard.

Whoever killed her chipped away at the rock to make it look as if the ground had given way. No other explanation made any sense. The authorities missed this only because they had come out to investigate an accident and not a murder. Kate hoped she had the evidence she needed.

As she rose to her hands and knees to creep away from the edge, a flash coming from the outcropping caught her eye. She ran to the supply room and grabbed a pair of binoculars for a closer look. If the sheriff and his deputies weren't skilled in the science of trajectory, maybe a tip broken from a shovel would be convincing enough.

****

A crew of five men from the sheriff's department worked to retrieve the piece of metal as Kate, Jack, and Fred watched. Finally, Deputy Fitzroy turned to Kate. "Your theory is feasible, Ms. Caraway."

The yellow crime tape was back up, and within two hours, Sheriff Montego, Detective Kraus, and another detective named Snell were combing the area. Kate, Jack, and Fred were standing nearby when Deputy Fitzroy drove up. The figure in the passenger seat had such a startling appearance that Kate did a doubletake.

"Is that a CPR dummy wearing a BCD?" Kate asked.

"What?" Fred asked.

"Buoyancy Control Device," said Deputy Fitzroy, pulling the dummy from the car. "It's a scuba diving vest, and this is CPR Cindy. We added the vest and four extra pocket dive weights. How much did Mrs. Thurston weigh?"

"About one-hundred ten pounds. Why?"

"We're going to check if your theory is correct, Ms. Caraway. Cindy's going to tumble off the ledge under several different scenarios. Each time we'll pull her back up. If Mrs. Thurston was pushed, we'll know

167

shortly."

Fred turned around and went back inside.

"Sorry, I know this is hard," Deputy Fitzroy said. "I didn't mean to make light of the situation. When we're finished, a detective will want to talk to you again about your fall, Ms. Caraway."

Chapter Thirteen

Shortly after two o'clock, Detective Randy Kraus made himself comfortable in the den and wiped the dust off his wingtips. When satisfied he'd done all he could, he folded his handkerchief and stuck it in his jacket pocket. "Tell me again about what went on here last weekend, before Mrs. Thurston died."

Kate and Jack went over every detail: the argument between Emily Ann and her children, the announcement that she'd decided not to sell part of her acreage, and her decision to marry Fred Marlow. Laurie and Brian leaving Emily Ann's house to stay in the village, the unlocked lion's cage, which resulted in Fred's mauling, Emily Ann's scrapbook with the letters and article, and finally her apparent suicide note.

"Suicide note?" Detective Kraus said. "You found one?"

"I did," Fred said. "It was with the letters and the article." Without waiting for more questions, Fred continued. "I couldn't believe Emily Ann had killed herself. I didn't want it known if she had. Besides, I'm sure she was murdered. I was afraid if you had what might be construed as a suicide note, you'd end the investigation. I almost burned it."

"Mr. Marlow—"

"Here it is." Fred said. He handed Kraus an envelope.

The detective slid on a pair of latex gloves, removed the letter, and read it. "What did she mean about not going through it again and letting you down? Was it the cancer?"

"Emily Ann was—we both were—optimistic about her prognosis," Fred said. "She had a new doctor. The treatments seemed to be working. She never viewed cancer as a death sentence."

"Then what was it?"

"I honestly don't know."

Detective Kraus studied Fred for a moment then returned the note to the envelope. "I've read the report, Ms. Caraway, but I want to hear from you what happened on Iceberg Point."

Kate told her story over again, but this time she didn't feel as foolish.

"You didn't see anyone at all on the point? While you parked the car? Walked down the trail?"

"I was alone. There were several fishing boats and the couple on the sailboat who saw me and called the sheriff, but I didn't see anyone hiking around the area."

"Tony and Sandra Cappelli, the couple on the sailboat. Sheriff Montego spoke to them. They were on their way to Victoria. We have their cell number. I'll call and ask if they remember seeing anyone operating that plane, and I'll interview the fishermen who were on the water that day. Before I do, I'd like for you to show me where the incident happened. It's unlikely we'll be able to retrieve the remains of the remote-control plane. Unfortunately, we've had a full moon since then, and the high tides probably washed the pieces out."

"And the cigarette butt," Kate said. "I don't believe it made it all the way to the bottom. It could have landed on an outcropping."

"We'll check," he said. "Detective Snell will be in shortly. He's interviewing Mr. Bower. Then he'll want to go through the house again, especially Mrs. Thurston's office, since whoever broke in was looking for something. As soon as Snell gets here, you and I can leave for the point." Then he turned his attention back to Fred. "You said Evan Thurston was contesting the will. Have you heard from his lawyer?"

"Not yet," Fred said. "But I expect to. I've known Evan only a short time but suspect he's not easily deterred once he sets his mind to something."

"Evan's having financial problems," Kate said. "I spoke to a friend of mine who's the personnel director where Evan works. He's been fired, or I should say, he chose to leave rather than take a demotion. But even if he was responsible for his mother's death, he didn't push me off Iceberg Point. He was in Seattle at the time."

Detective Kraus frowned. "Sounds like you've been doing your own investigation."

"I knew Emily Ann didn't accidentally fall, and I knew she wouldn't commit suicide. She was excited about expanding Eagle Crossing and beaming at the idea of marrying Fred. She was a woman in love. She was not distraught."

Just then, the back door opened, and a tall, stocky man in a Seattle baseball cap pulled down tight, shading his eyes, walked in. "We're finished outside," he said.

"Detective Todd Snell." Kraus introduced everyone. Snell nodded. Unlike Detective Kraus, who wore neatly pressed slacks and a blue dress shirt, Snell wore khaki pants and a denim shirt, which were scuffed and stained from crawling around on the ledge.

"Ms. Caraway, you were at Jacob Bower's house right before you called us," Snell said.

"That's right. Emily Ann mentioned that he was a bit wary about the lion's arrival. We hadn't had a chance to talk to him and reassure him that he was safe. So, I went to see him."

"Well, he's not there now."

"He'd been drinking heavily, Detective Snell, before and while I was there. It's possible he's either passed out or not answering the door."

"There's no car in the carport."

"That's not good," Kate said. "Someone in his condition shouldn't be driving."

"Any idea what he drove?"

"An SUV, but I didn't pay much attention. A Subaru, I think—dark green, fairly new. The piece of metal, was it what I suspected? The tip a shovel."

"It was. The crew is still looking for the shovel. Sheriff Montego wants me to get started on the office and then see about the neighbors—the folks living along Alec Bay Road. Farmers are up bright and early. Not too many people drive out here without them noticing. But that was several days ago. I hope they have good memories."

****

Detective Kraus drove Kate to Iceberg Point. "Tell me about Ray Steiner. Is he still working at Eagle Crossing?"

"He is. Emily Ann paid him through the end of the month. He puts in a full day on Mondays and is here a few mornings during the week."

"Was he working that morning Mrs. Thurston

172

died?"

"No. I don't believe he's here on the weekends at all."

"Did Mrs. Thurston say much about him?"

"Just that he keeps to himself. But Fred said Ray was unreliable when he first started working at Eagle Crossing. He occasionally came in late. But once Emily Ann had a serious talk with him, Ray began showing up on time. He doesn't work directly with the eagles. I think he does odd jobs—repairing and cleaning cages. Oh, he does have his own set of keys to the cages and sheds."

The houses along Agate Beach were alive with activity—late-season vacationers coming to the island to enjoy the weather before the fall rains became an almost daily occurrence. Detective Kraus drove to Bat and Ball Lane all the way to the trailhead. He parked off the road. Kate imagined the detective's wingtips striding through the woods on their hike when he grabbed a pair of sneakers from the back seat.

"Detective Snell has the right idea. Dressing down has its advantages, but I'm an old dog who doesn't like new tricks. It drives my wife crazy. Our dry-cleaning bill is pretty hefty. Ready?"

As they hiked along the trail, Kraus continued with the questions. "Where did you park when you came out here?"

"In the small lot across from the beach," Kate said.

"Notice anyone around?"

"Just some kids playing in the house along Bat and Ball Lane."

"Okay. I'll check it out after I take you back. Let's retrace your steps. Lead on."

Kate took him to the reference marker and then along the trail to where she'd seen the sea lions. On the way back, they stopped at the spot where Kate had fallen. Kraus looked down and studied the area. "You're damn lucky you weren't killed. That's some drop."

"I *was* lucky. After bouncing around, I landed near that Madrona tree, grabbed on, and crawled into a crevice. You can't see it from here. That's why I wasn't able to see who was standing on the trail above me."

Kraus slipped his cell phone from his pocket and snapped several photos while Kate sat back on the dirt mound. She had no desire to stand on the ledge. She'd already spent too much time here. Kraus finished searching the area and made a call. "Snell, you and Fitzroy get down here when you're finished at Mrs. Thurston's. Tell him to bring his rappelling gear. I want him to scale this cliff wall and the rocks below. He's to look for a cigarette butt and anything that's left of that remote-control plane." He finished his call and turned to Kate. "I want you to sit here on the trail like you were doing before you fell. I will walk around and climb some of the higher points to see where the guy could have been standing. He had to have been watching you for some time."

The wind gusted across the point. Kate pulled her jacket tight around her and tried to make herself comfortable on a tuft of grass. She thought about Ray Steiner. He had never seriously entered the picture as a murder suspect. She couldn't imagine any motive for him. Maybe he had a loose screw. Maybe the confrontation from a few weeks ago with Emily Ann had been smoldering. But he wasn't working that morning. If he'd planned to push Emily Ann to her death, coming on a morning when he wasn't scheduled to work made sense. But how did the lion figure into the picture? Kate felt sure that something else caused Emily Ann to leave the house that morning. She'd pass her ideas by Detective Kraus when he returned.

Twenty minutes later, Kraus hurried to where Kate was sitting. His face was flushed, and his sleeves rolled up above his elbows.

"Found it. Walk over here, and you can see it in those trees." He pointed to a grove of evergreens, but Kate didn't see anything unusual. "A deer blind built up in that tree." He pointed again. "See it?"

Kate looked to where he pointed, and there it was, well hidden, about fifteen feet up. "Deer hunting's allowed on the island?"

"Not anymore. That's old man McGeary's property. That blind hasn't been used in decades. I'm going to climb up. Once you see me, start walking along this trail. Walk back and forth several times. Stop and squat down where you are now. I want to see if you're visible from that perch."

"Right." Kate watched as Kraus trotted across the field into the woods.

Slats were nailed to the tree, leading up to the blind. Kraus carefully climbed to the top, slipping once when a rung gave way beneath his weight. He waved at Kate, and she started hiking along the trail. She kept him in view the entire time. When Kate reached the spot where she had fallen from the cliff, she could still see him, but he disappeared when she squatted down. A few minutes later, Kraus returned. The knee of his slacks was ripped, and his shirt was stained with

175

perspiration circles under the arms.

"That's the place, all right." He picked at a splinter in his right palm. "And someone's been up there recently. Probably our guy. I saw you clearly. I could even see the top of your head when you sat down."

"Good work. Are you okay?" Kate said.

"I'm fine. My wife's going to be pissed as hell, though. These are new slacks." He grabbed his phone, called his partner to tell him about his discovery, and instructed him to comb the area. "Let's go," he said to Kate.

On the way back, Kate shared her theory about why Emily Ann rushed from the house that morning. Detective Kraus listened.

"She was not a careless person, Detective. If Emily Ann saw the lion wandering around, she'd have asked Jack and me to help. People working with wild animals know better than to tackle a situation like that alone. When I looked in her bedroom, it was obvious she'd left quickly. The book she'd been reading rested on the floor. Hangers and shoeboxes in her closet were askew. You were at her house. You saw how neat and orderly everything was."

"You think she noticed something wasn't right and went to check it out?"

"I don't know. Maybe Emily Ann remembered that she'd forgotten to lock the cage the night before. We stayed up late. With the trouble she had with her family and the anticipation of Fred arriving the next morning, it's understandable that she could have been distracted. I often do that—remember something I had forgotten as soon as I wake up. I also remembered something that morning Emily Ann died. It woke me up. It was her scream. I was too groggy for my brain to register. But I can hear it now, and I'll never ever forget."

Detective Kraus was silent for the rest of the hike when he finally said, "It could have been your imagination."

"It wasn't."

"It was just the three of you at the house that morning, you, your husband, and Evan Thurston. Tell me about that morning again."

Kate recognized the implication and chose to ignore it. "I had slept later than usual. Jack had taken our greyhound for a walk. All was quiet downstairs. Emily Ann was an early riser, but since we'd stayed up so late the night before, I didn't give her absence much thought—at first—but I couldn't help but feel something wasn't right. I set the coffee to brew and took Emily Ann's two dogs for a walk up to the facility. That's when I found her."

"And you *immediately* assumed that she had fallen."

"Wouldn't you?" Kate snapped.

"Go over it again."

Kate closed her eyes and let the events of that morning unfold for the umpteenth time. With the dogs carrying on as they did, Kate feared for their safety, scampering so close to the edge. Then peering over the cliff, seeing Emily Ann's body lying on the rock below, trying to convince herself that she was imaging things. "At first, I thought she'd fallen, that this can't be real. That Emily Ann wouldn't be so careless to stand on the lip of the ledge. We'd spoken the afternoon before about Emily Ann building a retaining wall around the ledge."

"Any reason for that?"

"Some erosion along the area, but I think with the expansion of her rehab facility, she felt it was the safest thing to do."

"Did anyone else know of her plans to build the retaining wall?"

"I'm not sure. Emily Ann's children weren't involved with her work. I'm sure Fred knew. Maybe Ray Steiner."

"Tell me again about the blowup during Friday night's dinner." They had reached the trailhead and stood by the entrance. Kraus rested his foot on the gate. Kate told how Laurie and Evan reacted to Emily Ann's two announcements: her decision to keep the ten acres to accommodate the new mountain lion wing of Eagle Crossing, and her plan to marry Fred Marlow.

"How did Mrs. Thurston react to their disapproval?"

"I believe Emily Ann expected it, but their hostility was a surprise."

"Why?"

"Why?" Kate looked at him. He was working on that splinter with a pocketknife.

"If her kids were generally supportive and if her son had been pushing her to sell the land, surely, she wouldn't expect them to be delighted with the news," he said. "That being the case, why bring it up during a nice dinner with friends from out of town who hardly knew her family?"

Kate immediately felt defensive at being asked to justify Emily Ann's judgement. She kept her voice calm when she finally answered. "Emily Ann and I have been friends since I was a little girl when we lived in Austin. It's possible that she wanted me there for moral support."

Kraus snapped his pocketknife shut and slid it into his pocket. He turned his attention to a stream of smoke curling up from a house whose only visible presence was the top of its chimney. "Wait in the car for a few minutes. I want to pay Marcus McGeary a visit. See if he saw anything that day you were here. He doesn't miss much when it comes to his property."

Kate climbed into the passenger seat but kept the door open. Even though the temperature was a cool 65 degrees, Kraus's car had been sitting in the sun. Moments later she heard angry voices coming from the woods, and then a loud slam. Kraus emerged from the trees, brushing a pine needle from his hair.

"That was quick," Kate said.

"Ornery old goat. He doesn't exactly put out a welcome mat. No help there."

"What'd he say?"

"I showed him my identification through a crack in the door. He flung the door open, called me a jackass, and accused me of smashing his only good still. McGeary must be near a hundred. Still thinks he's living during Prohibition. Snell and I will go door-to-door, cover all the houses along Agate Beach Road and Bat and Ball Lane."

Kraus backed his car down the road and as soon as he was pointed in the right direction, his radio crackled.

"Kraus here."

"Got something, Randy," Sheriff Montego's said. "Someone blazed a trail straight from Watmough Bay Road through the woods up to the cages. Snell's combing the place for footprints and fibers. Fitzroy's looking for tire tracks."

"You're thinking a local," Kraus said.

"Not necessarily," Sheriff Montego said. "It could be anyone who knew the layout of the property and was familiar with Mrs. Thurston's routine. I need Snell here. Take Ms. Caraway back. You'll have to interview the folks at Agate Beach by yourself. We can't waste any more time. This case is more than a week old."

"Got it. How did CPR Cindy do?"

"We'll have to retire the old gal. She lost a few limbs over the ordeal, but she confirmed our suspicions. Mrs. Thurston was pushed hard. I'm surprised the killer didn't fly off the ledge just from the momentum."

"We're on our way back," Kraus said.

"Emily Ann was pushed. I knew it. She would not kill herself. Does that let my husband and me off the hook?" Kate said.

Kraus cackled. "No one's off the hook yet."

Chapter Fourteen

Kate stood at the kitchen sink, cleaning feeding syringes, when Jack walked in from Emily Ann's office.

"Ready for this?" he said.

"I'm not sure. What's up?"

"I just got off the phone with Sheriff Montego."

"I'm listening."

"He said that you can stop worrying. Early this morning, Ray Steiner was roused from his bed and arrested for Emily Ann's murder."

"My God! How did they find out it was him?"

"Tire tracks. There were two mismatched tracks from a car parked on the side of Watmough Bay Road up from the house. They came from the Steiners' old Cadillac. Not many people have two different brands of tires on their cars. One wasn't even the right size."

"There's got to be more evidence."

"There is. Fibers plucked from bramble bushes leading from the tracks to the cages matched those of Ray's jacket. He was booked at the San Juan County Courthouse and sent to Bellingham to await his trial. He claims he's innocent."

"What's his motive?"

"Montego said something about Ray's history of violence. He'd gotten into a serious scrape once before. Served time for attacking a local farmer with a pitchfork after the guy accused Ray of stealing carved pumpkins off the front porch right before Halloween. The farmer's grandkids carved the pumpkins. Earlier, he had teased Ray that one pumpkin, in particular, looked just like him. You have to admit, Kate, the man is pretty strange."

"Sounds like the farmer is just as strange," Kate said.

"Well, Ray did have that confrontation with Emily Ann about missing work."

"But that was weeks ago. Ray may have reacted during a heated argument with the pumpkin man, but a premeditated murder doesn't sound like something Ray would do."

"I'm not sure about that," Jack said. "Think of the way he acted when his wife was screaming obscenities and pounding him with pinecones. He seems exactly the type to stew over something and then blow later."

"What about my incident? Why would Ray push me off the cliff? Those people barely have enough money to feed the kids, much less buy an expensive toy plane."

"The sheriff didn't mention that."

"I'm going to see Paula Steiner," Kate said.

Jack stared at his wife. She ignored him and started going through the kitchen drawers. "Emily Ann has a notebook in here somewhere with contact information," Kate said. "Here it is." Just as she was about to pick up the phone, it rang.

"Hello," Kate said as she jotted down the Steiners' number and address.

"Ms. Caraway? This is Brian Fuller. I never got a chance to thank you for checking on Laurie on

Monday."

"Hi, Brian. How's she doing?"

"Not good. Laurie's taking Emily Ann's death pretty hard. Is it true the cops arrested that the crazy guy this morning? The one who worked for her. Laurie was just starting to accept what had happened, and now knowing that her mother was murdered has worsened the situation. Not only that, Evan's not helping. He's contesting the will by claiming Emily Ann was unstable."

"But there's no longer a question of suicide," Kate said.

"Yeah, well…Evan believes that because Emily Ann's cancer returned, she wasn't thinking clearly. He claims that Fred Marlow was taking advantage of her, playing on her emotions."

"Can't you try and talk to him?"

"Well, I did where Laurie's concerned."

"What do you mean?"

"Evan wants her to come to his attorney's office and make some sort of official statement concerning Emily Ann's odd behavior. I told him to bug off and leave her alone for a while. We'll both be getting a little money from Emily Ann's estate. I don't know why he's in such a hurry to get more. As far as contesting the will, I have to agree with him. I mean, Emily Ann meets this man a few months ago, and the entire course of her life changes."

"I wouldn't go that far, Brian. Emily Ann was expanding her rehab facility and getting married, not changing her entire life."

"Anyway, I'm checking Laurie into a treatment facility. Her depression is scaring me."

"What about Ben?"

"My mom will fly out here to give me a hand. I just wanted to let you know. I'll be on the road a lot, and I don't want Evan badgering my wife."

"I'll check on Laurie while I'm here, Brian. I'm not sure how long that will be."

"That won't be necessary. She just needs some rest. Just wanted to call and say thanks."

He hung up before Kate could ask the many questions forming in her mind.

Jack chuckled and rose to give his wife a kiss.

"What's so funny?"

"It seems like ages ago when we first met Dickhead on the ferry," Jack said.

"*Dickhead* is too nice a name for him."

Before Kate could give Jack the details of Brian's call, the phone rang again.

"Fred Marlow, please."

"May I ask who's calling?" Kate said.

"Is this Ms. Caraway?"

Something about the gravelly voice rubbed Kate the wrong way. "You answer my questions first," she said.

"Considering you've no business staying in that house, I don't have to answer any of your questions. But because I'm a reasonable man, I'll oblige you. Name's Jason Perkins, Evan Thurston's attorney."

"Mr. Marlow is not in. Give me your number. I'll have him call you." Kate copied it.

"Tell Mr. Marlow—"

Kate hung up. "Things are about to get ugly. That was Evan's attorney."

"Fred can handle that. I've got to remove some

stitches from a big cat. I'd ask you to help, but I'm afraid you'd want me to accompany you to the Steiner household afterward. I'm not up for that."

Kate grabbed her bag and car keys. "I think you have the easier task."

"Aren't you going to call first?"

"Sometimes surprise visits are better."

"I'm going to get the dart gun."

"Wouldn't it be easier to put a tranquilizer in the cat's food?"

"I did. The dart gun is for you."

Before going to see Paula Steiner, Kate decided to check with Detective Kraus. She pulled up in front of the substation where three patrol cars were parked. The substation was not much larger than the ticket booth at the ferry station. Kate poked her head inside. Deputy Fitzroy was seated behind a small desk, and two other deputies were leaning against the wall, leaving little room for anyone else.

"Morning. I'm looking for Detective Kraus," she said.

"Our good detectives are having breakfast at Sunnyside Cafe in the village," Deputy Fitzroy said.

"Thanks," Kate said and turned to leave.

"Hope things can get back to normal at Eagle Crossing," Deputy Fitzroy said, "now that we got Steiner behind bars."

Another deputy chuckled. "It was only a matter of time. That guy's bad news."

Kate refrained from saying that normality at Eagle Crossing would never be possible without Emily Ann.

****

Detectives Kraus and Snell were just finishing

breakfast when Kate walked in.

"Sunnyside Cafe Huevos," Kraus said, pointing to his almost-empty plate. "Best thing on the menu."

"Just ate," Kate said. "Mind if I sit down?"

"I was coming to see you." Kraus lifted his cup and nodded at the waitress. "Coffee?"

"Yes, coffee sounds good. So, Ray Steiner claims he's innocent."

"He didn't claim much of anything. His wife did most of the talking—shrieking is more like it. We almost took her in, too. I had to pull her off Snell's back for him to slap the cuffs on Ray."

"Paula Steiner was two sheets to the wind, and Ray was almost as bad," Snell said. "He never could hold his own with that woman."

"They must've been up all night." Kraus motioned to the waitress to bring the check. "There were two empty bottles of cheap bourbon on the kitchen counter."

"Any connection between my incident and Ray?" Kate asked.

"We're working on that. There's the possibility that we're dealing with two separate crimes."

"Seriously? No murder on this island for almost twenty years, then one person is killed, another is almost killed, the same *modus operandi*?"

"As I said, we're working on it. Did you and Ray cross paths?"

"I first encountered him on Friday afternoon after Jack and I got to the island. I walked up with Kenya, my greyhound, and frightened him. He said he didn't like dogs and rushed away. Then the day after Emily Ann was killed, he was there working. Paula drove up, and they had a fight in the driveway. But after that, I haven't seen much of him. My husband spoke to him a few times while they were working on the cages."

"What was their fight about?" Kraus pushed his plate away and pulled out his notebook.

"Something about Paula oversleeping and having to take the kids to school because they missed the bus. But also the car was out of gas, and she had to call her sister to drive them to school. She was also upset because Ray was still working for Emily Ann. She wanted him to see about another job."

"In other words," Snell said, "life as usual with the Steiners."

"If it was Ray, where would he get a remote-control plane?" Kate said.

The waitress brought Kate's coffee and refilled the detectives' cups.

"Yesterday, we found out who the plane belonged to. It was stolen from Jed Barberette's barn."

"And he just now reported it?"

Snell started laughing.

"Seems his wife, Debbie, didn't know Jed bought the plane," Kraus said. "He'd been hiding it and taking it out whenever she went off-island. She was in Blaine visiting her mother all last week. Jed had been flying it almost every morning. Friday when he went to tuck it away, before the Mrs. came home, he discovered it was gone. He thought it was one of his friends playing a mean joke. He expected the jokester to call his wife while he was at work. 'Hey, Debbie, tell Jed to come pick up his toy. He left it here last week.' The Barberettes live just down the road from the Thurston place. When Snell was interviewing the neighbors yesterday, Jed told him about the missing plane. It was a Taylor/Billings model. Sound familiar?"

"Now that you mention it, I did see a T/B logo on the wing," Kate said. "The plane was red with white stripes on the wing. I didn't notice much else since it was flying directly at me."

"That sounds like the one," Snell said.

"I take it you didn't find any pieces of the plane on the rocks?" Kate said.

"Nope. Tide took them out."

"How about the cigarette butt?"

"Didn't find that, either."

"We did find out the article about the mountain lion attack came from Bower," Kraus added.

"How?" Kate asked.

"Fingerprints on the article matched his."

"His fingerprints are on file? He doesn't look like the type with a checkered past unless it involved an alcohol-related incident."

"Nothing sinister. Seems Bower applied for a public-school substitute-teaching certificate after he retired. I guess he felt if he got bored, he could do something else."

"Have you talked to Bower?"

"Haven't found him yet."

Chapter Fifteen

Around ten o'clock, Kate pulled up to the Steiner trailer. The Cadillac was gone, but three other cars were parked in the yard, a yellow Chevy Nova minus the windshield, an ancient Nash Rambler minus the tires, and a beat-to-shit Toyota pickup that looked like it just might run. A thirty-foot trailer sat on crumbling cinderblocks and sagged on one side where the ground had given way. A satellite dish hung at a precarious angle off the side, and judging by the loose-hanging cables, any connection between it and a TV had long been severed. The front yard—strewn with junk— looked like a scene left in the wake of a tornado. Old clothes, shoes, liquor bottles, beer cans, broken bikes and trikes, plastic toys, lawnmowers, and unidentifiable pieces of rusted metal barely visible through the weeds were strewn over the entire yard. Naked and painted purple, a doll had ant-covered marshmallows stuck into its head where the eyes had once been. The remains of a blown firecracker stuck out of the doll's charred left ear. Had the doll's owner willingly given up the doll for the sacrifice, or had an evil brother stolen it to torture his sister?

Broken wooden pallets, laid end to end, went right through the middle of the trash-covered ground. Kate avoided the makeshift sidewalk and treaded her way through the debris. A cinderblock acted as a step to the front door. The welcome mat, a huge flat rock with a message painted in the same purple paint used to adorn the tortured doll, said, "Take yo filthy ass outta here." Next to it someone had drawn buttocks, complete with hair curling from the crack.

A wailing coming from inside the trailer caused Kate to rethink her strategy. Maybe Jack was right. Perhaps she should have called first. She had Paula's number, so why not? Kate pulled her cell phone from her bag and punched in the number. The Steiner phone rang inside the trailer. After the fourth ring, she heard a loud crash.

"Lisa, pick up the fuckin' phone. Can't you see I'm in pain here?"

"Don't get your panties in a wad, Sis. I'm mixing the juice. Hello!"

"Lisa?" Kate said.

"Who's this? If you're a shittin' reporter, you can just piss off."

"I'm not a reporter. My name's Kate Caraway. I'd like to come over and talk to Mrs. Steiner. I can be there right away."

"Who?"

"Kate Caraway. Ray may have mentioned me to Paula."

"You mean like the seed?"

"Yes, like the seed." Kate sighed.

"Hold on. Paula, it's a broad named Caraway, like the seed. She's a friend of Ray's."

"Seed! What seed? Lisa, you're crazy."

Geeze, Kate thought. *These women are smashed.*

"What does she want?" called Paula.

"How the hell do I know? She wants to talk to you.

She wants to come over."

Before Kate got a yes or no, Lisa hung up, and the sisters began shouting at one another again.

"Okay, announcement made," Kate said to herself and pounded on the door. Then everything went quiet. Kate waited. Finally, "Who is it?" someone slurred.

"Ms. Caraway," Kate said.

"It's the seed," Lisa shouted. "We should let her in since she materialized on the front porch like some alien from Star Trek."

The wailing from a few minutes ago turned to uncontrollable laughter as Lisa opened the front door. The smell of stale beer hit Kate in the face, causing her to gasp. She expected to see a woman resembling Paula Steiner, overweight and ghostly pale. Lisa, instead, resembled a modern-day Twiggy. Her low-riding jeans barely covered her pubic hair. At least a foot of skin showed between her jeans and halter-top. Lisa's pierced navel held a silver loop attached to a chain that traveled upward, disappearing under the halter. Kate shuddered at the image of what the other end of the chain connected to.

"May I come in?"

This simple request caused Lisa to double over with laughter. She rushed from the door, saying something about wetting her pants.

Kate's survival instincts kicked in, and she remained outside. While she considered her next move, the trailer began vibrating—heavy footsteps stomping toward the front door. Seconds later, Paula Steiner filled the doorway.

"I realize that this isn't a good time, Mrs. Steiner." Kate slipped Paula a card through a hole in the screen.

"But I really would like to talk to you about Ray. I'm staying at Mrs. Thurston's house. Please call me."

Paula stared at the card and burst into tears. "Ray didn't kill nobody, I tell ya. What am I gonna do now with him gone?"

"I understand, Mrs. Steiner. I may be able to help. Please call as soon as you can."

Kate left the two women to continue pickling their livers. Paula probably wouldn't even remember the visit, much less call. Kate wasn't sure why she even bothered, except that she and Paula had something in common—a strong belief in Ray Steiner's innocence.

****

Kate returned to Eagle Crossing and found a note on the kitchen table.

Fred and I are at the medical clinic. He's having stitches removed. I'm having a few put in. We're a fine couple of rehabbers, aren't we? Don't worry. I'm okay. Just a gash on the wrist. Lions still swipe even when they're asleep.

Love, Jack.

"Damn! What the hell else could happen?" Kate said to Kenya as the dog loped up and stuck her nose in Kate's hand. "What do you think about all this, girl?" Kate reached down and hugged her greyhound. Kenya tilted her head as if the answer was too obvious. Kate considered driving back to the village to see about Jack's injuries but decided to trust his note that everything was fine. Besides, she needed to catch up on paperwork. Part of animal rehab involved tending to the animals. Kate couldn't neglect updating the notes on their treatment and condition. She gathered up her notes and sat down at the computer in Emily Ann's office.

Before she opened the first file, the phone rang.

"Kate?"

"Michael! My God. Is everything okay?" Kate's stomach fluttered, and her heart leaped up in her throat. All thoughts of rehabbing eagles, contesting wills, and solving murders vanished.

"Everything's fine." Michael laughed. "How are you doing?"

"Cut the small talk. You never call to chat. What's going on? Where are you?"

"Where do you think? I'm in Nairobi for supplies. I called your number in Chicago and then remembered you were on vacation. I'm glad you have call forwarding since I don't have your cell number. I've just come from the park's office. There's been a complete regime change. Your case has been mired in red tape for so long it seems no one's interested in Kate Caraway and the poacher she shot. When the new director took over last week, he pretty much wiped the slate clean."

"What are you saying?"

"What I'm saying is it's safe for you to come back."

Kate had to remind herself to breathe. She and Jack had left Kenya just over a year ago. After a gun battle with poachers, Kate had been advised to leave the country and not return until things settled down. Her research permit gave her the right to protect the animals "at all costs," but that phrase was nebulous and left to interpretation.

"Kate? Are you there?"

"Yes. I'm here. I just needed to catch my breath."

"So when can we expect you? Things are running

smoothly, but we all miss you. We've made a few changes for the better. You know what they say about everything happening for the best. Besides, look on the bright side. Your flight from camp allowed you to raise money we desperately need. I think you'll be pleased with what we've done."

Bright side. You've got to be kidding. Kate kept her thoughts to herself.

Over the past year, Michael, Kate's right-hand man, had kept her informed of life at camp. Whenever he went to Nairobi, he'd phone with updates, and he would also e-mail reports from the park headquarters. But they never discussed the subject of her return. The question had always been on the tip of her tongue. Being somewhat superstitious, Kate kept quiet. If Michael had news that she could return, he'd tell her right off. After the first few times Michael called, Kate's depression returned in full force, causing her to relive the incident over and over—opening the wounds, feeling the shock and pain of her actions.

"You've caught me off guard, Michael."

"I know. Take your time. There's no hurry. I just wanted to give you the good news. What are you doing in the San Juans? How's Jack?"

"Would you believe me if I told you?"

"Try me."

"He's getting stitched up after a mountain lion objected to him pulling *her* stitches out?"

"How do you two do it? I thought you were leading the life of a city couple. You can't seem to avoid needy creatures."

Kate laughed. "It's a long story. I'm not sure I can handle the details right now. Jack and I've taken over a friend's rehab facility here on Lopez Island. I'll be here for a while, but I'll keep in touch. Michael, I don't know how to thank you for everything you've done."

"Hey, just keep Jack out of trouble and get your butt back where you belong. Gotta go. The boys here at park headquarters are frowning at me. I've tied up their phone long enough."

They hung up. Kate sat in stunned silence, willing her heart to slow. A thousand thoughts assaulted her at once. It took all her patience not to get online and book the first flight back to Kenya. Kate looked down at her dog, who had fallen asleep with her head resting on Kate's foot. "What would I do with you, girl?" Kate said. Kenya would never survive in the bush. She'd have to stay behind. So would Jack. He had signed a two-year contract with the team. Kate had not realized until this moment how easily they had settled back into a civilized life in Chicago. Despite unrest over her situation, despite her hunger to return to the life she'd worked so hard to build, despite Jack's promise to return with her, Kate knew that returning to Africa would not be so easy.

A loud popping noise caused Kate to jump to her feet. She ran to the kitchen and looked out the window. Sitting with its front tire in the flowerbed, the old Toyota pickup, minus its driver, let out another belated backfire, and the engine sputtered to a stop. Kate opened the kitchen door and watched Paula Steiner totter down the drive and up to the porch. Her hair hung wet from a shower. She had changed clothes, although the spandex outfit did little to improve her appearance. The odor of tobacco and booze was now barely detectable, and Kate was grateful for Paula's effort.

"I'm glad you came," Kate said.

Paula swept in and plunked down in a chair at the kitchen table. "I had to use Lisa's car to jump start the truck. The cops took our Caddy." Paula looked around, pulled a stick of gum from her shirt pocket, and began to unwrap it. "Nice house. I suppose you won't let me smoke in here? I know, stupid question," she said, shoving the gum into her mouth. She began chewing with such force that Kate feared Paula would crack a molar.

"How about coffee?" Kate offered.

"Yeah, coffee would do—strong. And two aspirin." She took a shaky breath. "I hope Lisa wasn't too rude. All her brains can fit in her left tit, and that's not saying much. Sorry about the seed thing."

"I've been called worse," Kate said. "You don't sound like you're from here."

"Nah. Macon, Arkansas. Met Ray when he was stationed at Little Rock Air Force Base. We moved here after he left the service. His grandmother left him that speck of land. We put a trailer on it, and before I could blink an eye, we had three kids and had settled into a nice rut."

"Tell me about Ray," Kate said, handing the woman two aspirin and a glass of water.

Paula swallowed the aspirin along with a wave of tears. "Ray didn't kill that woman."

"How can you be sure, Paula? The sheriff doesn't arrest someone unless the evidence is strong enough to stand up in court. Why was Ray parked on Watmough Bay Road? He wasn't scheduled to work that morning. And if he needed to see Emily Ann, why traipse through the woods?"

"I know all that. We had a fight the night before. I told him to get the hell out, not for good, you understand. He drove off. He told me he pulled over to sleep it off."

"Why here?"

"I guess 'cause no one ever drives out this road. Listen, Ray's not smart enough to kill anyone."

Kate let that last statement pass. "Was he on good terms with Emily Ann, I mean after she warned him that time about not showing up for work?"

"If you think that dressing down upset him, you're crazy. Just water off a duck's back. He gets more shit from me in five minutes. And that's a bunch of shit about him going after that farmer with a pitchfork. That old man was nuts. He's the one who picked up the fork and went after Ray. Ray tackled him and wrestled it away, but he got blamed for assault and spent three months in jail. Bullshit!"

Kate poured two cups of coffee. She put two scones on a plate and slid them into the microwave. Paula's eyes widened at the sight of the pastries. "These are a couple of days old, but if I heat them, they should be okay."

"Thanks. I should eat something."

"Paula, does Ray know how to operate a remote-control plane?"

"A what?"

"You know, one of those toy planes flown by remote control."

"Hell, no. I told you Ray ain't that smart. I had to take the chainsaw away from him. He tried to cut some tree limbs and zipped through the cable wires. Stupid ass almost electrocuted himself." Paula smiled at what

Kate deduced must have been a fond memory. *True love*, she thought.

"Why? What about a remote-control plane?" Paula asked.

"Not important." The microwave beeped. Kate placed scones and two plates on the table.

"You said you could help," Paula said, reaching for a scone. She removed her gum and stuck it on the side of her plate. "The last time Ray was in jail, we lost almost everything. I can't pay bills if Ray don't bring in a paycheck. Besides, the kids need their dad."

"I'll do what I can, Paula. Was Ray with anyone that night after he left the house?"

"He left after midnight, I think. He said something about going over to that clod Louie Fister's place. That's what he usually does when I throw him out."

"Where do I find Louie Fister?"

"Worthless piece of shit. He works at Fisherman's Bay Marina when he's not hanging around the Legion Hall."

"Paula, I'll see what I can find out. But I need to talk to Ray."

"Won't do no good. He don't remember nothing."

"He doesn't remember driving out to Watmough Bay Road?" Kate asked.

Paula shook her head. Her eyes filled with tears. "It looks bad, don't it?"

"What do you think about taking over Ray's work here?" Kate laid her hand on top of Paula's. "I'm sure Fred wouldn't mind. We need the help. That way you'd continue to have a paycheck for a while. The work's not too hard. I've no doubt you can handle it."

"I'd have to be home before the kids get home

from school. I don't like leaving them unsupervised."
Paula brushed scone crumbs from the front of her shirt
and shrugged her shoulders. "The job would sure help
since my fat-ass breadwinner's sitting in jail."

Kate remembered the purple doll with the blown-
off ear and suspected supervision of the Steiner kids
was by no means a nurturing endeavor, more likely
limited to the prevention of drawing blood and igniting
the trash heap surrounding the trailer.

Chapter Sixteen

Kate found the marina on her first pass down Fisherman's Bay Road. She parked in the resort lot and walked down the hill toward the water. A guy fitting Paula's description sat on the pier eating a sandwich. A large bag of chips and a liter of cola sat by his feet.

"Louie Fister?" Kate asked.

"Yep." He smiled up at her, showing dark gaps where teeth should have been. A sweaty, stained cap advertising a beer brand, pulled low, shaded his eyes. A faded T-shirt and cutoff jeans hung loosely over his skinny frame. He picked up the bag of corn chips and offered her some. It looked as if his fingers hadn't been washed in a week.

"No thanks. Just had lunch. Paula Steiner told me I'd find you here. I'm Kate Caraway. I'm staying at Eagle Crossing. Emily Ann Thurston was a dear friend of mine."

"Ray didn't kill that woman." Louie set his sandwich on his thigh and took a long drink of cola. "Ray's a crazy dude, but he wouldn't do that."

Kate sat next to him. She changed her mind about the chips and grabbed a fistful from the bottom of the bag "Did you see Ray that night? Paula said Ray might have come to see you after he left the house."

"Yeah, he came over. My wife won't let him in the house, so we stayed outside and drank some beers. I told him he shouldn't go driving anywhere. Told him to sleep in the car. He said he would. I left him there and went back inside."

"What time?"

"Late. Around one, maybe."

"Did he stay there all night?"

"Sheila, my wife, has to get up around four to go to work at the bakery. She said he was still there when she left. I woke up later, around nine, I guess. He was gone."

"Did you tell the sheriff this?"

"Sure did."

"Once Ray woke up from sleeping it off, why would he drive over to Watmough Bay just to go to sleep again? He'd have to pass his house on the way. Why not just go home?"

"And deal with Paula? Are you kidding?"

"But if he wasn't ready to go home, why leave your house in the first place?"

"You sure ask a lot of questions. Why do you want to know so much?"

"Both you and Paula believe Ray didn't kill Mrs. Thurston. I just might agree with you."

"Well, it don't matter what we believe. Ray's been arrested. That's that. He can't afford no bigshot lawyer." Louie shoved the rest of his sandwich into his mouth. "I gotta get back to work."

Kate stayed on the pier after Louie left. The intense sun made her wish she'd worn sunscreen, but the breeze over the bay cooled her face. She finished the chips and watched the shorebirds flitting about in a small preserve formed by Otis Perkins Spit. The slender sandbar divided the sound from a saltwater lagoon, creating a perfect breeding habitat for birds.

Then Michael's voice echoed in her head. "It's safe for you to return. And we are more than ready to have you back."

Kate closed her eyes and pushed that conversation from her mind. Instead, she listened to the raucous sound of seagulls fighting over a fish carcass lying in the nearby mudflat. The pungent aroma of shallow sea brought up a memory of the Texas coast—a summer location on Galveston Island, soon after her mother had died—very soon after. Kate ran barefoot along the beach, feeling the warm sand and the surf as it trickled over her toes. She remembered laughing for the first time since the funeral and then abruptly losing the sense of joy as the hurt came rushing back. That brief flash of joy made her feel that she'd betrayed her mother. The vacation was botched from that moment on. No matter what Ted Caraway did to cheer up his six-year-old daughter, the effort was wasted. Kate recalled the moment her father gave up trying to make things better and just stayed near, offering silent comfort. Kate felt it now—her dad's quiet comfort here at Fisherman's Bay, along with the seagulls and the ripe smell of the lagoon.

****

Kate wondered how Jeannie was holding up after dashing off Monday evening. If Emily Ann's friend was still down in the dumps, maybe they could offer one another some comfort. She'd meant to call yesterday, but with all that had occurred, she never got around to it.

When Kate walked into the library, she found Jeannie seated at the front desk, intently reading the computer screen. "We have two copies, Lindsay, but they're checked out, and there's a waiting list," she told a woman standing across from her. "I can put your name down, and we'll call when it's available."

The woman left. Jeannie looked up, startled to see Kate standing there.

"Hi," Kate said. "Do librarians get a coffee break?"

Jeannie's usual welcoming smile was absent. "Oh, Kate. Nice to see you. It's been crazy around here this morning. We've just had an elementary school class come for story time. I love that they visit, but it takes a while for my blood pressure to return to normal. I just can't leave right now. I'm sorry."

"I understand. I came by to see how you were doing after the other night."

Jeannie removed her glasses and rubbed her eyes. "Yes, well, I'm better now, I guess. I heard they arrested Ray Steiner. That poor family. How are they going to make ends meet? They've had a string of bad luck."

"Bad luck?" Kate said.

"Well, maybe the wrong choice of words. It's just that…I don't know what I mean."

"You're not the only one who feels that way."

"What?" Jeannie gave Kate a sideways glance.

"That they have the wrong man."

Jeannie flushed red. She looked around to see if anyone was near. "Listen, I have a book group starting up right now. I need to get ready for them. Let's visit sometime later, all right?"

Kate barely knew the woman, but Jeannie's brushoff cut deep. She left the library feeling worse than when she arrived.

****

Kate heard Jack and Fred laughing in the kitchen as she walked in. "For two sutured-up guys, you two are certainly cheerful," Kate said.

"Hey," Jack said. "Are you okay?" He walked over to kiss her on the forehead.

"I should ask you that." Kate picked up Jack's hand. "It doesn't look too bad."

"Four stitches and a tetanus shot."

"How about you?" Kate asked Fred.

"Some of the external stitches are out. Others aren't. Nasty scar, but otherwise fine." Fred started a pot of coffee. "Now that Ray's out of commission, I need to find some help with the chores," he said.

"Oh, that reminds me. I stuck my nose into your business. Paula Steiner came over around noon after she somewhat sobered up. She's convinced Ray is innocent."

"Of course, she is. She's his wife. What business of mine did you stuck your nose into?"

"She's in dire straits right now—caught me at a weak moment—and I sort of suggested that maybe she could take over Ray's job, at least for a while."

"You what?" Jack chuckled.

"She's sitting around that ramshackle trailer drinking all day with her wacky sister. She has no other income. I just thought…I realize now what a stupid suggestion that was. After all, her husband's accused of murdering Emily Ann. What the hell was I thinking?"

"I know what you were thinking," Jack said. "You think Ray's not guilty."

"I'm still having trouble with his motive," Kate said.

"You mean besides the guy being a bit loony?"

Fred said.

"To tell the truth, yes. After I talked to Paula, I went to see Louie Fister, Ray's drinking buddy. It seems after Paula threw Ray out of the house that night, he drove to Louie's. A few beers later, Ray passed out in his car. Then sometime after four, he woke up, drove past his house, and parked on Watmough Bay Road where he fell asleep again."

"That's if you believe his story," Fred said. "I don't mind Paula helping out. I don't have anything against her. She didn't ask for this trouble. If she wants to work, that's fine with me. Speaking of work, hungry animals are calling my name." He filled his thermos and started for the door.

"Wait a minute," Jack said. "If Ray parked on Watmough Bay Road the morning Emily Ann was killed, why didn't I see the car when I took the dogs for a walk?"

"It depends on where the car was," Fred said. "The road is winding and hilly. If Ray parked it around a bend, you wouldn't have seen it."

"Maybe. And it *was* foggy that morning," Jack mused. "I'll be out to help in a minute."

"No, I can handle this. Give that hand a rest." Fred hurried out the kitchen door.

"You think Fred's upset about me putting Paula on him like that?"

"No. He seems sincere in wanting Paula's help. He doesn't strike me as the type who'd hold a grudge." Jack took Kate by the elbow and walked her into the den. "Now, tell me what else happened today."

"That's not enough?"

"It is, but you're holding back. Have a seat and

talk."

"You're no fun anymore if I can't hide things from you. What does that say about our marriage?"

"That it's been a long, fruitful one. So, did you find out something?"

"I went to see Jeannie at the library. I needed a little comfort, and after Monday night, I thought she might as well. She didn't seem all that happy to see me, though. On Monday morning, she was hell-bent on figuring out what happened to Emily Ann."

"Regardless of what you believe about Ray being innocent, the sheriff did arrest him. Putting a face to the murderer opens up another level of grief."

"You might be right, but I can't help but feel there's more to Jeannie's despondency."

The Jack Russells bounded through the doggie door, followed by Kenya, who only managed to get her head and one shoulder through the opening.

"Better slide open the patio door and let her in before she pulls the frame out of the door." Kate laughed.

"I don't think she's ever had this much fun." Jack walked over and opened the glass door. "She'll be lonely once we go back to Chicago."

Kenya crossed the room in two gallops and landed gracefully next to Kate. The greyhound laid her sleek head on Kate's knee and then wriggled it around until she found Kate's hand. The message was quite clear. Kate accommodated her dog by massaging her ears. Kenya seemed to flow up from the floor onto the sofa without even moving. "Maybe it's time to get her a sibling," Kate said.

"Fine with me. Maybe a Chihuahua or a pug.

Something small for a nice contrast."

"Michael called this morning."

"Our Michael?"

"He said it's safe for me to return."

"Ah, so that's it. I knew something else was bothering you. But isn't that what you've been waiting to hear all these months?"

"How can I return to Africa right now? You've got another year on your contract. And there's no way we can take Kenya to live in the bush. And what if I get there and find out—"

Jack moved over to the sofa and squeezed in between dog and wife.

"Slow down. You're right. You can't manage it right now. I'm sure Michael isn't expecting you to show up at camp immediately after hanging up the phone. There are visas to get, and that's no speedy process. We'll talk about it and work it out. There are all sorts of possibilities."

"I guess so."

"Did you forget? I'm always right. Besides, I don't have to report to spring training until February. I can go back with you for a while. I'm sure Max and Olga will be happy to keep Kenya while we're gone. Didn't you tell me Rosa Linda and Daniel spent more time at the ranch than their apartment in Austin? That means Luna will be there too, and Kenya will be delighted to stay with her greyhound cousin. In the meantime, let's deal with things here. We'd planned to stay for two weeks."

"Jack, we can't leave now."

"No, but soon. Fred needs to get on with his life. Another few days at the most. Now, tell me what Michael had to say."

They talked for almost an hour. Kate never understood her initial response to keep her worries to herself. Jack was the world's best listener. He didn't try to solve her problems and only gave her advice when she absolutely needed it.

"Let's go for a walk," Kate said. "I haven't had any exercise all day, and neither have the dogs."

"Sounds good. How about going to that little park at the end of Alec Bay Road? Blackie Brady, I think it's called. Fred said there's a small cove where we could let the dogs off their leashes."

Blackie Brady Park was a two-mile hike from Emily Ann's place. By the time they got to the beach, the dogs were panting and content to sniff the shoreline at a leisurely pace. Kenya waded up to her chest to cool off then found a spot of sand in the sun on which to rest.

"If Ray's innocent, we're back to the family again," Jack said. He sat down on a driftwood log.

Kate walked around, selected several flat stones, and began skipping them across the water. "Yes, I know. And that's what's so puzzling. They were all here on the island when Emily Ann died, but not when I was pushed off the cliff."

"Do we know that?"

"Susan was teaching. Evan was at work. Jill confirmed that. Brian was on the road, and Laurie was at home sedating herself. Don't forget Jacob Bower. He still seems the most obvious to me. We now know that he was the one who gave Emily Ann that article about the mountain lion attack. He had means and opportunity, but the motive's weak."

"Is it?"

"His fear of the lions and the desire to disrupt operations seem weak to me."

"You're thinking like a levelheaded person."

"Right. That's because I am—"

"What I mean is…well, you saw the man. He appears to be in the advanced stages of alcoholism. Maybe during one of his intoxicated states or blackouts he killed Emily Ann. I'm not talking about premeditated murder. He saw her standing there that morning, rushed over, and pushed her off."

"But what about me? Why try to kill me?"

"Maybe he suspected you knew something or saw him. You were up on the cliff not long after Emily Ann was pushed."

"I see what you mean. I need to find out more about this guy."

Suddenly Dotty began barking, and Speckle dashed over to check out her sister's distress call. Kenya raised her head but stayed put. Her bored look said that Dotty and Speckle's discovery wasn't worth the trouble. Kate and Jack looked up to see the two dogs nipping at a live crab sidling across the shore. Before Jack could leash the dogs, the crab caught Speckle on the nose and hung on long enough to draw blood. Her barks turned to squeals, and Dotty retreated to a safer distance.

"Time to go," Jack said. "Tending to wildlife is enough for us. We don't need to add domestic animals to the rehab list."

"No." Kate laughed, pointing to Jack's bandaged hand. "We don't indeed."

When they got back, Fred had not yet returned from the cages. Kate checked her cell and saw that Jeannie had called but didn't leave a voice mail.

"Sounds like Jeannie's had a change of heart about talking to you," Jack said.

"I'll call her right now." Kate hit return call, and Jeannie answered on the first ring, suggesting they meet. "No problem," Kate said. "Do you want to come by here? I understand. I'll be right there."

Kate hung up and began to dig her keys out of her bag. "She wants to meet at Sunnyside Cafe. She has another meeting this evening and doesn't have time to drive out here. But I get the feeling that she doesn't want to come to the house."

"Maybe it's still too painful for her," Jack offered.

"Maybe," Kate said. "I'll be back as soon as I can."

****

As soon as Kate pulled into the parking lot, Eleanor Grommer came out of the bookstore next door. Kate smiled and waved but received a scowl in return.

Jeannie sat gazing out the window toward the bay.

"Nice view," Kate said.

"I never get tired of looking at the water. Have a seat," Jeannie said. "They have great desserts here."

"Just coffee for me, thanks," Kate said. "Seems like all I've been doing since I got here is eating."

"I can't keep this to myself any longer. I've been turning it over in my mind since I left Emily Ann's the other night. Maybe it's nothing. Maybe you can help me decide."

"What is it?" Kate asked.

"It's Fred. I'm afraid he's not telling the truth."

"About what?"

"About when he got to the island the weekend Emily Ann died."

"He flew in on Sunday right before noon."

"No, he didn't," Jeannie said, shaking her head. The waitress came by, bringing Kate's coffee and refilling Jeannie's. The librarian picked up her spoon and stirred even though she added nothing to her cup. "Fred was on the island Saturday night. I saw him. I'm sure it was him. I was leaving the golf course about 7:30, and I saw Emily Ann's Explorer pull out of the airport parking lot. Thinking it was Emily Ann, I tooted the horn, but it wasn't her. At first, I thought it was another SUV just like Emily Ann's. Then I noticed the Eagle Crossing logo on the side door. Fred was driving. It's probably nothing, right? I mean…him being here the night before."

Kate wanted more than anything to assure Jeannie that her concerns were unfounded, but that wasn't possible.

Chapter Seventeen

"Jeannie told me she saw Fred Saturday night," Kate said to Jack. "What does that mean?"

"It could mean he simply came in early," Jack said, playing devil's advocate. "He knew that Emily Ann was going to break the news to her family at dinner on Saturday evening, so he stayed away as planned. Or he was scheduled to arrive on Saturday and to not show up here until Sunday."

"I distinctly remember Emily Ann saying that because Fred had some business to take care of, he wouldn't arrive until late Sunday morning."

"Maybe he finished the business early." Jack took two beers from the refrigerator and sat at the kitchen table. "You think Fred killed Emily Ann?"

Kate reached for a beer. "I don't know what to think. But when Fred arrived on Sunday morning, he said that he had just flown in a few minutes earlier. And he was driving Emily Ann's SUV."

"He did say that, didn't he? So, he lied," Jack said.

"What's his motive?" Kate asked. "As soon as he and Emily Ann were married, this house and facility would be half his."

"Maybe he wanted more than half," Jack said, taking a long drink of beer. "Maybe he wanted the house and facility, but not Emily Ann."

Kate fought back tears at the thought that Emily

Ann could have been conned and murdered. "But Emily Ann was sick and not expected to live long. Fred could have just waited."

"He said her cancer was in remission."

"We have to talk to him," Kate said.

"And tell him what? That we suspect he murdered Emily Ann?"

"Where was he the other day when I had the encounter with the remote-control plane?"

"Let me think. You left just before lunch. I made sandwiches for everyone. After eating, we worked for a while, then Fred went upstairs to rest. I guess he could have left and returned without me knowing."

"Was he able to drive last week?"

"He could have driven, but he couldn't have hiked out to Iceberg Point, carrying a remote-control plane."

"Unless maybe his injury isn't as bad as he lets on."

"Eighty-something stitches is pretty bad."

"Maybe he had help, then! This is too much!" Kate said, slamming her bottle on the table. "I want to talk to him now!"

"Let's not act too quickly," Jack said. "Fred's going to know something's up. You're not good at hiding your feelings."

Kate picked up her beer. "I have some work to do in the office. I want to finish something I started earlier." She looked at her husband. "You, however, have the face of a master poker player."

"It comes from baseball—not poker. Speaking of which, I have some phone calls to make. There's a pitcher from Houston turned free agent. It's time to put in my two cents."

Kate went to the computer. Instead of adding data to the animal files, she executed a search on the Internet. She typed in the name *Macie Stevens*. Other articles on the child's death gave more information. The girl had been playing in her sandbox the morning of her scheduled birthday party. Her body was found about two hundred yards from the house. A neighbor, mowing his lawn, saw the lion dragging the girl down the middle of a dry culvert that ran behind his house. He chased after the animal, throwing rocks and shouting until the cat dropped the girl. The autopsy confirmed that Macie Stevens' neck had been broken. She died instantly.

Her grandmother, Joann Archer, was quoted in the article. "At first we feared Macie had been abducted by some crazy guy who preyed on children. Those perverts are everywhere these days. When I saw the huge footprint in the sandbox. I knew immediately what had happened. I warned my daughter about moving so far away from the city. People think the city is dangerous. Look what happens when you live in the suburbs."

Another article included a picture of Macie's parents, Robby and Hannah Stevens. Both were white-faced and shocked, holding on to each other, looking as if they would crumble if they let go. Then Kate noticed a familiar face in the background. She searched through Emily Ann's drawer, looking for a magnifying glass, and found an old pair of reading glasses instead. The magnification was strong enough for Kate to be sure. Jacob Bower stood off to the side, looking ready to bolt. The older woman behind the Stevens couple, probably Macie's grandmother, Joann Archer, judging by her resemblance to Hannah Stevens, appeared stone-faced, seething with anger.

Jo—Kate remembered the inscription in Jacob Bower's bird book—his ex-wife. Joann Archer must have remarried. Was the horrible death of his granddaughter what had caused him to move to Lopez Island to live by himself? Was that why he stayed inebriated? Was learning of Emily Ann's plans to bring mountain lions to the island what caused Bower to teeter off the narrow line between grief and insanity and push Emily Ann to her death?

"Hey, how's it going in here? I brought you a sandwich. You must be hungry." Jack set the plate down on the desk and walked up behind Kate. He massaged her shoulders. "Your look of concern has changed to a look of fright."

"That's because I have a good idea who pushed Emily Ann off the ledge."

Jack closed the office door, pulled up a chair, and sat down next to his wife. "How can you be sure?" he asked.

Kate pointed to the article on the computer screen. "Read this," she said.

"My God. How awful. That poor little girl. But how does that fit with what's happening here on the island?"

"Take a closer look. Your eyes are better than mine."

Jack leaned close to the screen. "Damn! It's Jacob Bower. Macie Stevens was his granddaughter!"

"Right. Bower must have written those threatening letters and included that article."

"Imagine trying to run from something that horrific only to find the cause of your trauma right next door.

215

That certainly gives him a strong motive for killing Emily Ann."

"And maybe for trying to kill me if he associated me with Emily Ann's cause. You know, another animal rehabber, bringing wild animals in contact with innocent people."

"If that's the case, we're dealing with a lunatic. Fred's in danger as well."

"Fred. We can't let him off the hook that easily. We have to tell him about Bower, but we also have to ask him why he lied about coming to the island the night before. Now's a good time."

Jack stood up. "Let's wait until the morning. Enough has happened today."

"Fine. But before we talk to Fred, I want to see what Bower has to say."

"What! You're not going over there again. You're lucky he didn't try something the last time you were there."

"I know. That's why you're going with me first thing in the morning."

"We can't just ring his doorbell and inform him we suspect him of killing Emily Ann."

"I'll ask for his help. I'll say a group of island citizens are concerned about Eagle Crossing's new acquisitions. Ask if he can speak out for our cause."

"And just stand by and see how this crazy fellow reacts? Let's hope he doesn't own a gun." Jack walked over and looked out the window. "It's starting to rain." He turned to Kate. "Fred's out on the deck. He's going to wonder what we're up to here in the office with the door closed."

"I'm going upstairs. I've had enough for one day."

Kate switched off the computer. Before she and Jack left the office, her cell phone rang.

"Hello."

"Kate, it's Susan. I just wanted to check in with you."

"Susan, glad you called. How's Laurie?"

"I'm on my way to visit her. She wasn't allowed visitors for the first few days. It's after hours, but since I'm family, they'll let me see her for a few minutes. Any developments there?"

"Maybe." She told Susan about Jacob Bower and the death of his granddaughter and filled her in on the rest, except for what Jeannie had told her about Fred.

"Could he have killed Emily Ann?" Susan asked. "But they arrested that other guy."

"Too early to tell. Call me tomorrow and tell me how the visit with Laurie went. I wouldn't mention this development, though. How's Ben?"

"He's still with Brian's mother. I phoned her yesterday. Ben's having a hard time. Sounds like Brian is, too. She said he feels guilty about being away. He calls every couple of hours."

****

The sound of the wind howling shook Kate from a deep sleep. She rose up and looked out. Against the dim glow of the moonlit sky, huge evergreens swayed and bent. Heavy winds across the islands were not unusual. Blowing forty to fifty miles per hour, they could last a few hours or several days. Kate dropped back into bed and pulled the comforter over her head. She was asleep in seconds.

****

"Kate, sweetheart, wake up." Jack patted her

shoulder.

"What…what time is it?"

"Almost seven. I wanted to let you sleep, but we have a problem."

Kate sat up. "What's wrong?"

"It's okay. Here's your coffee." He set a cup on the bedside table. "Last night's wind damaged several of the cages. Fred's up there now, but he needs our help."

"The animals?"

"All okay. Some of the birds' perches and nesting boxes were knocked down, and shingles were blown off the roofs. Branches and limbs are down, and there's building equipment strewn all over the place. Nothing we can't fix. Drink your coffee and get dressed. I'll be up at the cages." He kissed his wife and left the room.

"Damn!" Kate said to Kenya, who was still under the covers. "Never a dull moment."

Kate finished her coffee and slipped on a pair of jeans and a sweater. She pulled her hair into a ponytail and put on Jack's baseball cap. She went downstairs, found two thermoses, and filled them with coffee. On the way up to the cages, she stopped at the storage shed for a pair of gloves.

"About time you got your lazy butt out of bed."

Kate jerked around to see Paula Steiner dragging a pile of brush behind her.

"Paula?"

"Who'd you expect? Dorothy from the Wizard of Oz?"

"I didn't think you'd be working so soon."

"Neither did I. That idiot, Fred, called at six this morning. Told me if I wanted to work, I'd better get my ass up here."

"Might not be a good idea to call your boss an idiot."

"Oh, Fred don't mind. I already tried it out on him, and he barely flinched."

Kate's mouth fell open.

"Gotcha. Just kidding. My assignment, which I chose to accept, is to drag all this damn brush down here. We'll burn it later when the wind dies down."

"How does it look up there?"

"Like the big, bad wolf huffed and puffed. Some of them cats seem a little jumpy."

"You'll get used to them."

"Oh, I'm used to them just fine. It's them who's got to get used to me. I found that if I whisper to them, you know, like that horse-whispering guy, they seem to calm down some."

Kate and Paula made their way back up the trail. Fred and Jack were inside one of the owls' cages. The owl was perched on a tree limb wedged between the mesh fencing at the very top of the enclosure. Its nesting box was now a pile of boards tossed in the bottom of the cage.

"Give Miss Sleepy Head something to do," Paula said.

"Reporting for duty." Kate saluted.

Fred laughed. "You can feed the cats. We haven't had a chance to do that yet. I think the birds are okay for now. You can feed them, too, once Jack and I get these cages cleared. How does that sound?"

"Sounds like a good way to start the day."

For the next three hours, the four of them worked without stopping. Finally, Eagle Crossing looked like a rehab facility instead of a pile of rubble. The backbreaking work kept Kate's mind off Jacob Bower, but she couldn't help thinking about Fred and what Jeannie had told her about him last night. She would not let the day go by without confronting him.

Once Paula had finished clearing away the debris, she helped Kate with the feeding. "How did you get involved with this kind of work?" Paula asked.

"Started back when I was little. I tried to rescue every baby bird I found whether it needed rescuing or not."

"I guess this kind of work gets into your blood."

No shit, Kate thought. *Whether you like it or not.*

"Paula, can you run over to Bryson's Feeds?" Fred called. "He has an order ready to pick up. I have an account there, so just sign for the stuff. Take the Explorer."

"No problem," Paula said and almost skipped down the trail.

"I think she'll work out. Does a much better job than Ray." Fred arched his back and sighed.

"Looks like you've overdone it this morning," Kate said. "Why don't you take a break? There's not much more to do. Jack and I will finish."

"I won't argue. See you back at the house."

Kate turned and looked toward the trail that led to Bower's house.

"Ready?" Jack said.

"Stop that," Kate said.

"What?"

"Reading my mind. Let's go."

"Someone's here," Jack said as they approached Jacob Bower's driveway. A Saab station wagon was parked next to Bower's Subaru. "Think we should come back later?"

"California plates. If it's a relative, they may be visiting for a while. I don't want to wait any longer to talk to this guy."

Kate and Jack walked up to the front steps and found the front door wide open. Dry leaves had blown in and were scattered in the front hallway. On the floor in the entrance was a woman's leather handbag and a set of keys.

"This doesn't look good," Jack said and stepped in front of Kate. He knocked on the open door. "Mr. Bower?"

A loud screech echoed from inside—a woman sobbed. "No! Dad! Dad!"

Kate ran in behind her husband. Crumpled on the floor by an armchair, a young woman had her arms wrapped around Jacob Bower's legs. The man's head was leaning back on the headrest of a chair as if he were staring at the ceiling. A trail of blood from a bullet wound to his temple had dried on the right side of his face. On the floor by the chair lay a handgun.

"Call 911!" Jack shouted to Kate. "Ma'am, are you all right?" Jack took the woman by her shoulders and helped her to the sofa.

"He wouldn't answer the door. I had to use my key. I just walked in and found him in the chair."

While Kate made the call, Jack checked Bower's vital signs.

Kate hung up and sat next to the woman. She recognized her immediately from the article about Macie Stevens' death. "EMS is on the way," Kate said.

Jack walked over and sat down on the coffee table. "What's your name, ma'am?"

"Megan Rutherford. Dad's dead, isn't he?"

"I'm afraid so," Jack said.

"I was too late. I tried to get here sooner, but I couldn't get a flight until this morning."

"I'm Kate Caraway, and this is my husband, Jack Ryder. We're staying next door." Kate felt the woman stiffen.

"Next door? Not that place that has the mountain lion?"

"We were friends of the owner. She died a few days ago," Jack said.

"This was too much for him. I should have realized sooner. I was too late."

"You can't blame yourself," Kate said.

"Dad came up here to drink himself to death after what happened to my niece."

"Macie Stevens was his granddaughter?" Kate said.

Megan looked up, surprised, and then surprise was instantly replaced by a look of resignation. "I suppose Dad told your friend about what happened."

"In an indirect way, yes," Jack said. "We found an article about your niece's death among Emily Ann's things."

"It must have been terrible for your father when Emily Ann moved the lion up here."

"It was. My dad called me the first time a few days ago. I hadn't heard from him in months. He's been estranged from us ever since Macie's death. He held himself responsible."

"Why?" Kate asked.

"We were having a birthday party that day for Macie and my twins. They were all born on the same day. Dad was supposed to watch Macie. He and our mother were separated, and, when he found out that Mom was coming to the party with her new boyfriend, Dad went to his car and drank himself into a stupor, leaving Macie unattended. Next thing we knew, Macie was gone."

"I don't think Emily Ann ever realized what your dad was going through," Kate said.

"I should have gotten here sooner. I could have prevented all of this."

"You can't think that way, Mrs. Rutherford," Jack said. "Suicide's not the fault of those left behind."

"I'm not only talking about Dad's death."

A sound that was becoming all too frequent announced the arrival of the emergency crew. Deputy Fitzroy rushed in with a look on his face that said, "Not again." Behind him was Detective Kraus.

The crime scene tape went up again, and the fingerprint guys were at it. After Megan had answered countless questions, she asked, "What happens now? I mean, I have to make plans to bury Dad."

"Any time there's an unexpected death, we have to investigate," Deputy Fitzroy said. "It'll be a couple of days before we can release your father's body. It might be better for you to return home."

"No, I'm staying, but not here, not in this house. I'm sure there's a hotel on the island."

"Come to the house with us," Kate said. "We'll make some calls and find you a place. But you're welcome to stay with us."

"I couldn't do that. A hotel will be fine. I have to call my husband…and Hannah."

After calling her family, all of Megan Rutherford's resolve had been exhausted. Kate did not want to send her on her way to find a place to stay.

"I know of a nice inn in the village," Kate said. "I'll call and see if they have a vacancy. At least let us go with you and see that you get settled in."

Megan agreed, and Kate made the call.

Five minutes later, Kate drove Megan Rutherford to Windsong Inn. Jack followed in their Land Rover.

"Are you sure you'll be all right here by yourself?" Kate asked as she and Megan stood at the front desk waiting for the innkeeper.

"My husband's on his way. He's flying in and should be here in a few hours. I'll be fine. Thanks so much for your help."

A gray-haired man, who looked as if he'd just come in from doing yard work, stepped behind the front desk. Kate introduced herself and Jack.

"Sorry you had to wait. I was in the garden gathering some things for tonight's dinner. You must be Mrs. Rutherford. I'm Ned Hornsby." Rather than shake her hand, he patted it as if, in her grief, Megan Rutherford would break apart. "My wife will be down in a second to show you to your room. Ms. Caraway explained the situation when she called. I'm really sorry about your father."

A woman wearing a summer dress partially hidden by an apron came down the stairs.

"My wife, Sarah," Ned said. "Sarah, this is Mrs. Rutherford."

"Nice to meet you." She walked over to Megan and took her by the arm. "I'm sure you'll want to lie down, dear. Just come upstairs."

Megan turned to leave, and Kate handed her a slip of paper. "Here's my cell phone number and the

Thurston home phone. Please call if you need anything."

"Ms. Caraway," Megan said. "I'm sorry about your friend. I mean her...her accident."

"Thank you," Kate said. She was about to add that Emily Ann's death was no accident but held her tongue. She felt Megan Rutherford already knew that.

Chapter Eighteen

Ned Hornsby watched Megan Rutherford and his wife disappear upstairs before he spoke. "I can't believe we've lost two islanders this week. Sarah and I knew Emily Ann well. We didn't really know Mr. Bower though. Saw him in the market a few times. We're a small community, and anytime someone dies, we all feel the loss, especially under such tragic circumstances."

"Thanks for accommodating Mrs. Rutherford," Kate said. "And for finding a room at the last minute for Emily Ann's daughter and family last Friday night."

"Glad to help. Mrs. Fuller was distraught when she arrived. The whole family was. We put them up in a room next to our place. We live in the wing off the kitchen. It sounded as if they were up most of the night. They weren't a problem, mind you, but it was obvious that something had happened."

Ned Hornsby was clearly searching for the reason why the Fullers needed a place to stay at the last minute, but Kate was not going to discuss the family disagreement and add more fodder for the local gossips. Hornsby did not take the hint.

"That little boy of theirs sure is cute."

"Ben. Yes, he sure is. A little shy."

"Sarah and I were concerned that he may have been sick."

"Why?" Kate asked. "He was fine when they left to come here."

"You know kids. They can be fine one minute and sick the next. Sarah and I have five of our own. All grown and flown the coop. The little boy started crying early that morning, and the parents had a hard time getting him to quiet down. Not that they were a problem. It's just that we were right next door and couldn't help but hear. The little boy, Ben, most certainly woke up and got scared, finding himself in a strange place."

"I'm sure that was it, Mr. Hornsby. Thanks again."

"Don't worry about Mrs. Rutherford. We'll watch after her until her husband gets here."

Kate and Jack left the inn. The wind had stopped. Billowing white clouds filled the sky, leaving only a few patches of blue.

"Let's not go back to the house just yet," Kate said.

"There's that nice restaurant by the water at the end of the village road a couple of blocks from here. Want a glass of wine?" Jack took Kate's hand.

"Sounds good."

"I want to stop at the market to fill up with gas first."

"I'll meet you at the restaurant," Kate said.

Kate walked along a string of shops—an art supply store, a clothing store selling original designs, a craft store selling everything from wool yarn to accessories made from alpaca fiber. At the craft store's window, Kate stopped to read a flyer on the uniqueness of alpaca fiber when Eleanor Grommer came out carrying a bag full of yarn. The old woman didn't hesitate to walk over to Kate. "More trouble up on the hill at Watmough Bay,

I hear."

"Hello, Mrs. Grommer."

"People just don't listen. I told Emily Ann many times—"

"Mrs. Grommer, Emily Ann's gone." Kate felt anger well up—anger that lay just below the surface. She gritted her teeth to keep it down. "Can't you—"

"That woman never had her priorities straight. If she'd spent more time volunteering at St. Francis' Church and less up there with those birds—"

"I don't want to hear it, Mrs. Grommer! *That woman*, as you call her, was a dear friend of mine. How she spent her time was none of your damn business! She's gone now. Give it a rest. Besides, I think St. Francis may have been pleased with the work Emily Ann did, don't you?"

"Well, I never!"

"No? Then maybe it's about time."

"What's that supposed to mean?"

"Time to get a life, Mrs. Grommer, instead of meddling in other people's," Kate said and walked away smiling. When she reached the Bay Cafe, she sat down on the bench and waited for Jack. He pulled up and parked in front of the bike rental shop across the parking lot.

"You look pleased with yourself," he said.

"I just had a nice conversation with Eleanor Grommer. Do you mind if we walk instead of going into the restaurant? There's a stair-climb down to the beach. I'm not really in the mood for a glass of wine right now," Kate said.

"Sure. It's low tide. Let's go."

Private property bordered the small beach. Unless

one traced back and forth along the thirty or so yards designated for the public, a long stroll was not possible. Instead, they sat on the bottom step.

" 'If I can ease one life the aching.' " Kate pulled her hair back from her face.

"What?" Jack asked.

"I keep thinking about that Emily Dickinson poem Bower read at the funeral, 'If I Can Stop One Heart from Breaking.' I think he was referring to easing his own pain."

"For killing Emily Ann?"

"I think his daughter believes he did."

"If that's the case, the sheriff needs to know. Megan Rutherford should not withhold that information. But what I don't understand is her referring to Emily Ann's death as an accident. She obviously doesn't know that the authorities now believe it was murder."

"She knows." Kate turned and looked at her husband. "I'll talk to her again later. She's had enough for one day."

"We'd better get back. I'm sure Fred's wondering what's happened."

"Just a couple of hours ago, we'd planned to confront Fred about his lie." Kate stood and brushed sand from her jeans.

"We still should, even though there's a strong possibility that Emily Ann's killer is dead."

"I want to go home."

"I'm beginning to miss the big city, too." Jack stood up and wrapped his arms around his wife. "Just say the word."

Kate laid her head on Jack's chest. It wasn't

Chicago she meant, and going home wasn't as easy as *just saying the word.*

****

Fred was standing at the door when Kate and Jack drove up. "I was about to go looking for you two. I got out of the shower and heard the sirens. You were gone, and I didn't know what to think. I'm glad everything's okay."

"Sorry, Fred," Jack said. "We didn't mean to frighten you."

"Everything's not okay," Kate said.

In the den, Kate explained what had happened. Fred slumped into the sofa. Speckle and Dotty climbed onto his lap. He shook his head in dejection. "A few months ago, Emily Ann and I were strolling along Otis Perkins Spit. I proposed the idea of merging our two rehab facilities. She didn't hesitate. She loved the idea. And then I proposed marriage. And now she's gone, I'm tied up in litigation that'll last for months, and our neighbor kills himself because we're bringing lions to the island. It wasn't supposed to be like this. I don't know if I can pull this off."

"What do you mean?" Kate asked.

"After Emily Ann died, I was determined to continue with our plans because I knew she would have wanted it that way. I stayed busy building the cages and caring for the animals. Zach was here to boost my spirits, but now I don't know. What am I doing here? It really hit me in the last couple of days. I'm alone. Really alone. Unless you count these two mutts." He shook his head again and forced a laugh. "It'll be just me and Paula Steiner working here. And that thought is enough to make me want to head back to Santa Rosa."

"Give yourself some time," Jack said. "The work you do is important. You haven't had a chance to grieve. So much has happened."

"Too much. I'm going upstairs for a nap. It's been a hell of a day. I sent Paula home. I think that woman would have worked until she dropped. Good suggestion, Kate. Come on, girls." Speckle and Dotty followed him to the stairs. They were halfway up when the doorbell rang.

"Damn," Fred said. "So much for plans."

"I'll get it," Jack said.

Deputy Fitzroy and Detective Kraus stood under the archway of overgrown rose vines. "May we come in?" Deputy Fitzroy asked.

Kraus gave him a look that said, "You'll never make it as a cop with that too-polite attitude."

Not waiting for an invitation, Kraus stepped into the foyer. He glanced up at Fred on the stairs. "Glad you're all here. This makes my job easier. Jacob Bower was murdered. I need you all to answer some questions."

****

Specks of blue sky had disappeared under dark, heavy clouds, leaving Kate with a feeling of being sucked into a black hole. She, Jack, and Fred gave statements.

"The time of death was between midnight and four," Kraus said. "Anybody hear anything last night?"

"In that wind? Are you kidding?" Fred said. He ran his hands through his hair and then over his face. "I couldn't have heard a gun go off if it had been right next to my head."

Kraus looked out the patio window. Drizzle began

to fall, shrouding the evergreens and the view beyond. He tugged at his chin and seemed to ponder every nuance of Fred's words.

"Ever get up in the middle of the night to check on the animals?"

"Often," Fred said.

"How about last night?" Kraus spoke, sounding bored. But Kate couldn't help but notice the furtive look on his face—the look of a veteran detective whose mind saw all the possible paths laid before him, clear and distinct, but whose voice gave nothing away.

Fred followed his gaze and seemed to ponder Kraus' question. "I did. I couldn't sleep. I got up around, oh, two I guess, and went out to the cages. Except for some downed limbs, everything seemed okay."

"You had some damage, though?" Kraus said.

"We had some heavy gusts around five thirty, and I went to check again. That's when I found the place a mess."

"Do you mind telling us why you think Bower's death was murder, not suicide?" Kate asked.

"We don't think it was murder. We know. The medical examiner's report will confirm it. Bower's blood/alcohol level proved that he was too intoxicated, probably comatose, to have pulled the trigger. Besides, bullet's trajectory—its entry—shows that the gun was held above the body and fired at a downward slant. There were no powder burns on his hand. And lastly, Jacob Bower was left-handed. The shot to his right temple was not self-inflicted. We've traced the gun to a pawn shop in Everett. The gun was stolen during a break-in."

Kate expected more questions and was surprised when the detective snapped his notebook shut and announced he was leaving.

Half an hour later Kate stepped from the shower, pulled on a pair of sweats, and walked into the bedroom. Jack was propped up on a stack of pillows reading while Kenya's sleek, slim head rested in his lap.

"This morning everything seemed clear and simple," Kate said, towel drying her hair.

Jack set down his book. "You mean Bower killing Emily Ann and then himself."

"Exactly. Now there are two murders and an attempt on my life."

"Bower still could have killed Emily Ann."

"And Fred found out and killed Bower?"

"He certainly lacks an alibi for early this morning."

"Or maybe it's the other way around. Maybe Bower knew Fred killed Emily Ann, saw him that morning, and Fred killed Bower to keep him from talking."

"But if Fred's the one, what motive does he have for trying to kill you?"

"I'm too much of a threat. Knowing Emily Ann so well and being in the house, going through Emily Ann's files, maybe he's afraid that I'll find something."

"Then if Bower saw Fred push Emily Ann, why didn't he go to the sheriff?"

"Maybe Bower was blackmailing Fred." Kate threw the towel down on the foot of the bed. "This is crazy. If all this is true, then we're sleeping under the same roof as the killer."

Kate jumped at a light tap on the door.

"Come in," Jack said.

"I hope I'm not disturbing you."

"Not at all," Jack said and motioned for Fred to have a seat in the armchair.

He folded arms across his chest and stood by the window instead. "Thanks. I just needed to talk...I mean, I can't understand what's happening here." Then he looked around the room and smiled. "I expected your bags to be packed." The smile disappeared. "Listen, I know how it looks. And I couldn't help but notice...or feel your suspicion. For whatever it's worth, I didn't traipse up to Bower's house and shoot him last night."

"Could you clear up one point for us?" Kate said.

"What's that?"

She hesitated for a fraction of a second, feeling silly, feeling like a suspicious, paranoid old snoop. But anger replaced uncertainty at the thought of Emily Ann being conned by her lover and business partner and then murdered. She couldn't stop the hard, accusatory words from spewing from her mouth. "Jeannie Shuttleford saw you on the island the night before Emily Ann was killed. You were leaving the airport in Emily Ann's Explorer."

"Right. That's true. So?"

"So, Emily Ann said that you weren't scheduled to fly in until Sunday morning right before brunch. And when you got here that morning, you said that you had just arrived."

Fred looked from Kate to Jack and back to Kate. He sat down in the chair and seemed to deflate. "I did say that, didn't I? I was able to get away the night before. I called Emily Ann and told her that I had arrived early and would be staying the night at the Marina Inn on Fisherman's Bay Road. I suggested that I come on over and we'd make the announcement that night. She told me about how Laurie and Evan had reacted to the mountain lion. And that Laurie and her family had packed up and checked into an inn, and Evan was holed up in his room. It didn't sound like a warm and cozy atmosphere. Anyway, we decided to stick with the plan. I was driving Emily Ann's Explorer because she'd left it at the airport for me. When I said I'd arrived that morning, I wasn't thinking. So, does that prove that I didn't come up here early on Sunday morning and push Emily Ann off the cliff? No. But, Sunny June can prove I didn't."

"Who?" Kate and Jack said in unison.

"She's the owner of Sunnyside Cafe. I was up early that morning because I was anxious about meeting the family. I wanted coffee. The Marina Inn's gracious enough to provide little scented soaps and shampoo for its guests, but not coffee pots. So, I drove into the village, hoping to find a convenience store open. Funny. All the time on this island, I hadn't realized that there were no convenience stores. Sunnyside Cafe was opening in half an hour, so I waited in the parking lot. The woman who owns the place is Sunny June. Anyway, she brought out a cup of coffee. I was much appreciative and told her how nice she was. She just laughed and told me she was no such thing. She noticed me sitting in the Explorer and imagined she was seeing Kenny Rogers. The coffee was an excuse to get a closer look." Fred laughed. "I told her I was glad I didn't look like Kenny Rogers since he was dead.

"Don't think I don't know that I look like the most

obvious suspect. Emily Ann changes her will and leaves Eagle Crossing, her house, and her property to me. That and the fact that I wasted no time in moving in and setting up the operation. But Emily Ann and I had talked about 'what ifs' many times. What if her cancer flared again? What if she became too ill to handle this place? When you're staring cancer in the face, you tend to make plans to cover your bases. We spent hours discussing every possible scenario. It was her idea to leave the house and property to me. I strongly objected. We sort of compromised by incorporating the business as a nonprofit."

"That sounds just like Emily Ann," Kate said.

"I was in no hurry for her to start changing wills and stuff like that, but she insisted, not for my benefit so much as for the animals themselves. I don't have to tell you how dedicated she was to wildlife rehab. This was her life. She believed in what she was doing. Even to the point of alienating her own children."

"Sorry, Fred, but we had to ask," Jack said.

"I understand." Fred rubbed the small of his back. "No hard feelings. I don't believe that Bower killed Emily Ann, and I don't believe Ray Steiner killed Emily Ann, either. Now, let's get cracking and try to figure this out."

"I agree with you about Ray, but I'm not so sure about Bower," Kate said. "Something his daughter said this afternoon. I think she knows or suspects something. I'm going to see her in the morning."

"We need to think of factors that Emily Ann and Bower had in common," Jack said.

"They both lived here on the mountain top," Fred said.

"Their land is some of the island's most valuable," Kate added, rubbing her temples. "But I still think we're barking up the wrong tree. Listen, it's after two, and all we've had today is coffee. Let's go downstairs, and I'll make us some lunch. I can't think on an empty stomach."

As they got up to leave the bedroom, the phone rang.

"I'll catch it downstairs," Fred said.

As soon as he left the room, Jack said, "Feel better now that we know Fred's side of the story?"

"Actually, no."

They walked into the kitchen as Fred was hanging up the phone. "That was Susan."

"Everything okay?" Jack asked.

"Hardly."

"What's happened?" Kate said.

"Laurie left the hospital sometime last night. No one knows where she is. Susan's frantic. She called Brian, and he's on his way back to Seattle. But that's not all. Evan didn't show up for work today."

"Hopefully, they're together," Kate said. "Maybe…"

"Are you thinking what I'm thinking?" Jack said.

"Oh, no." Kate slumped down on the chair. "Not Laurie and Evan. Why would they kill Jacob Bower?"

"The most obvious answer is that they know or think they know Bower killed Emily Ann," Fred said. "But how could they have found out?"

"Me," Kate said. "I told Susan about Bower and his granddaughter, and she must have told Laurie when she visited her last night."

"I'm calling Detective Kraus." Fred picked up the phone.

Chapter Nineteen

Kate walked into Windsong Inn to see Megan sitting in the dining room with a man who looked equally forlorn. His light-brown hair curled just below his ears. A pair of wire-rimmed glasses framed his eyes, giving him an academic look. Kate imagined him in front of a class of college students lecturing on classic literature.

"Please sit down, Ms. Caraway. This is my husband, Sam."

He rose and shook Kate's hand. "Megan told me how helpful you and your husband have been. Thank you so much, Ms. Caraway."

"Call me Kate." She sat down at the table.

"Mrs. Hornsby is brewing some coffee. Would you like some?" Sam smiled.

"That would be nice, thank you."

Sam walked to the buffet and fetched another cup. Megan looked worse than she had when Kate and Jack had found her at Bower's house. Her skin was pasty white, and her lips were dry and drawn.

"I guess you know about Jacob," Sam said. "When the deputy came to tell us that Jacob hadn't committed suicide, oddly enough, we felt a small sense of relief, but it lasted only a couple of seconds. I don't know which is worse, murder or suicide."

Tears started to stream down Megan's face, and

Sam placed his hand on hers.

"I should have tried to help him," Megan said. "He fell apart when he and Mom divorced. I kept hoping he'd snap out of it, but things just got worse for him." Megan drew in a breath. "Why would someone kill him?"

"I know this is hard for you," Kate said, "but I want to know that as well. The sheriff's arrested a man named Ray Steiner for Emily Ann's murder, but my husband and I strongly believe that he's innocent. And now that your father's been—"

"He *is* innocent," Megan said. "I don't know who killed my dad or why, but I'm afraid Dad killed your friend."

"Megan!" Sam said. He seemed just as surprised at his wife's pronouncement. "What are you saying?"

"A few weeks ago, Dad called me for the first time in months. He was drunk. He was crying. I couldn't make sense of what he was saying. I…I hung up on him. He'd done that before, called after drinking himself silly. Then he called again a few days later. This time he was sober. He sounded different, scary almost. He said he'd stopped drinking and that he had to talk to Hannah, my sister, Macie's mother. Hannah's refused to talk to Dad ever since the incident. She never forgave him for Macie's death. You see, Hannah and her husband Robby had given up on having children. Fifteen years later, Hannah gets pregnant. Macie was a delightful surprise, and Hannah doted on that little girl. Sure, most parents do, but with Hannah, Macie was everything. The party that day was way over the top. Hannah had been planning it for weeks. She made enough cupcakes to feed every kid in town. She called me several times a day about what to include in the party favor bags for the kids. She spent weeks sewing Macie's birthday outfit. When I walked in the house on the day of the party, I could hardly move with all the decorations. Hannah was rushing around doing last-thing nonsense. Macie was outside playing in the sandbox. Hannah asked me to bring her in for a bath. But Macie wasn't there. She wasn't..." Megan broke down, sobbing.

"Honey, please," Sam said.

"I'll never forget the look on Hannah's face when we realized Macie had gone."

"Megan's right, Mrs. Caraway," Sam said. "Hannah was inconsolable. What do you say to parents whose only child had simply vanished?

"Dad had left Hannah's house after the police found Macie's body," Megan said. "He just ran away. I guess he couldn't face what he'd done. He never acknowledged his part in Macie's death. I knew Hannah wouldn't talk to him, so I never told her he'd called. I got to thinking about Dad's last call to me. It sounded eerie like he wanted to put things right before...before he died. I called him several times, and he never answered. That's when I decided to fly up here. When I saw him lying back in that chair, I knew—without a doubt—he was a classic case for suicide."

"Megan, we don't know what really happened," Sam said.

"But I do know. It's funny how the mind works. Sitting there with you and your husband yesterday, waiting for the police to arrive, I could hear that first conversation with Dad. The one when he was shit-faced drunk. It was like a tape was replaying in my head. He said something about killing her. I thought he was talking about Macie until he muttered on about being so angry that he'd wished she was dead. I was horrified. Last night I realized that he was talking about Mrs. Thurston. I'm so sorry, Ms. Caraway, but my dad killed your friend."

****

Kate felt wrung out after leaving the inn, but also relieved since Megan Rutherford decided to tell the sheriff about that telephone conversation with her father. Her story was sure to throw serious doubt on Ray's guilt and convince the county's prosecuting attorney that the case against Ray was too weak to keep him in jail. Kate ran these thoughts through her mind as she filled a washcloth with ice cubes. She took the aspirin from the cabinet, then ground beans for a fresh pot of coffee. Paula Steiner sat at the kitchen table, her head buried in her hands, and belched. Kate feared she'd become inebriated from inhaling alcohol fumes.

After returning from visiting Sam and Megan, Kate had gone to the computer to input more information about the new arrivals. She needed to involve herself in some mindless task while contemplating everything she'd heard. Fifteen minutes later, pounding on the kitchen door broke her concentration. Before she could get up to answer it, Paula let herself in.

"In here, Paula."

Paula stuck her head in the office. "I needed to talk to someone. Busy?"

"Nothing that can't wait."

Paula walked over to the computer and picked up the notebook Kate was using. The smell of alcohol told

Kate how Paula had spent her afternoon.

"What's this? It looks like some kind of shorthand or secret code."

"Abbreviations—labels actually for the animals that were brought in on Friday."

"F-A-UK-NR?"

"Female, adult, unknown injury, non-releasable."

"M-A-B-NR? Male, adult?"

"Blind, non-releasable."

"M-J-S?"

"Male, juvenile, shot."

"Releasable or non?" Paula tossed the notebook on the desk.

"Don't know yet. We like to think positive and assume every animal can be released. They only get the NR label if there's no doubt. Like the blind mountain lion—no way can we release him."

"I'm a F-SF-DB."

"Help me out, Paula."

"Female, shit faced, desperate bitch."

"You need coffee. Let's go into the kitchen."

The coffee was ready, and Kate filled two cups.

"You won't tell Fred, will you?"

"About you getting drunk? No, Paula, I won't. But if you're going to be the breadwinner, for the time being, you're going to have to lay off the bottle."

"Sometimes I just can't cope."

"You and half the seven billion other people on this planet, but getting drunk isn't going to help. You also have your kids to think about."

"Oh, they're all right. Lisa's watching them."

The thought made Kate shudder. But then she suspected the Steiner kids could indeed take care of themselves, seeing how the adults in their lives were drunk most of the time.

Ignoring the glass of water Kate had given her, Paula washed down four aspirin with her cup of black coffee. "It's the waiting that's killing me. Not knowing what's going to happen."

"Paula, I'm hesitant to tell you this. I don't want to give you false hope, but the sheriff may have another viable suspect." Kate related the conversation with Megan Rutherford. Paula listened intently as if Kate's words were a life raft.

"If Bower confessed to his daughter that he killed Mrs. Thurston, they should release Ray, right?"

"He didn't exactly confess. Besides, they need more than hearsay to expiate your husband."

"To what?" Paula choked on her coffee. "He hasn't even had a trial. How could they execute him?"

"Expiate…let him go."

"Hell, why didn't you just say that? You about gave me a frigging heart attack."

Kate had to smile. Despite Paula's drinking habits and foul mouth, Kate was beginning to like Ray's wife.

"You don't have any more of those scone things, do you?"

"No. How about a grilled cheese sandwich and a spinach salad? I've tried several times to eat today, but something always comes up."

"Well, since you're cooking, I guess I can't complain."

Jack and Fred came in and stopped in their tracks. From the look on Jack's face, Kate knew that the smell of alcohol still lingered.

Paula tried to hide behind her coffee cup and look

small.

"I was showing Paula how I enter data. She's going to stay and eat with us."

"Great," Jack said. "Fred told me that you have a way with the cats."

Paula shrugged her shoulders and turned slightly pink.

"If you're not careful, Kate's going to recruit you to work for her in Africa when she goes back," Jack said, winking at his wife.

With all the developments over the past twenty-four hours, Kate hadn't even had time to think about Michael's phone call. In fact, she'd almost forgotten.

"Can't you just see me in Africa?" Paula said.

"No, I can't," Fred said. "But I can see you putting in more hours here. You do have a natural ease with the animals."

Paula was unusually quiet during the meal. After they'd finished, Jack and Fred went back to the cages, and Paula volunteered to help Kate clean up.

"Spinach salad was good. I never make spinach at home. Kids don't like to eat a lot of green things. But you're right, you know."

"About what?"

"Me laying off the bottle for a while. It's just that I never had much else to do. I like working here. I used to work at a convenience store in Macon, and I liked it. I got to jaw with all sorts of people."

"I know what you mean. When I was in Kenya, I pretty much worked around the clock. When you work with animals, you learn to be prepared for anything at any time. Then suddenly I found myself back in the States without a damn thing to do. I thought I would lose my mind."

"You! Your life seems so perfect."

"Nobody's life is perfect."

"I need to ask a favor, but you've done so much already. I mean, just believing that Ray's innocent is a lot. Since he's been in jail, some people in town have been acting like I got a disease."

"I'm sorry, Paula. I know this must be hard for you. What's your favor?"

"I want to see my husband. So do the kids. But I can't drive that piece-of-shit car of Lisa's to Bellingham. We'd end up broke down on the side of the road."

"How about if I take you tomorrow morning?"

"You mean it? But I'm supposed to work."

"I'm sure Fred wouldn't mind if you made up the time later. Besides, I'd like to talk to Ray myself."

"I'd have to take the kids out of school. But it's for a good cause, right?" Paula finished wiping the kitchen table and grabbed her things. She reached the door and turned around. "Thanks, Kate."

"See you in the morning."

****

Kate called Brian to find out the latest on Laurie.

"I canceled the rest of this week's appointments. I need to stick around here. I can't imagine where she's gone. I'm about to lose my mind."

"Could she be with a friend?"

"I've called everyone I know. No luck."

"What about Evan? He wasn't at work yesterday. Could they be together?"

"She's not with him either. That San Juan County detective was here this morning. They located Evan. He was with his girlfriend all day yesterday."

"Have you talked to him?"

"I tried this morning. Evan said that he had nothing to say to me, that it was my fault Laurie is missing, that if I hadn't been on the road so much this wouldn't have happened. Typical Evan, never offering a solution, but quick to blame. I don't know what I'd do if anything happened to Laurie. I know I can be overbearing at times, but I love my wife. When this is all over, I swear I'll be a better husband."

The sadness in Brian's voice rang true and brought back all the pain of everything that had happened since she arrived. Kate wanted to say something hopeful. Before anything came to mind, he spoke again.

"Kate."

"What?"

"It was obvious why Detective Kraus was here. He didn't come out and say it, but I'm sure...I'm sure he suspects Laurie."

"Of what?" Kate said, knowing the answer to her own question.

"Bower is murdered, and Laurie is gone. They think she may have killed him because she thought he'd killed her mother. She wouldn't, Kate. Laurie wouldn't do that. I know she hasn't been very...stable lately. It looks bad for her. Damn. Listen, I...I have to go in case...Laurie tries to call."

"Brian, if I learn anything, I'll call."

Chapter Twenty

Kate wrangled the Steiner kids into the back of the Land Rover while Paula finished getting dressed. The two boys' antics quickly turned from tickling to thunderous. If they hadn't been belted in, they'd be clambering over every inch of the SUV. Tommy, the oldest, had his hand down his little brother's shirt, threatening to rip his heart out like the bad guy in one of the Indiana Jones movies. The younger brother, whose name Kate didn't know, grabbed Tommy's hair and called him "puke breath." Kate turned around and said, "Listen, now—" Before she could complete her request for the kids to behave, Tommy let out an ear-piercing yell, and Kate learned the name of the middle child.

"Kennnnnny. You shithead."

Kenny had his teeth in his brother's arm.

"Get out!" Kate shouted. She jumped from the driver's seat and yanked open the back door. "Now!" Before she could assist the boys out of her SUV, she heard the screen door slam. She turned and saw a tiny version of Paula skip down the driveway toward them. The youngest child, a girl, had reddish-blonde hair the color of her mother's. She looked to be about five. Wearing a bright-orange T-shirt and green tights, she resembled an upside-down carrot. Her oversized flip-flops extended several inches beyond the heels of her

248

tiny feet. "Hi, I'm Brittany. Why are you yelling?"

"Gee, lady," Tommy called out. "Don't get your panties in a wad." He turned to Brittany. "Shut your damn face before I smash it."

Brittany started to cry.

"My panties are none of your business, Tommy. And you'll call me Ms. Caraway. If you guys want a ride to Bellingham to see your dad, you'll have to ride on top, strapped to the luggage rack. Now get out."

"You can't do that," Kenny said, but the doubt in his voice told Kate that she had his attention.

"You guys are small enough to all fit on top. Come on. You first, Tommy. Don't worry. I'm a careful driver. I advise you to keep your mouths closed so insects won't slap against your teeth." Then she looked up at the sky. "Hmmm. It does look like rain."

"You made your point...Ms. Caraway," Tommy said.

"Listen. You can make this worse for your mom, or you can help. And believe me, she needs your help. Wild animals act better than you, and don't make your sister cry again."

"They always make me cry," Brittany whined.

"If Brittany cries during this trip, you boys will stay in the car while we girls enjoy pizza before we come back. And no profanity and no name-calling."

"Got it," Kenny said.

A few moments later, Paula climbed into a silent car.

"Ready?" Kate said.

"W-S-RTG."

Kate cocked her eyebrows in Paula's direction.

"Woman, sober, ready to go. I thought my

offspring would have you screaming for mercy by now. You must have a way with kids."

"No shi—" Tommy edited himself. The drive to Bellingham was funereal quiet.

****

Kate had to wait her turn while Paula and the kids visited Ray. The crowd in the waiting room ranged from nervous elderly people to younger ones who looked as if they wanted to start a riot. Then there were a few whose jaded faces said, "Been there, done that." Kate sat next to a woman who'd fallen asleep in her chair. With legs stretched out in front and her chin resting on her lofty chest, her snores echoed through the small waiting room. Kate moved to the other side of the room and flipped through the selection of magazines resting on the counter. Nothing more recent than two years ago.

"Lola!" a female officer shouted. "How many times do I have to tell you that you can't sleep in here?" Lola yawned, stretched, and shot the finger at the officer. She stood and ambled out.

Kate followed and opted to wait on the street, but the atmosphere outside wasn't much better. A group of cocky teenagers shuffled by, smoking and cussing, causing other pedestrians to scurry to the other side of the street. A homeless man was asleep on the sidewalk. Next to him, tied with a tattered belt, a young German Shepherd-type puppy whimpered, obviously experiencing his first few days on the street. He trembled and ducked whenever anyone walked by. One of the teenagers almost stepped on the dog and tripped trying to avoid it. Then gaining his footing, the boy kicked the dog, causing him to jump into his owner's lap. The homeless man woke up and shoved the dog so hard he gagged on his makeshift leash. Then he kicked the dog himself. The kids started laughing.

Kate walked up to the puppy, squatted down, and extended her hand for inspection. The dog, expecting another rebuke, rolled over on his back in submission. His hairless belly was red and splotchy from irritation. Fleas were too numerous to count.

"Your dog's got a lot of fleas. They're making him sick. When was the last time either of you ate?"

"Fuck you, lady." The man rolled over and closed his eyes. The dog started whimpering again.

Kate folded a five-dollar bill and was about to put it in the cup, then thought better of it. She knew what the money would be used for. She looked over at the cowering dog. The hopelessness in his eyes almost too overpowering to take in. "I know how you feel, little buddy." Someone walked by and threw the dog a crust of pizza. He merely sniffed at the scrap and laid his head between his paws. Kate was not going to judge the circumstances that led to people living on the street, but exploiting puppies to gain a few extra handouts made her blood boil.

Her thoughts were interrupted by Tommy and Kenny walking down the street.

"How was your visit?" she asked.

Kenny shrugged. "Okay, I guess."

"Dad says the food sucks. I mean, it's pretty bad," Tommy added. He stuck his hands in his pockets, and his face hardened. "He didn't kill that woman. I know he didn't. What's going to happen to him, Ms. Caraway?"

"I'm not sure, Tommy. But if it makes you feel any

better, I agree that your dad didn't kill Mrs. Thurston. I'll do what I can to prove it."

"He wants to come home," Kenny said.

"He may never come home," Tommy shouted and took off running down the street.

Kate headed in the boy's direction when Kenny said, "It's okay. He won't go far. He does that all the time."

Just then Paula trudged down the steps of the courthouse, Brittany clutching her mother's hand, trying to keep up.

"Are you okay?" Kate asked.

"Mommy's crying," Brittany said.

Paula handed Kenny a few dollars. "Here. Take your sister to that 7-11 and buy her an ice cream."

Paula pulled a tissue from her pocket and blew her nose. "Ray looks bad. He's not eating." She ran her fingers through her hair and shook her head. "I don't know if this was such a good idea, the kids seeing their dad in jail." She swallowed back the tears. How in the hell did my life get all screwed up? I don't have no control over anything. Ray's right. I just sit back and watch as things go to shit."

"That's not true, Paula. You're doing what you can. You're working for Fred, earning some money."

"It's not enough, though. If I don't turn things around, what's going to happen to my kids? I've been stuck in a rut for so long, I don't know how to crawl out. Look." Paula pointed toward the 7-11. Kenny and Brittany were hovering over the homeless man's dog. Brittany petted him while Kenny let the mutt lick his ice cream. "Kenny's a softy. He always brings home hurt birds and frogs and things. Like you when you was little." Paula drew in a much-needed breath. "If you're going to visit Ray, you better go now. Visiting hours are almost over."

"Tommy took off down the street."

"He'll be back."

Kate wanted to offer Paula some words of encouragement, but before she could say anything, Paula walked over and joined her two younger kids.

The jailer brought Kate back to the visiting area where Ray waited. He glared at her from behind the Plexiglas. Dark shadows created cavernous depressions under his eyes—a contrast to his ashen-colored face. He had the look of a man who'd given up hope. Kate picked up the phone receiver, and after a few seconds, Ray picked up his on the other side. "You shouldn't have brought my family here."

"They really miss you."

"Yeah, well, they better get used to it," he mumbled.

"Listen, Ray. I'm here to help, but you're going to have to help me. Can you tell me anything that will give me something to go on? I talked to Louie Fister, and he told me about you two being together the night before Mrs. Thurston died. When did you leave his house?"

"Go away. I done said everything to my lawyer. I ain't saying no more."

Kate stared at Ray for a few minutes and finally said, "I've no intention of going away. Waiting is something I'm good at."

"Wait until you rot. I ain't telling you nothing."

"The sheriff may have another suspect in Emily Ann's murder."

"Good for him."

"If you can throw some light on this messy situation, remember something, anything, you might be able to walk out of here soon, and your daughter would have her father at home where he belongs."

Kate had finally struck the right chord. Ray seemed on the verge of tears. "You and Paula were stupid for bringing my girl in here."

"Maybe, but what's done is done. You need to help us get you out of here so you can be a father to her and not just some man she visits in jail."

He coughed and finally looked at Kate. "I don't know what I can tell you."

"What time did you leave Louie's place?"

"Around six, I guess."

"Why didn't you go home?"

"Paula threw me out the night before. I wasn't ready to come crawling back. Besides, I was still a bit woozy."

"Did you see anybody on your way to Watmough Bay Road?"

"No one's ever on that road. That's why I went. You think I'd sleep off a drunk in the Lopez Market parking lot?"

"How long were you parked there?"

"I don't know."

"You didn't see or hear anything?"

"I remember being cold. I guess that's what woke me up. I had trouble starting the car. It took a while, then I left."

"Emily Ann died between six forty-five and seven fifteen."

"Yeah, that's what the cops said."

"They also found threads from your jacket in

several places from the road to the cages."

"So?"

"So, did you walk through the woods up to the cages?"

"Hell, no. Why would I do that when I can take the trail from the house?"

"When you were working, did you ever see much of Jacob Bower?

"He'd come around some, but not much."

"Ever talk to him?"

"No."

"Any idea who would want to kill Emily Ann?"

"No. I told this all this to my lawyer." He snorted. "Some lawyer. Looks like he's still in high school."

"Did Bower ever ask about the lion?"

"I told you I never talked to the jerk! He'd look at me like he was too good for someone who cleans cages."

"He and Emily Ann ever argue about anything?"

"Not in front of me."

"You had words with her a while back."

"Sure as hell did! She chewed my ass in front of my kids because I was late to work." He rubbed his eyes. "But I wouldn't kill her over that." He ran his fingernail along a deep gouge someone had carved into the table in front of him, then shrugged his shoulders. "She had a reason to be pissed. She hardly ever lost her temper. Paula told me about the cancer. I guess Mrs. Thurston was having a bad day."

Kate saw the sincerity in Ray's face, an emotion, she suspected, that rarely surfaced. "Know a woman named Eleanor Grommer? She and Emily Ann weren't exactly friends."

"Old Eleanor? Yeah, she seemed to have had it in for Mrs. Thurston. Not sure why. Except that Mrs. Thurston was always doing good things for people. Everyone liked her. No one likes Old Eleanor, the old bat."

"Did you know Emily Ann got threatening letters about bringing the lions to the island?"

"Mrs. Thurston didn't tell me her problems."

The jailer came and nodded to Kate that her time was up. Kate looked at her watch. These fifteen minutes with Ray offered her nothing.

"You were parked there about an hour, asleep in your car," Kate said. "During that time someone came to Eagle Crossing, pushed Emily Ann off the cliff, and supposedly opened the lion's cage. It had to be someone who had a key or knew where the keys were kept."

"I have my set of keys. The cops took 'em when they arrested me."

"Ever give the keys to anyone?"

"No reason to."

Kate stood up to leave.

"I didn't have my jacket that morning."

"What?"

"The morning Mrs. Thurston died. I didn't have my jacket."

"Where was it?"

"Don't know. Lost it, I guess."

"But the sheriff found it on the back seat of your Cadillac."

"Oh." Ray blushed and shrugged his shoulders again.

Kate started to walk out when Ray said, "Thanks

for helping Paula get work. I hope she keeps her shit together. I mean, if I'm not around, she's going to have to take care of those hellions of ours."

****

Paula and all three kids had gathered around Kate's Land Rover. Tommy was sullen, his arms folded across his chest. Kenny and Brittany were bugging Paula about getting a dog.

"You guys hungry?" Kate asked. "How about pizza?"

Brittany forgot about the dog and started jumping up and down. "Cheese! I like cheese pizza. Can I have a soda, Mom?"

Paula looked at Kate.

"Soda and pizza. Let's go," Kate said.

****

Once back on Lopez, Paula asked Kate to stop at the market before taking them home. Tommy, who had not spoken a word since they left Bellingham, piped up, "Mom must be out of beer."

Paula jerked around, and for a moment, Kate expected to hear a string of expletives directed toward Tommy. Instead, Paula said, "I got other things to get, smart mouth." Everyone waited in the car while Paula rushed in. Ten minutes later, she returned with two full grocery bags.

"Let's go," Paula said. "Brittany's asleep."

Kate arrived at the Steiners' trailer and parked behind a rust-colored Ford Escort. The kids scampered out of the car as soon as Kate cut the engine. "Aunt Lisa's here," Brittany cried.

"Bitch better be sober. I ain't putting up with her shit tonight. I got too much to do," Paula muttered out of the side of her mouth.

"I told Ray to call you if he remembered anything."

"Thanks for everything, Kate. I don't know how much good it did. But at least Kenny and Brittany had fun. I'll see you in the morning if I can get that damn truck started."

"Call me if you can't. I'll come get you."

Paula opened the door and paused. She looked at Kate for a moment, then said, "Why are you so nice to us?"

A flurry of answers crossed Kate's mind, but her response was simply, "I like you."

Paula smiled. "Yeah, we kind of grow on people." She grabbed her groceries and followed her kids inside the trailer.

Chapter Twenty-One

Kate opened the kitchen door. The soft sound of Cole Porter, barely audible, greeted her with a feeling of calm, reminding her that everything was not one big jumble of chaos.

"How'd it go?" Jack called from the den. "You're in one piece, so I guess you survived the afternoon."

Jack and Fred were playing chess, listening to jazz.

"I feel like I just stepped into another world." Kate sat on the sofa next to her husband. "One where people play chess and don't cuss and don't yell and don't cry and don't try to pull one another's hearts out through their chests."

"Here." Jack handed his glass of wine to Kate. "Sounds like you need this."

"What I need is a bath. Twenty minutes in that jail, and I feel grungy."

"Learn anything helpful from Ray?" Fred said, his eyes glued to the chessboard.

"Not really. Ray seemed resigned to his fate. He admitted he drove and parked on Watmough Bay Road at the time Emily Ann was killed. He claims he passed out."

"You still believe he's innocent?" Fred said, putting a knight down and causing Jack to wince.

"His motive is too weak," Kate said. "He had an argument with Emily Ann weeks ago, and he decides to kill her? That's silly."

"He does have a history of violence," Jack said, frowning at the board. He tentatively moved a piece and held on to it for a few moments before releasing it.

"If you call one incident with a farmer who sounds crazier than Ray a history, I guess he did." Kate sipped the wine. "The problem with Ray is that he's not much of a fighter."

"He doesn't have to be," Fred said. "He has Paula. Checkmate."

"Damn." Jack retrieved his glass of wine from Kate.

"Looks like you've met your match." Kate laughed. "I'm going upstairs to take a shower. Any word from Brian about Laurie?"

"He called about an hour ago," Fred said. "No word. He didn't sound good. I don't think he's slept since she disappeared."

On the way up, Kate decided to check her notes in the office. She hated being behind on updating the files—a task she planned to leave until the next morning. Kate wanted to get an idea of how much needed to be done. Fred and Jack had neatly stacked the data sheets by the computer. With Emily Ann's files on each animal on the computer as well as on printed copies, it should take Kate only a couple of hours. However, since the new animals had arrived, she had not taken the time to make a new file folder for each one. She decided to do that now rather than wait until the morning. Kate pulled open the drawer and took out nine new folders. Each animal had been identified with a number, and Kate wrote these numbers on the files. As she replaced them in the drawer, she noticed several folders in the back, each with a first name as the label.

Emily Ann's letter files. Kate had forgotten all about them. Emily Ann had been an avid letter writer, and she'd made a copy of each letter before she sent it. There were enough letters here to make a book. Kate pulled out the file with her name. She opened it and was immediately taken back more than twenty years. The first letter was written to Kate right after Emily Ann had left Austin. Kate didn't have to read it. She could still almost recite it word for word. It was vague and evasive, giving Kate no clue as to why Emily Ann moved across the country. Kate replaced the file and was surprised to see one labeled "Ted." She wasn't aware that her father had received letters from Emily Ann. The idea was ridiculous—of course, he would have. And there they were—several of them, making up one of the thickest files in the drawer. Kate couldn't help herself, and the open file now spread across her lap. Emily Ann had written in answer to Ted's letter. "Yes," she agreed, "it is time to meet Kate."

Suddenly Kate was back in the kitchen in their house in Hyde Park, listening to the oldies on the radio. The Lovin' Spoonful singing about a beautiful morning had Kate joining in. Her hands were covered in flour as she stretched the pizza dough across the pan. Hamburger and mushroom—her father's favorite. It was a Friday night, and Kate had planned to surprise him and have dinner ready when he returned from the university.

She recalled the incident as if it were yesterday.

Her dad walked in and set his stack of student papers on the dining room table. "Smells good."

"You're home early. I wanted to have the pizza

ready when you came in."

Ted Caraway gave his daughter a tight hug. "You're too good to me, you know."

"Maybe you should raise my allowance."

"I just might do that." He picked up a spoon and tasted the browned hamburger. "Hmmm, just the right amount of garlic. Do you have any extra mushrooms?"

"This is enough." Kate frowned. "It's the amount I always use."

"I have a favor to ask."

Kate looked at her father. He'd turned slightly pink. "What?"

Ted Caraway was never at a loss for words. "I've invited someone to dinner. She's a vegetarian. Maybe you could leave the meat off one half." Her father smiled.

"A woman? You invited a woman to dinner? Dad! Way to go!"

"Her name's Emily Ann. I think you'll like her."

That was an understatement. Kate and Emily Ann hit it off immediately.

As Kate replaced the letter, she noticed another written years earlier and dated April 7, 1981. An icy chill washed over her as if a poltergeist had blown into the room. Ted and Emily Ann had known each other almost two years before Kate's mother died. She picked up the letter and read it. Any hope Kate had about their early relationship being merely platonic was shattered. "Oh God," she whispered and closed her eyes to keep the tears from spilling.

"Stupid! Stupid! Stupid!" Kate pounded her forehead with the palm of her hand. She felt like an idiot. How could she have missed it? Her father and

Emily Ann had been having an affair while Kate's mother was still alive.

Kate went to the kitchen and poured herself a glass of wine. Jack and Fred were deep into another game of chess. She returned to the office. The alcohol began to soothe her nerves. What happened between her father and Emily Ann was none of her business, but the pain of their deception cut deep. Kate replaced the folder and was about to shut the drawer. Then she noticed a folder with Evan's name on it. This one contained fewer than half a dozen letters. Kate scanned the contents and found nothing of importance. A folder with Susan's name held several letters. Kate checked those as well. It was clear that Emily Ann had an easier time communicating with her daughter-in-law than her son. In Brian's folder were two letters—the first one written after Emily Ann had met her future son-in-law. She had written to tell him she'd enjoyed meeting him. The second one welcomed Brian into the family. Finally, Kate opened Laurie's folder. It was empty.

"Hey, I thought you were going upstairs to take a shower," Jack called from the doorway.

"I am." Kate closed the drawer and turned off the lamp. "Actually, a bath sounds better."

"I can help you with that paperwork in the morning if you want," Jack offered.

"Thanks. There's not much. We can have it done in no time."

Jack followed Kate upstairs. She went into the bathroom, filled the bathtub with hot water, and added bath foam. She left her clothes in a pile where they fell and slid in under the suds.

"Want some company?" Jack said. He held up the

263

bottle of wine.

"Sure. Think we can both fit in this tub?"

"It'd be a tight squeeze. Although, I don't mind giving it a try sometime. I thought I'd sit here on the floor, and we'd finish this bottle." Jack gathered up Kate's clothes and put them in the clothes basket.

"I'm ready to go home," Kate said.

"It wasn't exactly the two-week vacation we'd planned, was it?"

"No. It sure wasn't."

Jack sat down, and Kenya ambled in. She circled three times and lay in the doorway.

"We can go anytime you're ready. But I can't see you leaving Ray to his fate, not as long as you believe he's innocent."

Kate spread the soapsuds around on the surface of the water. All thoughts of Ray and his arrest were pushed to the back of her mind along with all the other unsettled issues that hounded her like a pack of lost dogs, yowling and whining to be tended to.

"What's on your mind?" He grabbed a washcloth from the towel rack and a bar of soap and picked up Kate's foot.

"Dad and Emily Ann knew each other even before Mom died."

"How did you find that out?"

"Emily Ann kept a copy of every letter she'd ever written. One written to Dad was dated 1981."

"You didn't read the letter, did you?"

"I read enough. Jack, they were having an affair while Mom was still alive. Why all these secrets? Why—"

"Kate, let go of this. Things happened between

them that you'll never understand, sweetheart. You're not meant to."

Kate tried to choke back the tears but couldn't. "I don't understand anything anymore. Emily Ann didn't just leave Dad—she left me, too. Why? I wanted them to stay together. I needed her. Then the next thing I hear, she's married and has a family."

"Kate—"

"And I…can't help thinking that one of them killed her. I'm so confused. I'm sure Evan suspected his mother had a relationship with Dad and blames his parents' divorce on him. And now he sees Fred as another interloper. There's so much bitterness in this family."

"Kate, that makes no sense. What happened between your dad and Emily Ann happened before Evan was born. You're not thinking straight. You've had a long day. We both have."

"A day that seems like a week."

"You'll feel better in the morning."

Kenya raised her head and barked. "See, even Kenya agrees. Now drink your wine, and give me your other foot."

Chapter Twenty-Two

The next morning Kate rose early. She needed work to keep her mind busy, or she risked falling victim to her emotions. She didn't wait for Paula to call and ask for a ride. At eight thirty she dialed the Steiner number. On the fourth ring, Lisa answered and sounded out of breath.

"Yo."

"This is Kate Caraway. I'm calling to see if Paula needs a ride to work."

"Work! You need to come get this crazy sister of mine before she works me to death." Before Kate could ask what Lisa meant, she hung up.

Kate had a few minutes before she had to leave, so she dialed Detective Kraus' number.

"Kraus here."

"Detective Kraus. This is Kate Caraway. I'm calling to find out if—"

"I can't talk about how we're proceeding on the investigation, Ms. Caraway."

"Yes, I know, but I hope you can at least tell me if Megan Rutherford's story is being taken seriously. I mean, Ray's family is just barely hanging on."

"We're taking everything seriously. I can't be at two places at once. I have only one other detective on the case, and we've done little else since Bower's murder."

"I understand, Detective Kraus. I'm going to see Paula Steiner in a few minutes, and I was hoping to give her some encouraging news."

"I'm not in the counseling business, Ms. Caraway. I'm trying to solve two murders and an attempt on your life. They're most likely tied together, but I haven't found that thread. Until I do, and until I can be sure Ray Steiner isn't woven into the tapestry, he stays put. Sorry."

About a quarter mile from the Steiner place, Kate came upon what looked like a row of giant pumpkins lined up along the road near the driveway. As Kate got closer, she realized that the pumpkins were Halloween trash bags filled to capacity. She pulled into the driveway, and if it weren't for the Toyota pickup and Lisa's Escort, Kate would have thought she'd driven to the wrong house. The yard was well on its way to becoming free of trash. Paula was out front filling another bag. She waved over her shoulder when she noticed Kate. Tommy was mowing the lawn. Kenny and Brittany were sorting through a pile of rubbish. On the rock-step, drinking a cup of coffee, sat a brooding Lisa.

"Glad you're here," Lisa called to Kate. "Now maybe I can stop working."

"No way, sister," Paula called. "While I'm at Eagle Crossing, you and the kids better finish up here. When I get back, I expect this yard to look decent." Then she walked over to Kate. "What do you think? The place is starting to look halfway normal."

"You must have started at the crack of dawn," Kate said, stepping out of the car.

"Started last night," Lisa said. "Paula threw so

much shit away, the trailer's almost empty."

"Give me time to clean up, and I'll be ready," Paula said as she went inside.

"What'd you do to my sister?" Lisa reached inside her shirt pocket and started to pull out a cigarette, then apparently thought better of it and put the pack away. "I had a couple of six-packs waiting for Paula when she got back from Bellingham, but she didn't want any. She said there'd be no more drinking or smoking in this house, and then she put me to work."

"Wow! I don't know what to say," Kate said. "This place looks incredible."

"I guess Paula feels she needs to get her shit together. Can't really blame her. The party can't last forever."

"You must be exhausted," Kate said to Paula when they climbed into the car.

"No. I actually feel pretty damn good. I got a burst of energy. I knew I wouldn't be able to sleep anyhow. But you don't look too good. What's going on?"

"I was hoping to have good news about Ray, but it seems that the investigation gets more complicated."

"I have hope," Paula said.

Kate looked at the woman sitting in the passenger seat and marveled at her. Her husband was in jail for murder, she lived in a trailer that looked as if it were about to blow apart with the next windstorm, and she now had to support three kids alone.

"It seems you do." Kate smiled.

"I ain't gotta choice. I made some decisions last night while I was cleaning up. Whether Ray gets out of jail or not, I have to turn things around, and, by God, I will. Now, what else is happening? You can't be this mopey about the Steiner family problems. Spit it out."

"You're pretty pushy this morning."

"Yeah, well, I'm on a roll."

"Where should I begin? Laurie Fuller disappeared yesterday morning, and no one's heard from her. Brian thinks that Detective Kraus suspects her of killing Bower."

"Laurie Fuller? Mrs. Thurston's daughter? But why?"

"I'm not privy to the investigation. But opportunity comes to mind. The gun used to kill Bower was stolen from a pawn shop in Everett near where Laurie had been admitted."

"Why would she kill Bower?"

"Not sure, unless Laurie believed that Bower had killed her mother."

"Believed? Maybe she knows something. Maybe that's why she's been a basket case ever since her mother was killed. Maybe she finally snapped and decided to take matters into her own hands."

"You know, Paula, if you don't make it in the wildlife rehab business, you could hang out a psychic shingle because I was thinking the same thing."

As soon as they arrived at Eagle Crossing, Paula hopped out of the Rover and started up the trail to the cages. "I'll be down later, and we'll talk some more."

"Sure," Kate said. "I'll join you after I get some paperwork done."

"Maybe you can think of a reason to get rid of the guys, too." Paula turned and smiled at Kate. "And then we can talk about what's really bugging you."

****

Kate walked into the house just as Jack was

coming downstairs. "Good. I was waiting for you to get back. Don't get comfortable. Fred gave us a task. Go put on your hiking boots. We have quite a hike ahead of us."

"What's up?"

"Something that should make you smile. Those two eagles are ready to spread their wings. And Fred wants them released at the top of Chadwick Hill."

"That does make me happy. But there's no way I'm climbing up that rockface, and neither are you. I kind of like you, and I want to keep you around a bit longer. It's too dangerous."

"Don't worry. We're going up the back way through the woods. Fred said it was about a forty-five-minute hike. He gave me the directions. Carrying two cages will take us twice that long. I've got a backpack with water, a couple of protein bars, and a thermos of coffee. If we leave now, we should be back in time for lunch."

Five minutes later, Kate and Jack placed the two cages in the back of their Land Rover.

"The entrance to the wooded trail up Chadwick Hill is half a mile down on Watmough Bay Road. There's a place to pull off. You'll see the trail to the right. I've hooded the birds, so they should be fairly docile on the way up," Fred said. "Once you get to the top, let them stay in the cages for a few minutes before you release them. Why am I telling you this? You know what to do."

****

The trail wound upward through the woods. It took them working in tandem to heave the cages up and over rocky slopes. This made for slow going, like playing leapfrog. At this rate, the trek would take much longer than predicted. Then the trail leveled out, and they were able to trek at a steady pace for a good twenty minutes until the trail turned steep again. An hour into the trek, Kate's shoulder and leg muscles started to protest. "That coffee's calling me," she said. "Let's take a break."

"Good idea."

They set the cages down and used a fallen tree for a bench. Jack poured each of them a cup of coffee. He handed Kate hers, smiling.

"What are you grinning at?"

"You. Your face is red, and there are pine needles in your hair. You're absolutely beautiful." He scooted closer and kissed her on the cheek. "We make a great pair, don't we?"

"We do. It's been a while since we've done something like this."

"Not the type of thing you can do in downtown Chicago. Have you given any more thought about Michael's phone call?"

"A lot. But if we go back…what about your job?"

"I don't have to report to spring training for a few months."

"There's Kenya."

"I know. There's a lot of time for planning. We don't have to work everything out right now."

"But there are just so many questions to answer. So many things are uncertain."

"There're no guarantees, Kate. But if Michael thinks it's safe for you to return, then maybe you should trust his judgment."

"Maybe. Let's get the birds released." Kate

finished her coffee, put the cup away, and picked up the cage.

She looked toward the trail. "That's some hill up ahead. We'd better get going."

By the time they reached the top of Chadwick Hill, every muscle in Kate's body burned.

"We're almost there," Jack said.

"Almost? We can't get much higher than this," Kate said.

Jack pulled a piece of paper from his pocket. "According to Fred's notes, there should be a rope swing up here somewhere. Take a break, and I'll see if I can find it."

"What's special about the rope swing?"

Jack looked at his notes again. "East of the swing about fifty yards, the woods thin out. There's a large denuded rock where the cliff drops off. The wind drifts are perfect for release."

"Oh, great. A steep cliff, just what I need."

Kate sat down on a boulder. She pulled out her water bottle and splashed water on her face, thankful for the cool breeze fluttering through the trees.

"Found it," Jack said. "Not too far from here is a safe place for you to stand while I release the eagles. I assume you want me to do the honors since standing on the edge of the earth is not your thing."

"Be my guest. You release. I'll prepare the birds."

Jack donned the thick leather glove and held the first eagle by its talons. The bird flapped its wings, and Jack slowly released his hold. Like a kite taken up by the wind, the eagle rose with ease and grace and seemed to hang for a moment and then slanted to the left and flew out over the water.

Every time Kate released an animal back into the wild, the moment caused her heart to swell and a lump to form in her throat.

"Beautiful," she said. "Absolutely beautiful."

A few minutes later, the other eagle joined the first, and both were now soaring over Watmough Bay. Jack looked down and started laughing.

"What?" Kate said.

"Come over here and take a look."

"Are you kidding? I'm not getting any closer to the edge."

"Come on. It's okay. I'll hold your hand."

"Although that sounds nice, it's not very comforting for an acrophobic." Kate edged her way over and stopped about ten feet from the edge. "I don't see anything."

"There's a group of kids on the beach. They must have watched as I released the eagles. They're clapping." Jack waved and gave them the okay sign. Just as he turned to leave, something else caught his attention, and he stopped.

"Let's go," Kate said. "It's almost noon, and I'm starving. I must have burned a thousand calories clambering up this hill." When Jack didn't follow, Kate turned around. "What is it?"

"I can see Emily Ann's house and the cages from here."

"Really?"

"Look." Jack pointed. "Can you see them from where you are—that red color in those trees."

Kate scanned the hillside. "Oh, yeah. I see it. It's Emily Ann's roof. And there's Bower's house. It looks like maybe Megan Rutherford is over there. I can see the smoke rising from the chimney."

"I don't see it," Jack said.

"Right over there." Kate pointed. "In that clump of trees."

Jack studied the area for a few seconds, then jerked the binoculars from the backpack. "Holy shit!" He grabbed Kate's hand and dragged her back toward the trail.

"Jack, what?"

"That smoke isn't coming from any chimney! The woods are burning!"

Kate and Jack scrambled down the trail. Ten minutes later, the wail of sirens rose from the road below. Bower's two acres melded into Emily Ann's property. If the wind blew in that direction, the fire would spread unbelievably fast, and the entire hillside could go up in a matter of minutes—the woods, the houses, Eagle Crossing, the animals. Kate prayed as she scampered down the trail after Jack, running as fast as possible. Kate lost her footing going down a steep incline, and, unable to right herself, she tumbled down the rest of the way. Jack was several yards ahead. With adrenaline shooting through her veins, Kate jumped up and didn't stop to check for damage. Not twisting an ankle was all that mattered and, assured that she was okay, she continued after Jack.

The sirens grew louder and seemed to scream with an urgency that became worse with every passing second. Kate willed the noise to stop. She willed the fire to go out, for everything to be under control as soon as she and Jack came down off Chadwick Hill. When they entered the clearing near the road, Kate knew her wishing and praying had been in vain. Emergency vehicles had blocked Watmough Bay Road. What had been a thin trail of gray smoke half an hour ago was now a tower of flames with smoke blackening the sky.

From where she was, she had no way of telling exactly how far the fire had spread. As the crow flies, they were less than half a mile from the house. All she could think of was getting to the cages. By the time she reached the Rover, Kate realized that might be impossible. Jack was standing by the car arguing with a deputy from the sheriff's department. Kate ran up to them.

"You can't drive that car up there, sir. It's too dangerous. We're evacuating everyone living on that hill."

"I understand," Jack said, trying to catch his breath. "We're staying at Eagle Crossing. We have several animals that have to be evacuated. We can't just stand here and watch."

"Stay here. I'll be right back." He rushed over to his patrol car and grabbed his walkie-talkie.

"Jack, what's going on? We've got to get up there! Kenya, Fred, the animals!"

He pulled Kate to him and held her. "I know."

While they waited for the deputy to return, Sheriff Montego's patrol car sped around Alec Bay Road and slid to a stop. "Get in!" he called to Kate and Jack. "Deputy Jaegar, drive the Rover and follow us." As soon as they slammed the doors, Sheriff Montego began weaving through the melee of vehicles. "We've got fire choppers coming from the mainland. Deputy Fitzroy just called down from Bower's place. It's gone! The fire department is cutting a fire line just beyond where the house was."

"What about the animals?" Kate cried.

"Don't know. We'll find out soon."

When they pulled into the driveway, they met Deputy Fitzroy leaving with what looked like a land version of Noah's ark. Kenya, Dotty, and Speckle were riding in the back seat behind the plate glass divider, looking like three canine criminals off to the slammer. Kate jumped out of the patrol car just as it was coming to a stop.

"I've got the dogs and one cat," Fitzroy said. "Fred said the other cat was still in the house. I'm taking them to Barberette's place down the road. I'll be back as fast as I can." Kate looked up as Fred came hobbling down the trail from the cages. "Thank God you're here. The firefighters are up there cutting a fire line. But we can't count on that working. We've got to get the animals out of here. The fire's about two hundred yards away, but if it jumps the line, it'll race across this hill in minutes."

"Where's Paula?" Kate yelled, running up the trail.

"She trying to get the birds into the transport cages. She's not having much luck. They've flown up into the tops of the enclosures. She needs help."

"I am on my way," Kate said.

"Jack, we need to tranquilize the cats. I'm going to use the pistol instead of the rifle. We've got to work fast. Once they're out, we'll use the tarps to carry them to whatever vehicles we can find. Your Land Rover, the Explorer, Paula's pickup, and whatever squad cars are available. Barberette has chicken coops he's no longer using. He said we can move the cats to his place. He's at the cages with Paula now."

On the way up the trail, Kate heard the thumping of the helicopters and prayed they'd be able to douse the fire. When she arrived at the cages, Kate found the osprey's cage wide open and Paula clambering up the rickety steps nailed to the side of a dead tree up to the rafters.

"I can't reach it," Paula yelled and slipped off a rung, catching her footing and tearing a hole in her jeans.

Knowing that the flimsy steps would not hold Paula's weight, Kate called for her to come down. "I'll do that. Get the two eagles in that first cage." Paula didn't hesitate. She climbed down and rushed out.

Kate had just placed the bird in a transport cage when an EMS crew clambered up the trail with a stretcher, followed by Sheriff Montego.

"What's happened?" Kate ran up to him.

"A woman's body."

"Dead?" Kate immediately thought of Megan Rutherford. "Who was it? Was she in Bower's house?"

"Don't know who yet. She wasn't in the house. One of the firefighters found her slumped in an SUV— a Grand Cherokee parked at the base of Bower's driveway," he called over his shoulder and ran up the trail.

Laurie Fuller. What the hell was Laurie Fuller doing at Bower's place? Kate wanted to follow the sheriff, but she needed to get the rest of the birds.

"I've got all the eagles." Paula ran over. "How many birds are left?"

"Just the falcon. See if you can get one of the deputies to help you carry these cages down the hill."

Suddenly the wind shifted, and the air filled with smoke. The falcon had managed to climb up to the very top of its cage and tuck itself inside its nest box. If Kate hadn't known the bird was there, she would never have seen it. The trees inside this cage didn't have steps nailed to them. Kate needed the ladder. She ran back to the shed just as Jack and Fred were carrying a sedated mountain lion down the trail.

"We've got three more to go," Jack said. "How are you doing?"

Kate couldn't stop now to tell them about Laurie Fuller. "I need the ladder to get the falcon. Then we're finished with the birds."

Kate had trouble wedging the ladder close enough to the box. Several branches had been crisscrossed around it to provide a woody habitat for the bird. After several tries, Kate secured the ladder and starting climbing. When she reached the top, she needed a moment to allow her eyes to adjust. The inside of the box looked like a black hole. The falcon nervously scratched from one side of the enclosure to the other. Kate slipped on the leather glove and slowly felt around inside. The enclosure stretched to five feet across and eighteen inches high, giving the falcon enough room to dodge Kate's attempt at grabbing it. Frightening it any more would cause it to flail around and possibly injure itself. Using her gloved hand to feel her way across the floor of the box, she hoped to grab hold of the bird's talons with one hand and then slip the hood over its head with the other. In order to do that, she'd need to crawl part way inside. Although the glove would protect her hand and arm, what she also needed was a helmet in case the bird went into attack mode. No time to search for any more protective gear now. She continued to feel her way inside.

The falcon crouched in the far corner. "It's okay,"

she whispered. Kate grabbed a long narrow pole lying across the floor to move it out of the way. She slowly pulled it toward the light. Despite the hot smoke filling her lungs, a cold chill shot up her spine.

Chapter Twenty-Three

Paula rushed up to meet Kate and took the falcon's transport cage. "That's it," Kate said.

"They just brought that woman down from the Bower place." Paula wiped the sweat from her forehead with her sleeve. "They're loading her in the van right now."

Kate ran down the trail. She reached the EMS van just as they slid the stretcher inside. Detective Kraus stood at the rear of the van. Before Kate got any closer, she saw that it was indeed Laurie Fuller.

"What happened to her?" Kate asked Kraus. "Why was she up there?"

"Not sure, but she seems heavily drugged. Unfortunately, with the fire, we haven't been able to search the area. Too risky."

Kate brushed her hair from her face. "I'm glad you're here. I found something you need to see."

He turned and looked at Kate. "What?"

"A shovel."

"A shovel?"

"Right. One with a broken blade. It was wedged up inside one of the bird boxes. I left it there."

"Show me."

Kate's eyes were beginning to burn, and her throat felt scraped raw. She looked at her watch and was surprised to see that only an hour had passed since she and Jack had arrived with the deputy.

"Any word on the fire?" she asked Kraus on the way to the cages.

"Seems the fire line is working. But it's still too early to tell. It depends on the wind, which has already shifted directions several times in the last half hour. The choppers managed to douse the worst of the flames, but there were small pockets still burning. Laurie Fuller was lucky. If one of the firefighters hadn't found her when he did, she'd be gone. The Cherokee was at the base of Bower's driveway."

"I can't imagine what Laurie was doing here."

"We'll find out. If she pulls through, that is."

They made their way up to the falcon cage. Kate pushed the door back for Kraus to enter. He pulled a latex glove from his pocket, stood for a moment, and looked up toward the box.

"Another ruined pair of trousers," he said and started climbing the ladder. Once at the top, he pulled out a penlight and examined the shovel handle and blade. He pulled his radio from his pocket and called Sheriff Montego. "I need some help up here at the bird cages. We have the shovel." He snapped off the radio and turned to Kate. "I'll take it from here. You'd better go back down. It's still too dangerous to be up here."

Kate left the detective and went in search of Jack. She found him just as he was about to drive off in the Land Rover with a sedated lion in the back.

He called out the window. "Be back in a moment. Got to move fast before this cat wakes up."

Kate saw Fred sitting on the porch steps. She walked over and joined him. "That's the last one." He nodded in Jack's direction. "They're all at Jed

Barberette's barn down the road." He reached down and started to rub his legs. "I think I overdid it."

"You probably need to have that leg looked at."

"I'll be fine. I'm going to Barberette's to make sure the animals are okay. We were lucky. We could have lost the entire lot."

Fred struggled off the porch. "You shouldn't stay here."

"I'll wait for Paula, then we'll leave here, and I'll go to the medical center to check on Laurie."

Fred nodded, hobbled to his SUV, and turned around as he climbed in. "The other cat, Tortuga, is still in the house. At least I think she is. If you see her wandering around outside, let that crazy cat in. You won't be able to catch her."

"Will do," Kate said.

Paula came limping down the trail, face red and breathing hard. "Out of shape. That's another thing I'm going to change."

****

Kate and Paula drove to the medical center in Paula's pickup. When they arrived, they learned that Laurie had been airlifted to the hospital in Bellingham. She had not regained consciousness.

"What was that woman doing up at Bower's place?" Paula asked. "Some of those firefighters were talking about the fire being arson. Do you think she started it?"

"I don't know, Paula." Kate couldn't bear that thought. "We've still got a lot of work getting the animals situated at Barberette's farm. You've already put in a lot of time today. Why don't you drop me off and go home?"

"Lisa's there. I called her and told her to watch after the kids. Let's get busy."

For the next four hours, they got the animals settled in. One lion almost didn't regain consciousness, and for a few tentative minutes, it looked as if they were going to lose her. Fred gave her an injection of adrenaline while Paula monitored the cat's vital signs. She worked as if she'd been doing this for years. Kate was amazed at Paula's ability to pick things up so quickly.

Debbie Barberette came out to the barn around seven thirty that evening and insisted the group come to the house for a break. She'd made sandwiches and coffee. Jack was still securing a cage and announced he'd be in shortly. Everyone else went inside for the much-needed rest. When Kate sat down at the kitchen table, what little energy she had left seemed to drain out through her feet.

"Hopefully, we'll be able to move the animals back to Eagle Crossing in the morning," Fred said. "I'll have Jack check the cages one more time tonight, and Paula can check on that sleepy lion. But we'll need feed for tonight and a few other things."

"Make a list," Kate said. "I'll go get whatever we need."

"Sounds good." Fred wolfed down one sandwich and reached for another. "I'd go with you, but—"

"You need to rest that leg," Kate said. "I'll be back shortly."

****

Kate pulled up to a dark, quiet house. The sky had turned the bluish-gray that lingers long after sunset. She looked up toward the cages where the evergreens cast deep shadows, making it difficult to see. She switched on the outside lights, but the electricity was out. Using a flashlight, she gathered the supplies then went inside the house to look for Tortuga. Without dogs, cats, and people, the house had an eerie feel, almost as if it had been abandoned long ago rather than just a few hours. Kate's cell phone rang, breaking the silence.

"Kate. It's Susan. I have some news about Laurie."

Laurie, my God, Kate thought. With everything that had happened, she'd forgotten to call Susan.

"Laurie had been staying at a motel. She showed up at Evan's this morning distraught and on the verge of a breakdown. Evan took her upstairs to his guest room and went down to call her doctor. He wasn't gone for more than ten minutes. He went back upstairs, and she was gone."

"How did you find out?"

"Evan's here. Maybe you should talk to him."

Before Kate could respond, Evan was on the phone. "Kate. I'm afraid my sister may be in trouble. I think she's on her way to Lopez. In fact, she should be there by now."

"Evan. Laurie was here. But I have some bad news."

"My God! Tell me she's okay."

"She's just been taken to the hospital in Bellingham. She was found unconscious in her car."

"Goddamn-son-of-a-bitch! I'll kill the motherfucker!"

Before Kate could learn more, Evan hung up.

Kate redialed Susan's number. The phone was busy. She waited a few minutes and tried again. She opened the refrigerator and pulled out a bottle of water. Her throat felt as if she'd swallowed hot sand. After a long-needed drink, Kate dialed again—busy. *Damn. Who could he be talking to?*

Closed up, the house felt warm. Kate walked into the den to open the patio door when she heard the deck creak. Then she saw him and quickly snapped off the flashlight. He stood just outside the window, not ten feet away. He looked around as if to make sure he was alone. He turned and stared directly at Kate. She froze. Then she realized that he couldn't see her in the darkness. She looked down and saw that the door was unlocked.

If she tried to step away, the slightest movement would catch his eye. Before Kate had time to act, he walked over and reached down to open the door. That's when she saw the butt of the pistol sticking out of his waistband.

Kate's pulse beat so loudly she was sure he'd hear. If he opened the door and found her standing in the empty dark house, he'd know, and she couldn't let that happen. She grabbed the doorknob first and pulled the door open.

"Brian! You scared me. When did you arrive?"

Even in the darkness, Kate noticed the moisture on his upper lip shone. He hesitated, and instantly his facial expression changed from desperate to amiable. Her bluff caught him off guard, buying her some time if only a few seconds.

"I didn't know anyone was here. I had a late appointment in Anacortes when I heard about the fire. Luckily, a ferry was leaving, and I was able to get on. I wanted to make sure everybody was okay. I forgot my key and hoped the patio door was open." He pulled his jacket over the gun and reached for the light switch.

His lie was weak. He would have seen Kate's Land Rover parked out front. She saw in his face that he knew he'd screwed up, but she ignored his blunder.

"Electricity is out. It was a close call. This entire place could have gone up in flames." Her voice was too shaky this time to tell another convincing lie.

He walked in and closed the door behind him.

Kate heard the lock click.

"We just came in to check on the house and get some supplies. Jack and Fred went up to check out the cages. They should be back any minute now."

"Jack and Fred are up at the cages now? In the dark?"

Kate detected a slight smirk on his face. Careful not to look him in the eye, she turned her back and walked into the kitchen.

"They have flashlights. Thanks for your concern, Brian. You know you and Laurie are welcome here anytime. Fred wants Emily Ann's family to feel that this is still home." What a stupid thing to say, she chided herself. Her voice sounded hollow as it resonated in her head, but she needed to keep talking. She chanced a looked over her shoulder.

Brian glanced out the kitchen window, looking for what Kate suspected were the beams of the flashlights bobbing through the bushes. He sat at the kitchen table. Kate could see his confidence return. Her bullshit story hadn't worked. "Oh, I don't think so, Kate. Laurie could never come back here and feel at home. It's just as well that Fred has ownership now. Emily Ann wanted it that way, right?"

"But not if it meant excluding her family."

Brian laughed. "Do you really believe that? My

mother-in-law went to great lengths to exclude her family, as you call us." He slammed his fist down on the kitchen table. The saltshaker tumbled over. "Did you know I asked my mother-in-law for help? A little loan to take the edge off. My business is in a slump. Nothing bad. It happens. Just a slow period. Laurie doesn't know this, but Emily Ann turned me down. She said she was stretched too thin. Laurie insisted we ask for help that weekend we came to visit. We argued over it. She was sure her mother would help. What a joke. But that's not what's important here. I don't care about the money, not like that money-grubbing prick, Evan. What I care about is far more important."

Kate backed away a few steps. If she tried to run for the back door, she feared he'd shoot her in the back. She glanced around the kitchen for something she could use. Everything was neatly put away. Knives in drawers, skillets hanging over the island, nothing within reach.

"Where's your husband and my almost-father-in-law, Kate? You said they were on their way down? You didn't lie to me, did you?"

"Listen, Brian—"

"No! You listen!" He stood up, shoving the chair aside. "You think your dear friend Emily Ann Thurston was such a caring, selfless person, dedicating her life to these fucking miserable animals as if they were all that counted. I wasn't quite the husband she wanted for her precious daughter. I was too right-winged, too conservative, too—"

"Brian, Emily Ann didn't feel that way. She—"

"How do you know how she felt? You show up after several years and think you have everything and everybody figured out. Did you know my dear sweet mother-in-law committed murder? She killed my child! My very own child!"

Sweat ran down Brian's face. His shirt was damp. "I almost had Laurie convinced of what kind of person her mother really was." Brian slipped the gun from his waistband. "But I know now that she's just like her mother."

"The letters—Emily Ann's letters to Laurie," Kate said.

"Right, the letters."

"When did you find them?"

"That first night we arrived. The night Emily Ann made her joyous fucking announcement. Ben pointed me in the right direction. He'd wandered off, and I found him in Emily Ann's office. He'd pulled open the drawer of her desk. I picked him up, and as I was closing the drawer, I noticed the file folders labeled with everyone's names. I was surprised to see so many letters to Laurie. She'd told me that she and her mother hardly ever communicated anymore. She lied to me." He brushed the sweat from his forehead. "I took them with me to read later. After we'd checked into the inn, I went out to the patio and started reading. Let's see. How did my mother-in-law put it? Something like, 'You've only been married a short time, honey. You've plenty of time to start a family. You're young, and I want you to be sure about everything. About Brian and your marriage.' I was furious but proud of Laurie for not listening to Emily Ann. My wife knew how I felt about abortion. Then I saw the date on the letter, one month after we'd married. Laurie was pregnant. I didn't even know. She'd told her mother, not me. Emily Ann took Laurie to a clinic, and well, you see, they killed my first child—my wife and her mother." He set the gun on the table in front of him and rested his hand on the chamber. "What kind of family is this?"

Kate stood still, barely daring to breathe. Brian was no longer talking to her. Saying anything would only draw attention to herself. And what could she say that wouldn't make the situation worse?

"I couldn't believe what I'd read. Then I remembered that Laurie came to stay with her mother a few weeks after the wedding. She told me that Emily Ann was ill. That must have been when she went for the abortion. I lay awake the entire night at the inn, planning what I would do." He turned the gun around in circles. "Laurie was passed out on tranquilizers. I drove up here early that morning. When I saw that sot, Ray, sleeping it off in his car, I laughed—what luck. I took his jacket, walked through the woods to the cages and down the trail to the house. No one was up, so I waltzed into the kitchen and grabbed the cage keys, then went back to the cages and waited." Brian glanced out the window again, looking into the past. His face turned grim. "Shoving Emily Ann off the cliff was so easy. Just as I had finished cleaving the rock away with the shovel, you walked up. I was sure you saw me, you and that Bower guy. You both came traipsing by, so I hid. When you went to call the sheriff, I unlocked the lion's cage and left. Then you started snooping around. I tried to steer you in another direction—Bower's direction—with the letters about moving the lions here. But when that didn't work, I couldn't chance it. I realized I had to get rid of you…both you and Bower."

"And the suicide note."

"Right. Like I said, I had it all planned out until you fucking screwed it up. Let's go." He picked up the gun and pointed it at her. "Through the den, to the deck. Move."

"Brian, the police know you're here. They've found Laurie and have taken her to the hospital. She'll tell them everything."

For a moment, he seemed to take heed of what Kate was telling him. "Oh, no, she won't. Laurie won't be able to tell anyone anything. You're the only one who knows I'm here. Laurie drove the Cherokee up here, see. Laurie blamed Bower for murdering her mother, so she killed him and started the fire."

"No one will believe that, Brian. I'm telling you Laurie didn't die in that fire."

He laughed. "Once I get rid of you, I'll be in the clear."

"Evan knows what you did. Laurie told him of her suspicions."

"It's Evan's word against mine. There's no evidence to connect me to anything. There's no reason for me to have killed my mother-in-law. I've destroyed Emily Ann's letters to Laurie, eliminated those who knew. If anyone had a reason to kill Emily Ann, it was Evan. He's the one who's in desperate need of money. Let him accuse me. Sure, we all have motives. Me, Laurie, and Evan. Their motives are stronger than mine. You see, Kate, I've planned it from every angle. Naturally, I'll be a suspect. After all, I'm part of the *family*. The police know that Laurie and Evan had been harping on their mother to sell the land. The police know that Evan's gotten himself in a financial bind. The police know that Laurie's unstable. My only motive is that I'd asked Emily Ann for money. But you're the only one who knows that—you and Emily Ann, and she's dead. And you won't be around to repeat it, either."

"When Laurie comes to—"

"She's dead!"

"She was still alive, Brian, when they carried her down."

"You're lying."

"They've also found the shovel you used to chip that rock. You hid it in the falcon's cage."

"It doesn't matter. The only one who can connect me to that is you."

"I'm not the only one who can connect you to the remote-control plane."

"That plane is long gone. Besides, people often fly those planes at Iceberg Point. So, I used to have one. I don't know. Big deal."

"They'll figure it out."

"The police will have their suspicions, but in the end, it's Laurie they'll blame."

"And what will happen to Ben?"

"My son will be better off with just me. But that's none of your concern. You won't be around to worry about it, will you?"

"This isn't going to work."

"Move!" He grabbed Kate by her arm and twisted it behind her back, shoving her into the den. "Open the door and get outside." He shoved her again.

Out of the corner of her eye, Kate saw the hump of a shadow on the table in the moonlight. It moved slightly and then stopped and arched its back. Kate faked a stumble toward the table. As if on cue, Tortuga, claws extended, jumped from her perch right onto Brian's arm.

Kate grabbed a chair and shoved it into Brian's face. He fell against the table. The gun hit the floor and discharged. Kate dove for the gun, but Brian was quick. He grabbed her leg, and she fell. Kicking as hard as she could, Kate managed to land a hard shot at Brian's face. She heard the crack of cartilage and knew she'd broken his nose. Brian held tight. Kate scrabbled for the gun, but Brian grabbed her other leg and pulled her back, then threw an arm around her throat. Kate reached behind her and seized a handful of hair, pulling as hard as she could. Brian shoved his other arm at the back of her head and Kate feared he'd snap her neck. She let go. He flung her to the side and went for the gun.

Kate grabbed the closest thing to her—the floor lamp. She swung, jerking the plug from the wall, and hit Brian square in the middle of his shoulders just as his hand wrapped around the gun. Kate swung again and caught him on the side of the face. The metal base of the lamp slashed a gash into his cheek. She swung a third time just as Brian aimed the gun at her. Before he could squeeze the trigger, she knocked the gun away, threw the lamp at him, and ran to the kitchen and out the door.

She scrambled into the Rover, but the keys were not in the ignition where she left them. She took off up the trail. If she could get far enough ahead, she hoped to lose him in the woods.

"Kate! Stop! Come back. We can work this out."

She darted off the trail and headed through the trees for the road. Brian Fuller shouted, pleading for her to listen to what he had to say as he scrambled after her.

"Please. I mean it. I wouldn't hurt you."

Who is this guy kidding? Kate thought as she knocked the brush out of the way to run deeper into the woods. The acrid smell of charred forest was thick in the air, burning her throat and lungs with each breath. As she reached the top of the rise, she saw the damage done by the fire. The few trees left standing smoldered in the darkness. The top of the hill looked as if it had been bulldozed. What was left of Bower's house, the chimney and the stone walkway leading to the bare remains of the front door, were barely visible in the darkness.

"Kate! I've come to my senses. Please. You were right. I need to think about Ben."

He moved closer, nearing the top of the hill. Kate ran across the denuded area, heading for a section of brush spared by the blaze. As she jumped over a fallen tree, her foot caught. She stumbled and fell. Brian crashed through the brush a few feet away. If she didn't find shelter, he'd be on her in a flash. Kate clambered on all fours and took cover behind a boulder just as a shot rang out, exploding off the rock not a yard from her head.

Although the bullet came close, Kate doubted he'd seen her. But she couldn't chance staying put. He'd be across the burned area in just a few seconds. Kate hunkered down and ran toward a denser patch of growth. Entangling herself in creepers, she pushed her way through. Then not a few yards to her left, the beam from his flashlight shone toward her.

Kate dove to the ground just as the light swung in her direction. She lay still and hoped the brush cover was enough to hide her. He'd be upon her any second.

She felt around on the ground for something to use and wrapped her hand around a tree limb as another beam of light waved over the brush in front of her. Brian stepped lightly and paused, gasping for breath.

"Listen. I don't want to kill you."

Kate jerked.

"The gun went off by accident." He walked closer. "I know you can hear me. Listen. I'll throw down the gun."

Kate heard a thud.

The beam of the flashlight inched its way in her direction.

"Are you okay? Please say something."

Kate's heart thumped louder with each approaching step. She saw him clearly now. He stood less than six feet from her. The gun was still in his hand. Suddenly, he jerked to the right and froze. He snapped off the flashlight and stepped back.

Kate listened for whatever spooked him. After a few seconds, she heard it—voices coming from the Bower property. Brian bolted toward her. She jumped up and struck him across the shin with the branch. He went down but kept hold of the gun.

"Over here!" Kate called to the three firefighters coming over the hill. "Hurry!" she yelled again and ran toward them. Just as she reached them, another shot rang out, slitting the bark of a tree not two feet away.

They all dropped to the ground.

"What the hell's going on?" A man dressed in Nomex shined a flashlight at her.

"Turn those flashlights off," Kate cried.

Half an hour later, Sheriff Montego found Brian Fuller right where Kate had last seen him. Blood seeped from the gunshot wound to his right temple.

Chapter Twenty-Four

The room smelled of antiseptic and apprehension. Whoever decorated it must have been careful not to select a style and hues that inspired too much hope. The boxy, mid-century pumpkin-and-moss-green tweed sofas were worn to a shine. Prints from Bellingham's early 20th century hung on the almond-colored walls. The room was too stark and bright to be anything but what it was—a hospital waiting room, a place where people waited for news that could change their lives. Dawn spilled from the only window through the cracks in the blinds. Kate had been sitting with Susan at Bellingham General Hospital since they'd arrived two hours ago.

The door finally opened, and a woman walked in. "Mrs. Thurston?" she said, looking from Kate to Susan.

"Yes," Susan said, jumping to her feet. "That's me."

"I'm Doctor Newly. Mrs. Fuller just came out of her coma a few minutes ago. Things are looking pretty good." She smiled.

"Can I see her?" Susan asked.

"No more than five minutes. Your husband's still with her. Tell him to go home and get some rest. He sat up with her all night."

"I will," Susan said and left with Dr. Newly.

Kate went in search of her first cup of coffee when

she met Evan coming down the hall. He looked ready to keel over.

"Come with me," Kate said. "The cafeteria couldn't be any less comfortable. I hear they brew some jolting coffee. You look like you could use some."

On the way to the cafeteria, they ran into Sheriff Montego and Detective Kraus.

"How's your sister?" Sheriff Montego asked.

"She just came to," Evan said. "But she's not up for questioning. Can't you wait?"

"Afraid not, Mr. Thurston," Kraus said. "We need to get her statement as soon as possible."

Evan huffed and stormed down the hall. Kate followed and found him into the cafeteria standing near the window, staring out on the rainy day.

"Cream or sugar?" Kate asked.

"Black."

A moment later, Kate handed Evan his coffee. "Your sister's a brave woman, Evan. It might take a while, but she'll be fine." Kate wasn't sure if she believed her own words, but she felt better saying them. And, so it seemed, did Evan.

He sipped his coffee. "You really think Laurie will be okay? Her own husband tried to kill her. He killed our mother and Bower, and he almost killed you. I…I should have seen it coming."

"That would've been impossible, Evan. Don't blame yourself."

"Who else can I blame? She's my little sister. I've done nothing for the last few years but look out for my own interests."

"Blame only makes things worse. Laurie has you…you and Susan."

Evan stiffened and shot Kate a sideways glance. "I've really screwed up there too. I've lost my family and my job. I have a lot of making up to do."

"You might not want to hear this, but I'm sure Fred will help any way he can."

"No. That's not an option. I'm still suing." Evan set his coffee down and paced. "My lawyer seems to think I don't have much of a case, but I'm going ahead anyway."

"Maybe you don't have to."

"What do you mean?"

"Rather than dragging this thing to court and spending a lot of time and money, maybe you and Fred could settle."

"Settle?"

"Fred may be willing to offer a monetary settlement."

Evan folded his arms across his chest. "I'm not interested in negotiating with Fred Marlow."

"Listen. Your mother poured her heart into her work. She loved Fred, and she was happy with him. He's carrying on with her dreams. If your lawyer doesn't think you have a case, then try and approach it differently. Just think about it, Evan. Settling could solve some of your immediate problems and allow you to go on with your life. Laurie and Ben will need your help. Putting the past behind will make things easier."

He took a deep breath and let it out slowly. "Are you always this logical?"

Kate laughed. "I wish. I should listen to my own advice."

Susan walked over. "Coffee any good?"

"Strong—its pH is off the scale," Evan said.

"How's she feeling?" Kate asked.

"She seems somewhat relieved that it's all over," Susan said. "Detective Kraus and Sheriff Montego walked in as I was leaving."

"I'm going back to her room. I want to be there when they question her." Evan picked up his coffee and left.

"I think she suspected Brian all along," Susan said. "That was probably why she continued taking the tranquilizers. Too bad she had to carry that secret by herself. It must have been torturous."

"Now that it's over, it's easy to look back and see things more clearly," Kate said.

"What do you mean?"

"Little things," Kate said. "Things that are easily pushed aside. Ned Hornsby said something at Windsong Inn the day Jack and I took Megan Rutherford there. He said Ben was crying early that morning. He thought the boy was sick. Brian couldn't handle it when Ben cried."

"You noticed that too. Do you think Ben was sick?"

"No, I think Ben was unattended. Laurie was sedated, and Brian wasn't there. He'd driven to Eagle Crossing."

"And Laurie could have awakened and realized he was gone."

"I suspect so. That's why Laurie went home and pulled the wallpaper off the wall in Ben's bedroom. At first, I thought they were cartoon-style drawings of birds on the wallpaper."

"They were animated pictures of planes." Susan shook her head. "I remember Brian saying he tinkered with remote-control planes in college. You're right. Laurie knew." Susan pushed her hair away from her face. "She's going to have a rough time of it. I'll help any way I can."

"I know you will. Now that it looks like Laurie will be okay, I'm going back to Lopez."

"Thanks for everything, Kate."

"Stay in touch."

****

Two days after Brian Fuller killed himself and attempted to kill his wife, Eagle Crossing was up and running again. The animals, on edge after the evacuation were comforted by the normal feeding routine and began to settle down. Speckle and Dottie experienced a delayed reaction to all that had happened since the morning Kate discovered Emily Ann's body at the bottom of the cliff. Dottie was too skittish to leave the house and had to be coaxed. Speckle reacted to her sister's mood by keeping her tail tucked. Even Kenya took to moping around the house.

Kate had just hung up from talking to Michael in Nairobi when Paula walked in. She pulled a bag of coffee beans from the freezer as comfortably as if she'd lived there for years. "You look like you just lost your best friend."

"Maybe more than just a friend."

Paula dumped the beans in the grinder. "I'm gonna have to get me one of these." After the beans were done, she said, "I'm listening; what's the problem?"

"That was a colleague from my research camp in Kenya. He was pushing me to come back as soon as possible."

"Why in the hell did you leave in the first place?"

"I almost killed a man."

Paula's howl shook the windows. "You! You almost killed a man? An accident, right?"

"No. On purpose. I aimed the rifle. I pulled the trigger. I wanted him dead."

"No shit! I gotta hear this."

"He was a poacher. I'd just driven up on an elephant slaughter. The cow was already dead. She left a pair of twins, four months old. One had gotten shot in the crossfire. It was bleeding from its flank but still running around its mother's body, wailing. The elephants were part of my research group. I lost it. Something snapped, and I opened fire."

"Damn! Did you hit him?"

"In the leg. The guy survived, I was told."

"You need to work on your aim. I would of kept firing until the asshole was good and dead, then for good measure, I would of kicked him in the nuts."

"I'll remember that, Paula." Kate laughed. "But Jack and I had to leave camp in the middle of the night. We flew back to the States the next morning."

"Would you have been arrested?"

"Actually, that was uncertain. I had a license to protect the elephants at all costs, including shooting at poachers. But we'd recently found out that guards working for the park service—men hired to watch for poachers—had been poaching themselves. We filed a complaint, and many of them were arrested, including the park service chief. The man I shot was his brother."

"You're shittin' me?"

"Things had been coming to a head for a while. So rather than risk getting the entire research project canceled, Jack, my staff, and I decided it would be better if we left until things cooled down. I just didn't realize I'd be gone for over a year."

"Then things must have cooled down."

"Somewhat. But the situation there is always volatile."

Paula poured two cups of coffee. "You surprise me. I don't think of you as being so damn wishy-washy."

"Wishy-washy?" Kate's head jerked up. "I'm wishy-washy?"

"You don't strike me as the type who doubts herself. I see you as someone who calls the shots. Sorry, wrong choice of words. Someone who kicks butt and asks questions later."

"Really?" Kate smiled. "Sometimes I think of myself as a twit."

"I knew a twit once."

"What happened to her?"

"Him. I married him." Paula topped off Kate's cup. "I can go to Africa and kick butt for you."

"I don't doubt that."

"So, you want to go back?"

"In a New York minute."

"Jesus. Quit sitting around here and go already."

"It's not that easy."

"Why?"

Kate didn't feel like explaining the details to Paula, but the woman gave Kate a look that said she wasn't leaving until she got the whole story.

"You got the money to go?" Paula said.

"Well, yeah."

"Jack doesn't want you to go?"

"It's not that either!" Kate stood, walked to the

sink, and dumped out her coffee.

"Well, damn, Kate." Paula rolled her eyes. "It doesn't seem like you have a problem, now, do you?"

"How am I supposed to make a major decision about my life with everything that's gone on here?"

"Oh, don't be a FTNR." She walked toward the door to leave.

"FTNR?"

"Female, twit, non-releasable."

Chapter Twenty-Five

Kate spent the morning doing laundry before packing their suitcases for their trip back to Chicago. A phone call came in asking if Eagle Crossing took opossums. Kate referred them to the Parks and Wildlife Department. Another called about an addled raccoon found in a neighbor's storage shed. Seems the animals residing at Eagle Crossing weren't the only wildlife displaced by the fire.

Kate and Jack spent the afternoon helping Fred put the final touches on two more new cages. The conversation centered around Fred's plans for expanding the facility, which included a stone wall running the length of the cliff and another one surrounding the area where the cats were located. Additional security lights, not just at the facility but around the house itself, were installed. Fred wanted to make sure that when Laurie visited, she wouldn't have to worry about Ben's safety. Kate felt certain that family visits were a long time down the road, but she kept her feelings to herself.

They'd finished up a couple of hours earlier and went to the house to clean up before the guests arrived. Kate turned the oven down to keep the roasted chicken from getting too dry. Fred brought in the burgers he'd cooked on the outside grill. "Your black bean burger is on the left," he said.

Jack came in and pulled a beer from the refrigerator. "I thought you were drinking wine," Kate said.

"I am. This is for Fred." He looked over at Fred. "Quick, before the others arrive." Leave it to Jack to call attention to the issue they had skirted for too long.

Tortuga sauntered in and gave Fred a dirty look. "Okay, I get the message," Fred said. "What really burns me is why Laurie, knowing that Brian killed Emily Ann, would defend him."

"If you understood how much Ben having a devoted father meant to her, and the fact that Laurie had been on tranquilizers since Emily Ann's death, it might make sense," Kate ventured. "That first night when Jack and I arrived, Laurie was talking to me about Brian's large family and how close they were. She was bitter about her father abandoning her and Evan, remarrying, and starting a new family. She didn't want the same thing to happen to Ben."

Jack refilled her wineglass. Kate savored a sip and continued. "Besides, at first she wasn't sure it was Brian. But after that day I visited her in Seattle and told her about my accident with the remote-control plane, she couldn't ignore her suspicions any longer."

"And she still kept quiet," Fred said.

"It wasn't until Susan called her about Jacob Bower's death that Laurie knew Brian had to be stopped. That's when she called Evan and told him to come get her. She'd been staying at his apartment, struggling about what to do. She finally decided to come to Lopez and tell the sheriff. But before she could do that, she ran into Brian, and it almost cost her life. Somehow he managed to drug her and drive the

305

Cherokee up to Bower's place, then started the fire. She would have died in the fire if the firefighters hadn't found her."

"God. What would have happened to Ben, growing up with a father like Brian Fuller?" Fred asked.

The doorbell rang. "Enough on that subject," Jack said. "The party's here."

Kate went to open the front door and hesitated. The ruckus outside sounded as if a riot was taking place.

"Tuck in that shirttail, Ray," Paula shouted.

"I hate this shirt," he whined.

Kate opened the door, and a whirlwind of people rushed in, including, to Kate's surprise, Louie Fister.

Paula sidled up to Kate and whispered, as only Paula Steiner could, "We had to bring the slimeball, or Ray wasn't coming."

"No problem, Paula. This is Ray's party."

Ray walked in, looking like he'd just been scrubbed and shined. His hair was still damp and plastered down. He wore a fresh pair of jeans and a new white T-shirt, and his boots, though scuffed, were free of dirt. The kids followed their father inside. Kenny and Tommy, freshly scrubbed as well, ran immediately outside onto the deck where the dogs were. Brittany found Valentine curled up on the windowsill and knelt to pet the cat. Lisa paused on the back porch and put out her cigarette. Her low-riding jeans met just above the waistband with a faded Eminem T-shirt. The T-shirt covered most of her midsection but still left enough exposed skin showing that Lisa had chosen not to wear her belly-button-to-nipple chain.

Paula set a cake box on the kitchen counter. "It's Ray's favorite, German chocolate. I also brought some vanilla ice cream." She opened the freezer. "Like my dress?"

Paula wore a light-blue-and-white cotton-print dress and flip-flops. Her hair was wrapped in a twist, with a few ringlets cascading down the side.

"You look nice," Kate said.

"I bought the dress yesterday. Thrift shop, five dollars."

"A great find."

"I ain't proud."

Kate didn't for one minute believe that Paula was.

"So, you're leaving the day after tomorrow?"

"On the afternoon ferry," Kate said.

"Will you come back for a visit someday?"

"I most certainly will, Paula. And thanks."

"For what?"

"For putting things in perspective for me."

"No problem. Hey, ever need advice, you know where to find me."

Kate laughed and hugged Paula.

Ray made the mistake of sitting in the middle of the sofa. Within seconds, Dotty jumped into his lap and Kenya crawled up alongside him. Neither was intimidated by Ray's frozen posture, or perhaps they didn't care. Dotty licked Ray on the chin.

"Your husband looks terrified. I'll shoo the dogs back outside," Kate said.

"Leave 'em," Paula said. "Shock therapy. Ray needs to get over his fear of dogs."

"Are you sure?"

"Absolutely. But I'll make it a bit easier on him." Paula grabbed a beer from the refrigerator, walked over, and handed it to Ray. "Here, big guy. Drink it slowly and enjoy it. It's the only one you get for the rest of the day."

The doorbell rang, and Kate went to answer. She opened the door to Jeannie Shuttleford and behind her an uninvited guest. Jeannie shrugged her shoulders.

Eleanor Grommer elbowed her way to the door. "I heard a party was going on here, and I'm crashing it. I hope you don't mind," she said to Kate. Before Kate could respond, Eleanor pulled something from her purse. "Here, give this to Fred What's-His-Name. It's a check. A donation to Eagle Crossing. Tell him to put better locks on those cat cages." Then she walked into the house, her clunky heels echoing down the hall.

"Sorry, Kate. She showed up as I was leaving the library and insisted on coming."

Kate stood on the deck watching the glimmer of sunlight reflecting on the water below. A westerly breeze swirled leaves across the deck. The pain of losing Emily Ann was lessening, but only a bit. At least Kate could leave here knowing the truth about what had happened. Sometimes knowing made things easier.

Fred walked up. "Want some company?"

"Sure. How are you doing?"

"Still miss her."

"You must've been reading my mind."

Fred shrugged. "This barbecue for Ray was a nice idea. You've had a lot of nice ideas. Like suggesting that I hire Paula. That's worked out well."

"She's really something. Pray she stays sober."

"She will." Fred picked out a pine needle that had fluttered into his beer glass. "I got a call from Evan's attorney today. Seems like we may be able to work out a deal. But I'm sure that's no surprise to you."

"I can't take much credit. I caught Evan at the right time and put a bug in his ear."

"Thanks anyway. Maybe one day Evan can accept me as part of the family."

Kate looked at Fred.

"Right." He laughed. "When hell freezes over. But I'm going to work on Laurie. I think with time I can get her to come around. Besides, she's going to need someone."

"Susan will be your best ally."

They stood silently for a few minutes. The crows complained from a Madrona tree nearby.

"Jack tells me you're planning to return to Kenya."

"It's temporary. I'm not sure how long I'll stay. I just want to check things out."

"You must be excited."

"Excited. Apprehensive. Terrified, actually."

"You'll be fine. If things don't work out, I can always use a good rehab person here."

Kate reached over and kissed him on the cheek.

Leaving Jeannie, Eleanor, and Paula in the kitchen to bicker about how to store the leftovers, Kate went into Emily Ann's office, turned on the computer, and started a search. Within five minutes, she had the information she needed.

"Want some company?" Jack stood in the doorway, holding a plate of German chocolate cake.

"Sure, but I can't eat another bite."

"The cake's for me. I don't know about you, but I'm ready to get back to Chicago. I need a place where I can relax."

"Chicago's hot, sticky, loud, and crowded this time of year."

He laughed. "Sounds good to me."

"There is one thing I want to do in the morning. I'll need the Land Rover."

"Sure. I have enough to do around here. Where are you going?"

"It's a surprise."

"That's scary."

"A nice surprise, I hope."

"I don't want to hear anymore."

****

Finding a parking place in downtown Bellingham was almost as bad as finding one in downtown Chicago. Today, just any parking place would not do. Kate cruised up Lottie Street and then over to Central. After her fourth pass in front of the coffee shop next to the courthouse, she began to get discouraged. Maybe she was too late. Maybe the man had moved on and was now wandering around in some other city. Maybe Seattle or even San Francisco.

A car was pulling out of a space on the corner of Lottie and Commercial. Since she hadn't yet located the guy, Kate decided to take advantage of the parking opportunity and continue her search on foot. The downtown area was not that large. She could walk down each of the main streets in about an hour, and if that's what it took, she'd do it. If she couldn't find him, then so be it. But she'd try. She started at the courthouse and walked to Prospect, where the street ended at a large fenced-off construction site on East Maple. Then she turned up Grand. The buildings prevented any breeze off the water, and with the temperatures reaching the upper eighties, Kate was beginning to wilt and considered giving up. She stepped into the 7-11 for a bottle of water, and there he was.

"Come on, buddy. I don't have all day." The clerk watched impatiently while the homeless man counted out his cache of small change for a pack of cigarettes and a cup of coffee.

"My money's good, you jerk."

While he was haggling with the store clerk, Kate darted outside. She walked up and down the street, looking for the dog. No luck. Maybe someone else had rescued the animal. But who would want a dog that was malnourished and infested with fleas? Or maybe it had died, which might be best in the long run. Kate walked back toward the store and crossed an alley when she saw him. Tied to a dumpster, he was curled up in a tight ball, asleep. Kate ran back inside the store just as the man was leaving.

"Excuse me, sir." Kate walked in, directing the man back inside. "Can I buy you something besides coffee?"

"Get lost."

Kate ignored his request and grabbed him by the elbow. "Here. Sit down and stop being a pain in the butt. What do you want? Nachos, a sandwich, what?"

The man looked up, blurry-eyed, and belched. "Who are you, a goddamn social worker?"

"No, just someone who's trying to be nice to you. What'll it be?"

"Gimme twenty bucks."

"That's not food."

Several customers in the store were beginning to take notice of their interaction, and the man fidgeted. Kate turned to leave. "Have it your way."

"Nachos and a quart of beer."

"You can't drink beer in here." Kate went up to the condiment bar and started preparing the nachos. "Jalapeños?" she called to him.

"Why the hell not?"

She purchased a bottle of tea as well and set the meal in front of him. "It's hot outside. Enjoy your food in here."

He mumbled a thank-you as Kate rushed out the door and down the street. She had only a few minutes, but if the dog became frightened, all the time in the world wouldn't help. He was lying in the alley just as Kate had last seen him. She approached the dog slowly and squatted a few feet away. He raised his head and started to tremble.

"Hey, boy. It's okay. I won't hurt you." She extended her hand, and the dog backed away and whimpered. "Sweet boy. Want to come with me?" He sniffed her fingers, and Kate was able to scratch behind his ear. "Like that?" She slowly untied the belt. "Come on, boy." At first, he pulled back, but Kate tugged, and he began to trot along beside her. Rather than walk back in the direction of the 7-11, Kate turned down the alley to the next street. The dog stopped a few times to scratch at his fleas but seemed resigned to follow. When Kate reached the Rover, she opened the back and placed the dog in Kenya's traveling kennel. She gave him a quick dusting of flea powder and prayed she wouldn't have to fumigate the Rover.

Kate drove in front of the 7-11. The man was gone. She cruised on and spotted him several blocks past the alley where he had left the dog. He was jawing with several other homeless people and obviously hadn't yet discovered his loss. Kate suspected that this dog wasn't a constant companion and was likely left alone for long periods of time.

Kate did not feel one ounce of guilt over stealing the dog. Soon the man would have another to entice people into giving him handouts. But at least this one would no longer be exploited. This dog would be spending his time in the newly cleaned yard of the Steiner family. Maybe not living in the lap of luxury and having to learn to protect himself against the rambunctiousness of the Steiner boys, but Kate had no doubt the dog would be appreciated and cared for—after he and Ray went through a period of adjustment.

Shortly before noon, Kate pulled up to the Anacortes Vet Hospital. An hour and two hundred and fifty dollars later, the dog had been de-fleaed, de-wormed, vaccinated, groomed, and given a clean bill of health. He even seemed pleased with the blue bow attached to his new collar.

****

Kate found Ray Steiner under the hood of the old Cadillac, banging the engine with a wrench and spewing profanities. He looked up from his repair job. "Paula's inside taking a nap. Go on in and wake up her fat ass. Tell her to come out here and help me with this."

"I heard that, Ray." Paula stood behind the screen door, a cup of coffee in her hand. "I told you to tow that piece of junk down to the automotive shop. You don't know what the hell you're doing. Tell him, Kate. The jerk never listens to me."

"I'm staying out of the family argument. I just came by to let you know that Jack and I are leaving in the morning and to bring the kids something to remember us by."

"Well, your timing's right. The school bus is pulling up." Paula opened the door and stepped outside. Brittany climbed out of the bus and ran over to hug Kate. Tommy hopped out behind his sister. Kenny flew out last and swung his backpack at his brother, knocking him to the ground. Tommy kicked Kenny in the shin, and a fight ensued. Paula watched, shook her head, and rolled her eyes. "See what I have to put up with," she said. "If you're on your way to Africa, please take me with you."

"Chicago's our first stop. We'll see what happens after that." Kate opened the back of the Land Rover, and the dog hopped out and ran over to Brittany and licked her face. "I probably should have asked you first, but it's too late now," Kate said. "He's yours if you want him. He's been vaccinated and cleaned up, and he comes with a free ten-pound bag of dog food and a cushy bed."

Brittany jumped up and down. "Mommy, Mommy, can we, can we have him?" Kenny and Tommy stopped fighting and joined their sister.

"This poor dog won't have it easy. You know that, don't you?" Paula laughed. "And he's going to have to learn to defend himself against those two hellions."

Ray popped up from under the hood, ran into the house, slamming the door behind him. "And Ray's gonna need an adjustment period."

Kate drove away, glancing in her rearview mirror in time to see Kenny and his new dog engaged in a tug-of-war with what looked like someone's sneaker.

****

The ferry leaving Lopez Island was almost empty.

Jack parked and cut the engine. "A lot different than the day we arrived. Are you staying here or going up top?" he asked Kate.

"I'll be up in a minute. I packed a book I want to read, and I need to dig it out." Just as she stepped out of the Land Rover, a guy next to her emerged from his monster-size work truck. He looked like he'd spent the day logging.

"Hey. Humane Society license plate," he called to her and pointed.

Kate felt her hackles rise. The man smiled and gave her a thumbs up. He wiped his hands on his jeans and reached into the back seat of his rig. He pulled out a large black bag. Kate mistook it for a purse, then the man reached back inside the cab. He lifted out a reddish-blonde dog that looked like a cross between a Chihuahua and a Pomeranian. It couldn't have weighed more than five pounds. He gently placed her inside the bag. "Not supposed to take dogs up top, but she gets lonely down here by herself, so I hide her. I got Missy from the animal shelter on San Juan Island. Best dog I ever had."

Kate laughed and followed the man and Missy up to the passenger deck.

CPSIA information can be obtained
at www.ICGtesting.com
Printed in the USA
LVHW021954231022
731365LV00007B/202